# OPERATION LIGHT SWITCH

Published by Mission Point Press
2554 Chandler Lake Road, Traverse City, MI, 49696
MissionPointPress.com

MISSION POINT PRESS

ISBN: 978-1-943995-33-2
Library of Congress Control Number: 2017949038
Printed in the United States of America.

# JOHN WEMLINGER

# OPERATION LIGHT SWITCH

*To Teresa,*

*Finally... a woman who likes the cover! Enjoy the read!*

*Best,*

*John Wemlinger*

## MISSION POINT PRESS

# DEDICATION

FOR MOST OF my time in the service (1968 – 1995), we were lucky. The enemy was the Soviet Union, and we lined forces up and down the border between East and West Germany to defend against their potential invasion of the free world. But all of that changed with the fall of the Berlin Wall, the breakup of the Soviet Union, and the ever-increasing rise in extremism. The enemy today is literally anyone who resents America for any variety of reasons: perhaps it's our wealth; perhaps it's our freedom, or some combination of these. They can come at us out of seemingly nowhere. Making matters worse, these bad actors are not bound by even the simplest set of moral principles. Innocent men, women, and children are mere incidentals to them.

Like it or not, it is the US military that stands as their principal opposition. Yet, since the creation of the all-volunteer force following the Vietnam War, our military is the smallest it's been since the years between the two World Wars.

This book is a tribute to the remarkable flexibility and amazing agility of the US armed forces. It is dedicated to the men and women of America's army, navy, air force, marine corps, and coast guard, who every day must sift through the rhetoric and defend American interests around the globe. May our political leaders never overlook the difficulty or the danger of what you are asked to do.

I salute each of you.

# FOREWORD

*OPERATION LIGHT SWITCH* is a rewrite of a book I first published in 2003 entitled, *A Path to Innocence, A Road to War*. If I were to try and tell you what I have learned about crafting good fiction since then, this foreword would turn into another book.

As history has unfolded in front of me over the last seventeen years, the story I told in that first effort never left me. In 2003, the United States invaded Iraq. Recall the hype that surrounded Defense Secretary Donald Rumsfeld's much publicized campaign euphemistically called "Shock and Awe." Recall the pictures of armored columns, miles long, rolling toward a Baghdad that had already been bombed back to the Stone Age. Now recall what the wars in both Afghanistan and Iraq settled into. What started out as a hunt for Osama bin Laden turned into another miserably long military slog. The only reason we haven't lost 58,000 or more lives in these latest wars is because military medicine has advanced to such a level that fatal wounds are quite rare.

We should be able to recognize guerilla warfare when we see it. Vietnam should have given us that perfect vision. The enemy is indistinguishable from the civilian population they hide amongst. In this kind of an environment, thunderous armored columns are ineffective compared to one human being on the ground, watching, listening, and reporting. The way of warfare has changed. The role of elite Special Forces has become critically important in the post-Cold War world. Small, highly mobile, well-equipped, and well-trained groups that can blend into the neighborhoods where the guerillas hide, and soldiers and marines that can become trusted advisors to foreign armed forces are the wave of warfare's future.

*Operation Light Switch* is a case study in future war. An enemy pops up from nowhere. Intelligence collection is critical, often risky. Secrecy is paramount. But how nimbly Washington can react is just as critical. The current political climate in America, the deeply divided nation we live in, creates its own set of problems. Will the lives of American fighting men and women be valued above political careers? The answer is unclear to me, and that is unsettling. A good story in 2003 is now even more compelling in 2017. I hope you enjoy the read.

# OPERATION LIGHTSWITCH

# 1
## FREEDOM

Rifling quickly through the papers the prisoner handed him, the military policeman removed the one he was looking for and wordlessly pointed to the door. As it opened the grease on its hinges failed in the Kansas winter air, and the door groaned loudly. Cleveland Abraham Spires stepped through. Behind him, he heard the hinges groan again and the door clank shut.

He was free.

Situated on the western edge of Fort Leavenworth, the US Military Disciplinary Barracks was located on a bluff overlooking an expanse of field that separated it from Fort Leavenworth Army Airfield. The airfield was out here because it was noisy. The century-old prison was where it was because to put it any closer to the main part of the sprawling military installation would shatter the gentility of the good folks who lived and worked there. Cleve gazed down toward the airfield. It had been a decade since he'd been able to see things at a distance without iron bars intervening between him and the view. He watched a gust of wind roll toward him like a wave across the prairie grass that covered the field and the gently sloping bluff. He drew in a deep breath and waited for it to cascade over him. In a previous life, it would have refreshed his spirit, but not now.

The bus station was five miles away. It was cold, but he chose to walk. It would give him time to think.

IN A PARKING lot across from the prison, Tetsu Agaki hunkered down lower in the seat of his rental car and pulled the newspaper up in front of him. Glancing down at the picture in his lap, he looked again over the top of the paper at Cleve. He had his mark. Now all he had to do was figure out where he was headed. These were the delicate moments of his job. His first rule was, *never let the mark see you.* But, if he hung back too far he might lose him forever. His client wanted to know where Spires was going and what he was doing. Why? Agaki had no clue, but payment was contingent on results.

He let Cleve walk a few hundred yards, then drove past him. He exited the post's main gate and pulled into a drug store parking lot where he would be able to see him coming. At this point it was simply a tedious waiting game.

THE HARSH WINTER wind tore at Cleve's trench coat and rippled his trouser legs, but, lost in thought, he was oblivious to the cold. He put his hand in his coat pocket and felt the five crisp one-hundred dollar bills in there. This was all he had to show for the last ten years of his life.

*Go home.* But it wasn't that easy. Ten years ago, Command Sergeant Major Cleveland A. Spires, a highly decorated Special

Forces operator, had been court-martialed, accused of smuggling guns into Okinawa, Japan, from Thailand and of killing an airman, whom the government claimed had been his accomplice in the smuggling operation. The motive had been revenge. The airman, a security policeman, was supposed to clear a shipment containing contraband onto Okinawa's Kadena Air Force Base. But he'd gotten drunk, fallen asleep, and missed the shipment. Another security policeman had found the guns and ammo hidden in a pallet of personal military gear that was not supposed to contain either guns or ammo. His trial lasted a week. He was found guilty. It took another week for the court-martial board to agree on his sentence. They reduced him to the rank of private, E-1, costing him his hard-earned command sergeant major's retirement. If it had ended there, it wouldn't have been so devastating, but it didn't. They sentenced him to ten years' confinement.

He was almost 50 years old, but, for him, his life had ended ten years ago. His father had died while he was in prison. His mother was in Cleveland, Ohio, his hometown. They exchanged letters. Every month she accepted a collect phone call from him during his incarceration. These almost always ended with his mother in tears. His last communication with his wife, Liott, was a letter she had mailed to him nearly nine years ago. In it she'd said that she and their son, Daniel, were returning to Chuk Ra Met, Thailand, the small, remote farm village of her birth about twenty kilometers northwest of Korat. Daniel was getting into trouble for fighting in school. Kids were teasing him because he didn't look like them, his mother spoke English with an accent, and anything else that kids could think of to be cruel and unfeeling. When he fought back, she decided it was time to go home. Liott knew that this decision to return to Chuk Ra Met would make it impossible for her and Cleve to communicate. Modern conveniences had bypassed Chuk Ra Met. There was no electricity. Water came from a few common wells in the village center. Cooking was done over charcoal. The men farmed rice paddies and banana groves using ox-drawn plows and carts. News of the outside world only filtered into Chuk Ra Met when a villager went to Korat and brought it back, and this did not happen with any regularity. Mail service in or out was infrequent and unreliable. In the letter she'd mailed from the airport she'd said, *"Come to us when you can. Daniel and I love you very much."* She signed it, *"All my love, Liott."* It had torn his heart out. He'd failed all of them so miserably.

A strong gust of wind buffeted him. He leaned forward into it. The worst part of all of this, the part that had gnawed at him every hour of every day, was that he had not committed the crime of which he'd been accused, tried, and sentenced.


IT WAS NOT by accident that Colonel Lucas Johnson was standing at his office window. Colonel Lon Jeffers, a friend and the commander of the US Army Disciplinary Barracks, had called him a few minutes ago at Johnson's request and told him that Spires had just been released. Lucas could see Cleveland Spires as he trudged toward the installation's front gate.

Spires had only recently come back into Johnson's life as unexpectedly as he'd come into it ten years ago when then-Major Lucas Johnson was appointed president of a seven-member General Court-martial Board that tried and convicted Spires. A year ago, Johnson, newly assigned to Fort Leavenworth, had gone to the prison's barber shop for a haircut. He had heard they were inexpensive and it would be difficult even for a student barber to screw up a simple high-and-tight. As he took a seat waiting his turn, he peered down the row of a dozen prisoner/student barbers and spied Cleve Spires.

Little scared Lucas Johnson, a combat veteran who'd seen action in Somalia, Afghanistan and Iraq, and as he looked back on that day in the prison's barber shop, he'd never been able to explain to himself why he'd done what he did. But when he saw Spires standing behind a chair cutting another soldier's hair, Johnson got to his feet and walked out of the place only to pay three times the price for the same hair cut at the Post Exchange. Perhaps it was this sudden and unexpected proximity to Spires that had done it. More likely, however, it was because the court-martial had always bothered him. Special Operations was a small community and those that excelled became well known. Though they'd never served together, Johnson had heard nothing but superlatives about Spires. During the trial, Johnson had taken the time to familiarize himself with Spires's record. What he found in there bore no congruity with the man who'd stood bolt upright in front of him as Johnson read the board's guilty verdict to the military judge. But the facts were the facts. The murder weapon, a 9 mm Beretta that had been reported missing from the First Special Forces Battalion's arms room at Torii Station, Okinawa, had Spires's fingerprints all over it. It had been recovered from a small wastewater pond near where the body had been found on a remote section of the sprawling US air force base.

The defense contended that the fingerprints were there because Spires had conducted an inspection of the battalion's arms room the day before the airman was killed. That might have been enough to establish a reasonable doubt, but there was one other piece of evidence that Johnson and the other six members of the court-martial board had to consider. Acting on an anonymous tip, the Air Force Office of Special Investigations at Kadena and the army's Criminal Investigation Division at Fort Lewis, Washington, had begun monitoring Spires's stateside mail received at the post office on Fort Lewis, Washington. Ten days after the discovery of the body on Okinawa, a package containing fifty thousand US dollars arrived at Fort Lewis, mailed from the army post office on Okinawa the same day as the murder. The package was addressed to Command Sergeant Major Cleveland Spires.

The smuggling charge was dropped due to insufficient evidence. Spires couldn't be linked at all to the pallet of gear in which the contraband weapons were found. But there was still the matter of the murdered security policeman. Spires's court-appointed defense attorney argued that the victim, even though he was off duty at the time of his death, was carrying an unregistered weapon. When the body had been discovered, a stolen .38 caliber pistol was also found tucked into the waistband of the victim's pants. It nearly made Spires ill when he heard his attorney say, "If you must find that my client fired the weapon that killed the victim, you must conclude that my client's actions were in self-defense." The move, though it likely saved him from a life sentence for premeditated first degree murder, certainly condemned Spires to a jail sentence.

As Johnson stood at his office window staring down on Spires, the old questions returned. *What the hell happened to you? You were one of the best NCOs in the entire friggin' army. You might have even had a shot at being the Command Sergeant Major of the Army. What were you thinking? That no one would find out? That the possibility of getting caught was so low it was worth the risk? I don't get it. Explain it to me.* Now, after all these years, with Spires just in front of him, a few hundred yards away, Johnson was tempted to bolt after him.

But he didn't. What would be the point? It was over and done with. Spires had served his time. He was leaving Fort Leavenworth and the army. Shaking his head, Johnson turned his back on the window. *Good riddance. He's gone. You're back to command in six months and far away from here.* There was a beep from the phone on his desk. It was his secretary notifying him of a meeting in five minutes. Johnson shrugged his shoulders and returned to his duties.


AT THE BUS station, Cleve studied the schedule. As he took his place in line at the ticket window, he gripped the money in his pocket. His mind raced. Five hundred dollars wasn't much. There was a bus leaving for Cleveland at two o'clock this afternoon and as he turned to see what time it was he noticed the man behind him in line was Asian, probably Japanese, based on his experience in that part of the world.

"How may I help you, sir?"

She was attractive, polite, and patient as Cleve stood in front of her continuing to study the schedule of departures. Finally, he asked, "How much is a one-way ticket to Cleveland, Ohio, on that two o'clock departure?"

Well trained, she launched into a spiel about some special travel pass that would allow him unlimited travel over the next six months to any location in the lower-48 United States, all for the great price of $500.

Politely he responded, "No. Thanks. What is the fare to Cleveland, one-way?"

"Yes, sir," she said, punching a few buttons on her computer's keyboard. "The fare will be $75. The bus departs here at 2:00 p.m. and is on schedule. That should get you to Cleveland tomorrow at 11:00 a.m. Would you like me to print that ticket for you?"

He nodded and handed over a one hundred dollar bill. They exchanged smiles as he collected his change and his ticket. When he turned to leave the ticketing area, he noticed that there was no one in line behind him. The Japanese man who had been there was gone.

# 2

## BILLY DRISCOLL

As soon as Tetsu Agaki saw Cleve Spires lay down the money for the ticket to Cleveland, he'd done an about face and exited the bus station without looking back. He and Spires had locked eyes for a split second, a mistake Agaki immediately regretted, but it had happened. He wasn't about to let it happen a second time. Now, at the Kansas City airport, he'd purchased a one-way ticket to Cleveland. For the last hour, he'd just been hanging around the boarding gate waiting for the first boarding call. When it came, he took out his cell phone and pulled up his employer's number.

Agaki didn't like Billy Driscoll at all. He was, in Agaki's estimation, brash, crude and downright rude, a typical American, he thought, but the money Driscoll was paying him, results based, of course, was better than any money he'd made working for the Yakuza, so he was willing to look past what he didn't like. He waited until the second boarding call and then hit the *call* button.

Driscoll's cell phone, lying on the table next to him, buzzed. He was busy, but was expecting a call, so he reached for the phone. The naked Thai girl kneeling on the floor in front of him stopped what she was doing and looked up. He grabbed her roughly by her long, black hair and said in near-perfect Thai, "Don't stop. Don't you ever stop unless the customer tells you to." As he let go of her hair, she went back to work. "Hello," it was almost a snarl. In the background, Driscoll could hear faintly a public address system announcing a boarding call.

"Driscoll-san, it's Agaki."

"You got him?" Driscoll asked impatiently.

"Hai," Agaki began in Japanese, but then switched to fair English, a language he'd learned during a fifteen-year jail term spent in a prison just outside of Tokyo. "He is taking a bus to Cleveland, Ohio. I am in Kansas City and will fly to Cleveland in just a few minutes. I will intercept him at the bus station when he arrives. I am sorry, I must go. My flight is boarding," he said as he ended the call.

In his suite in the Windsor Hotel in Bangkok, Driscoll flew into a rage. Pushing the girl away, he stood, as naked as the day he was born, and shouted, "Dammit! The little bastard hung up on me."

The rant was in English and so the girl understood none of it. That didn't matter. It wasn't his words that would hurt her. She had seen him like this before, when she'd first arrived in Bangkok from her small village in the north. Her father had sold her to Driscoll because she'd become pregnant out of wedlock. When her baby bump began to show, she was disgraced. Her father, who also felt disgraced, decided that if she could no longer bring him a nice dowry, it was time to sell her. The one hundred US dollars he'd sold her for would buy him many things for his small rice farm. In Bangkok, the first order of business had been an abortion. Then she had to be trained. Both processes terrified her, but she was a survivor. In Thai, she asked, "Beelee, what is it?"

Driscoll glared at her, shaking his head. She thought he might hit her. The one other time she'd seen him angry like this, he'd hit a girl and broken her jaw. She hadn't seen the girl since, but knew she couldn't be working. The jaw had swollen quickly and become black and blue. Like that, she wasn't attractive to any man, so Beelee wouldn't keep her around.

Command Sergeant Major Driscoll muttered something in English and then paced around the room a couple of times. He tried to call Agaki back, but the calls went to voice mail immediately. *The little fucker turned off his phone. Wait 'til I get my hands on him.* He stomped some more, until his rage began to settle out of him. There was nothing he could do at this point. He could get mad as hell at Agaki, but the bottom line was he needed him. Driscoll was interested in knowing what Spires was going to do now that he was out of prison because Driscoll knew that Spires wasn't the one who killed that airman on Okinawa. He knew Spires wasn't the kingpin in a gun smuggling ring. He was the one who had stolen the 9 mm pistol with Spires's prints on it from the First Battalion's arms room. He was the one who had anonymously tipped off the Office of Special Investigations (OSI) about the cash in the mail. It had been Driscoll's fifty thousand dollars that sealed Spires's guilty verdict.

Ten years ago, Driscoll had thought the frame-up was genius on his part. He'd had to move quickly because he'd already been questioned by the Air Force Office of Special Investigations on Okinawa. Then-Sergeant First Class William Driscoll had been the one who had delivered the pallet full of personal equipment to the airport in U-Tapao, Thailand. He'd been the one who had signed the customs document indicating that the shipment contained no contraband. He'd pleaded complete ignorance about how the weapons had been stashed in the middle of the pallet hidden from sight by bag after bag of personal equipment that belonged to the Special Forces soldiers that would later board the plane for transport back to Okinawa from Thailand. He'd claimed never to have met or known the security policeman who'd been killed. At that point the OSI had no evidence of his involvement, but he was undoubtedly a person of great interest in the case. Because he had cooperated with the investigation completely, the army had only flagged Driscoll's records and advised his battalion commander that he could not leave the island of Okinawa until the flag on his records was lifted.

It was the same day that the OSI first questioned him that Driscoll happened to pass by the First Battalion's arms room, where he noticed Command Sergeant Major Cleveland Spires in there, apparently inspecting weapons. He noticed that Spires seemed particularly interested in the new 9 mm Beretta pistols that the First Battalion had just received to replace their decades-old .45 caliber hand guns.

The First Battalion's armorer, a buck sergeant, with two ex-wives and child support payments to each, had jumped at the ten grand Driscoll had offered him to steal one of the 9 mm pistols. The buck sergeant was responsible for maintaining a scrupulous inventory of weapons assigned to the First Special Forces Battalion. Driscoll had told the kid, "This is going to probably cost you your job. If it does, I'll give you another ten grand, but understand this—I'm going to kill somebody with the gun you give me. If you rat me out, I'll hunt you down like a dog when I get out of jail and put one between your eyes. Understand?" It had, in fact, cost the buck sergeant his job as well as all of his stripes for somehow letting that weapon go missing. But through it all the kid kept his mouth shut. Driscoll proved true to his word and gave him the extra ten grand. More importantly, though, the kid was absolutely sure that Driscoll would, at some point, kill him if he ever spoke to anyone about what he'd done.

Now, ten years later, what Driscoll wanted to know is, *What is Spires going to do?* If he was going to try and find out who framed him, then Driscoll wanted to see him coming. Billy Driscoll had a nice little gig going here in Thailand that he would protect at any cost. He had risen to the rank of command sergeant major and now in his current capacity as the ranking NCO in the First Special Forces Battalion on Okinawa, he had an official-duty reason to spend most of his time in Thailand. Since the fiasco with the security policeman and the botched shipment of guns, he'd laid low for a while. However, about nine years ago, he'd determined that the heat on him had relented sufficiently so that he could return to business as usual. The Yakuza paid him well for the guns, but even better for the drugs he ran out of Thailand into Okinawa. He'd used the money he'd made off of the smuggling operation to set himself up as the kingpin of a group of three bars in the sleazy sex districts of Bangkok. Between the three, he had over one hundred girls working for him. Each was paid based on the number of men they could talk into buying them overpriced drinks and ultimately lure into the bars' back rooms for sex. Billy Driscoll had a lot of money, all of it ill-gotten, and he'd never considered the fifty grand it had cost him to frame Spires anything but a good investment. Now, if he needed to kill again to protect his businesses because the guy he'd framed all those years ago was getting too close, he'd do it without any more qualms than the first time.

# 3

## GOING HOME

**W**ith the exception of an on-time departure from Leavenworth, Cleve Spires's trip back to Cleveland, Ohio, was the trip from hell. Nothing had gone as it should. There was not just one, but two breakdowns. The bus finally arrived in Cleveland at 4:30 a.m., nearly eighteen hours late. The delay gave Cleve more time to think about what he would say to his mother. He let everyone get off ahead of him and when the last of them exited the bus, he still sat there, staring out the window into the early morning darkness.

ACROSS THE STREET, Tetsu Agaki put the binoculars up to his eyes and watched as the passengers disembarked. When the bus had not arrived on time, he'd had his first panic attack. Busses, he discovered, are not like the airlines. There was no posting inside the station of delays, cancellations, etc. He had to ask the ticket agent yesterday morning, but he had not been helpful at all, except to inform him there had been some breakdowns and he thought the bus was probably back on the road, but could not give Agaki an estimated time of arrival.

He'd watched at least a dozen buses arrive and unload. *Where the fuck is he?* As this one unloaded and his mark did not get off, Agaki felt another pang of panic. *What if he changed his mind? What if he bought a ticket to somewhere else after I left the bus station in Leavenworth? What if he changed his mind along the way and bought a ticket to somewhere else?* He saw his big payday slipping away. He took the binoculars down and scanned the crowd standing around the driver as he pulled bags from the storage bins. He put them back up to his eyes. *Nothing!* As he lowered them, his frame of vision widened and he saw someone stepping down from the bus. Quickly he raised them up again. *There he is. Gotcha!*

CLEVE JOINED THE few people who were still waiting for the driver to unload their bags and looked around. Through a plate glass window he could see two men, homeless, he assumed, slouched asleep on the hard benches in the center of the otherwise barren room. Next to one was a shopping cart piled high with nothing that Cleve could discern was of any value or useful purpose. Each clutched a paper bag, bottlenecks protruding, close to his chest. The driver set Cleve's bag on the ground. Cleve retrieved it and gave him a couple of dollars for his trouble.

"Thanks." Surprise was evident in the driver's voice. No one else had made such a gesture.

"Yeah. You're welcome. Wasn't your fault."

Cleve was home now and a feeling of melancholy spread over him. He stepped inside the bus station for a moment just to regroup. Inside, he caught the ammonia stench of urine. Over three decades ago, he'd left Cleveland from this very same bus station as he embarked on his army career. Nothing had changed much. Urban decay was all around him. But then he reckoned that he had little right to judge either the poor condition of the station or the people occupying it. Thirty years ago, he had been a young man with no criminal record and nothing but promise ahead of him. Now here he was, a convicted murderer, an ex-con, returning home to his mother's house because he had no means to go anywhere else. Guilt swept over him. *What's the point? Why have you come back here?* Looking across the station, behind a thick wall of glass, probably bulletproof, he saw a lone ticket agent, propped on one elbow, watching television. He headed in that direction.

WATCHING SPIRES THROUGH his binoculars, Agaki felt the adrenalin surge of panic seize him. *Fuck! He's going to buy a ticket. Now what are you going to do? You can't risk getting close to him again.* He felt in his pocket for the roll of bills, thinking ahead that he might have to bribe the ticket agent, but, for now, all he could do was sit there and watch.

SPIRES STOOD FOR a long minute in front of the ticket window looking at the departure schedule, but not really reading it. *How long are you going to keep running away? You're here now. This is never going to go away until you face her, until you tell her how sorry you are.* He felt in his pocket for the four hundred dollars he had left. *Where are you going to go? Face her. Then get on with the rest of your miserable life.*

AGAKI BREATHED A sigh of relief when he saw Spires turn and leave. He watched him only briefly, but long enough to know that he was headed in the direction of his mother's house. Yesterday evening he'd already looked her up in the Cleveland area phone book and gotten the address to go with the name Driscoll had given him. He scouted out the surrounding neighborhood and generally became familiar with the area in which he thought he'd be shadowing his mark. The time to perform a reconnaissance like this was a rare luxury in his line of work. He pulled from the curb, turned down a cross street, cut over a couple of blocks, and headed for Ida Spires's house. This was all turning out to be much easier than he'd anticipated.

# 4

## PAUL STANLEY
## AND THE ASSOCIATION

This part of the deception never got easier for Paul Stanley. As he handed over the forged passport to the immigration agent, his heart was pounding so hard he could feel the thud at the back of his head. If he were caught, there would be no way to explain it away. The agent was thumbing through the document as if he were looking for something in particular.

Stanley could feel the perspiration running down his underarm. It was an eternity before the agent returned to the photo at the front of the passport, compared it to the traveler standing in front of him, picked up his stamp, pressed it down on the open page, and handed the passport back to him. US Army Major General Paul Stanley, director of logistics and security assistance at the United States Pacific Command, entered Japan through customs and immigration at Tokyo's Narita Airport as Mark Amial. Stanley had no idea who Mark Amial was or if he existed at all, nor did he care. All that mattered was that he'd successfully pulled off the deception once again.

Stanley grabbed his bag and followed the green line through Japanese customs with nothing to declare. Outside the terminal he stood in a short line for a taxi cab and when he told the driver he needed to get to Haneda Airport, on the other side of the sprawling megalopolis that was Tokyo, he was treated like royalty, as he should have been. The fare was going to be exorbitant, hundreds of US dollars. The money was inconsequential to Stanley.

Only eight people knew he was in Japan, and his boss wasn't one of them. Admiral Chet McKeever, commander of the United States Pacific Command, thought Stanley was on a hunting trip in the Canadian wilds and therefore out of communication until his return to civilization five days hence. McKeever had not liked having one of his principal staff officers completely out of touch, but Stanley had been hard at it for over a year now without a break and had done some really difficult work, in McKeever's estimation. So, he'd granted Stanley's leave request with instructions to give him a call when he was back up on the net.

Stanley's real destination was on Hokkaido, Japan's northernmost and least populated island. From Haneda Airport he would fly to Sapporo, where he would be met by a car and driver that would take him to his final destination, a hot mineral-springs resort called Kilomanjaro. There he would meet with one of the strangest mixes of men he could have ever imagined: a Japanese, a South Korean, a Thai, a Filipino, a Malaysian, a Vietnamese, a Chinese, and, last and perhaps the strangest of all, a North Korean. They referred to themselves as The Association, and other than that he knew very little about them except that each was well placed within their governments. In the last ten years he'd met with them on three other occasions, each meeting about three years apart. This meeting was out of that cycle, and Stanley had been surprised when the note from his handler, a Japanese man by the name of Seito Yamamoto, had arrived in the mail summoning him to this meeting. There was no question whether or not he'd be there. Paul Stanley owed these guys a lot.

Ten years ago they had literally pulled him back from the brink of financial disaster. A US-based HMO was closing in on him for nearly a quarter of a million dollars in unpaid medical bills owed for an estranged son's cancer treatments. At the time, Lieutenant Colonel Paul Stanley was tapped out. Alimony and child support payments for three failed marriages took almost all of his monthly salary. Bankruptcy was looming as his only option, and that would have caused his security clearance to be pulled. Career-wise, a field-grade officer without a security clearance is at the end of the road. There would be no more pro-motions, no more schools, no chance to command at the battal-ion or brigade levels and, certainly no chance to ever become a general officer.

Stanley never could determine how they knew about his dilemma and, at this point, he frankly didn't care. There had been only two rules. 1. Never mention The Association to anyone other than the eight men comprising it. 2. If he were ever in a position to influence military sales to any of their coun-tries, he would do whatever he could to make the sales happen. For his agreement, they'd placed a million dollars in an offshore account and given him access to it. He'd paid off the medical bills and not touched another dime of the money. He thought they liked that about him. As far as his career was concerned, getting out of debt had allowed him to rededicate himself to the army and to his career, and as a result he'd risen through the ranks to major general. While he didn't think a third star was likely, he was happy with how far he'd gone in the army, and he was equally pleased that over the last few years in particular, he'd pushed a lot of military sales their way.

His single frustration was how little he knew about them—which was squat, really. Seito Yamamoto, his handler, was the one who managed his attendance at these meetings. Stanley didn't know if they met on other occasions, how they had come together, or what they were trying to accomplish. At the meetings he would typically stay with them for only part of the time they were together. Yamamoto would politely say to him, "Paul, you are excused for now. If we need you, I will call you," and then he would tell him when they wanted him back. Stanley never questioned Yamamoto's directions, but all of it piqued his curiosity.

The governments of the men comprising The Association were rivals. North and South Korea hated each other. No love was lost between Vietnam and China. Malaysia, the Philippines, South Korea, and Thailand had strong alliances with the west, as did Japan. But when it came to Japan, virtually no country in Asia trusted the Japanese, a stigma still left over from World War II and reinforced by Japan's juggernaut economy. It wasn't difficult for Stanley to discern that Yamamoto was the *de facto* leader of this peculiar group, so, once, quite a few years ago, Stanley had tried to question him. He wanted to know what such a culturally and politically diverse group was really up to. They obviously had access to money, a lot of it. They'd given him the million dollars as if it were a mere binder fee. But, was it money from their governments? Or was it illegal money from who knew what? It worried Stanley, but not enough to make him stop, at least not yet. At first Yamamoto had been polite in his refusal to answer, but as Stanley had pressed, Yamamoto shut him down with a sternness quite uncharacteristic of the Japanese personality. Stanley had backed off.

It was February and a bone-chilling dampness had settled over Tokyo. Hokkaido would be even worse. As he settled back in the taxi for the long ride between airports, Paul Stanley had an unnerving thought. *Maybe I'm better off not knowing what the hell these guys are up to.* The cab gathered speed heading out of the terminal. He looked out the window as the bleak, winter countryside blurred past him. *No. You've done everything they've asked. Whatever it is they are up to, you've been a part of it. You're a part of them now and you can't stay in the army forever. Find out what you can and see if you want to be a part of it after you retire. You've come this far, why turn back now?*

# 5

## EYES ON HIS MARK

The house sat in the middle of the block, a typical row house built in the mid-fifties. Cleve's father had purchased it after returning home following a stint in the navy. Years later, just after Cleve had graduated from high school, he'd told his son to "Join the navy if you're going to sign up. At least you'll have a dry place to sleep and the food is decent." The irony in his father's belief that the navy was the only service that gave its people a *dry* place to sleep had not been lost on Cleve.

He stood for a moment in the swirling, pre-dawn cold in front of his mother's house. Looking up and down the street, he shook his head. Years ago, when they'd first been built, the houses were all identical: two stories with a basement, brick, fronted by a small yard bisected by a walk that led to four steps leading to a front porch. Now, most were abandoned, boarded up, with litter strewn about the barren yards. Only half of the streetlights were working. Yet in her yard, there was no litter. The sidewalks in front of her house and leading to the porch were shoveled clear, and he could hear the crunch of salt under his shoes. The porch was empty of furniture now, but he knew the aluminum lawn chairs that sat there in the summer would be neatly covered and stored in the basement. Her house numbers were clearly illuminated by the only porch light visible on the block. Through the window he could see the blinds his mother had always had there, drawn at this time of night, every slat perfectly in place. The immaculate condition of the home in an otherwise ramshackle neighborhood was testimony to the iron will of Ida Spires. No matter how bad things got around her, she would not let what was hers fall apart.

He stepped onto the porch and glanced at his watch: 5:00 a.m. *I should go somewhere until a decent hour. She's asleep now.* His stomach turned over. *Where?* He had no answer to that. He knocked too lightly on the front door the first time. Upstairs, asleep in the back bedroom, she couldn't have possibly heard him out there barely tapping, perhaps just another way his psyche was delaying this reunion. He braced himself and knocked again, louder this time, and in a minute he saw a light come on behind the drawn blinds. Seconds later, a dagger of light crossed his face as his mother spread wider the narrow opening between two slats. As quickly as they had parted, they closed, and from the other side of the door he heard faintly, "My God!" Her fingers frantically slid the chain lock free of its channel and he could hear her struggling with the dead bolt's mechanism that wasn't moving fast enough this one hundred thousandth time she'd unlocked it. The door swung open and he could see her now, backlit in the doorway. Her features were unchanged, exactly as he'd remembered her.

"Cleve...land," her voice cracked as she said his name. Tears quickly brimmed over the edge of her eyes and streamed down her dark cheeks. She stepped toward him, and the gulf that had existed between them closed as quickly as water closes around a hand dipped in a pool.

He tried to say something, but even the simplest of words, *"Mom,"* stuck in his throat and he couldn't get it out. Her head lay against his chest and he could feel her gentle sobs. There were no words, yet the comfort they took from one another equaled volumes. Cleve knew then and there that he was home. He regretted his earlier indecision. He was glad that he'd come here.

She pulled him into the small foyer. Everything was as he remembered it. "Cleveland," he couldn't remember the last time he'd been called that, but it is what she'd always called him, "you're home." Ida patted her son's chest as if reassuring herself that he wasn't some mirage conjured up in a dream. "I'll bet you're hungry. I'll make us some coffee and then breakfast. I can't believe you're home." She led him down the hallway into the kitchen at the back of the house. He took a deep breath and smelled the same smells he'd smelled as a boy growing up here. It was as if everything inside this place had stood still while he and his mother had aged thirty years. He followed her down the hallway into the kitchen just as he'd done as a little boy after being called in from play. There were so many things he wanted to say to her, so many things he wanted to know.

FROM HIS CAR parked down the street a few houses, Tetsu Agaki held up the binoculars and witnessed the reunion between Cleve and Ida Spires, its poignancy lost on him. Now, he judged, he'd better get hold of his employer and update him. He figured Driscoll was worried, not that that bothered him, but Spires's bus had been eighteen hours late. He chuckled at the thought, but this was all about the money, and Driscoll was his client, paying him very well for information. He reached for his cell phone.

It took six rings for Driscoll to answer half a world and half a dozen time zones away and then came the roar, "Listen to me, you little son of a bitch, don't you ever hang up on me again. You wouldn't do that with your buddy Fujiwara, so don't think you can get away with it with me. Fujiwara doesn't pay you anywhere near what I am..."

Agaki, anticipating the tirade, moved the phone away from his ear until Driscoll finished, then calmly began, "It was unfortunate I had to hang up, but they were boarding and I had to catch that flight. It was the last flight that day to Cleveland."

"Well, what the fuck took you so long to get back to me? That was two days ago."

"His bus was delayed."

"Bullshit! Listen you little bastard, if I find out you're milking me for more money, I'll break your scrawny little neck."

Agaki seethed at this threat, but took comfort in knowing he still had the upper hand. "Driscoll-san, I work at your pleasure. I will return to Japan today if that is your wish."

"Fuck you, Agaki. Tell me what he's doing."

"It appears he has come home to Mother. I just observed a most touching reunion at her doorway."

"How sweet."

"Yes. I will continue to watch him for the next few days and try to determine if he intends to stay here."

Driscoll did some quick math and figured he already owed Agaki either twenty or twenty-five thousand dollars plus his travel expenses. "Listen to me you little shit, if I find out . . ."

Agaki was smiling, "Again, Driscoll-san, I shall return to Japan today if that is..."

Driscoll hated anyone having the upper hand, but he had to

be sure Spires was staying put. "No!" he roared into the phone. "You keep your ass right there where you are and watch the bastard. Call me in two days and let me know what's going on."

"Hai," and he pulled the phone away from his ear still smiling. This time it was Agaki's turn to do some quick math and it didn't take him long to determine he could milk this deal for about fifty or sixty thousand US dollars. Driscoll had been right that this was the best money he'd ever made and so far, it had been pretty easy money. There was only one qualm Agaki had about the entire deal, and he'd been reminded of that when Driscoll mentioned the name of his old friend, Cato Fujiwara.

IDA SPIRES STOOD at the counter slicing some onions to mix with his scrambled eggs. He'd always liked them that way. "I haven't made scrambled eggs like this since your father . . ." Her hesitancy to complete the thought gave way to an awkward silence.

"I . . . I'm sorry I wasn't here when Dad..."

She turned to him, shaking her head, and held up her hand. "Cleveland, don't be sorry. There's no need. You couldn't have changed a thing even if you'd been here." She turned back to her slicing. "He died in his sleep in the middle of the night. I was lying right there next to him. I didn't know anything was wrong until I tried to wake him up the next morning. It had to be one of the most peaceful deaths God could ever grant a human being."

As a feeling of complete uselessness swept over Cleve, all he could do was hang his head and begin to weep.

She walked over to him, put one arm around his shoulders and patted his chest with the other hand. "It's OK, Cleveland. He's in a good place now and he knew you loved him."

"I loved . . ." The rest of it stuck in his throat.

Ida helped him out. "I know that and so did your father. If we would have believed any of it, it would have killed both of us long ago, Cleveland." She gave that a moment to sink in and as he was regaining his composure, she added, "I don't know how and I don't know when, I just know the truth will come out someday."

It was his turn now to reach out to her as he stood and pulled her close to him, ashamed of how badly he'd underestimated his parents' love.

She patted his chest again. "Now let me get this breakfast on the table. You must be starving," she said as she returned to her cooking.

While Ida finished making breakfast, he listened for other sounds in the house, but all he could hear was her gentle humming and the scrape of the wooden spoon against the heavy cast-iron skillet as she stirred the egg and onion mixture. When she slid a huge plate of scrambled eggs and bacon in front of him and sat down at the table, he asked, "Have you heard from Liott and Daniel since they . . .?" Just the thought of them choked him up.

It was the question she knew he was eventually going to ask. For the last hour, since she'd seen him at her front door, she had begun mulling over how she was going to answer, and she knew it was going to hurt. Putting down her fork, Ida looked up from her breakfast as tears began to fill her eyes. She reached across the table and covered one of his hands with hers. "Cleveland, it's not your fault that they couldn't manage here."

"It's all my fault, Mom. I lost my family when they sent me to prison. Now that I'm out, I'd just like to know they are safe."

"It wasn't your going to prison that made them leave," his mother offered.

Drowning in his loss, he sat there, not comprehending what his mother had said.

"Cleveland . . ." she paused until he looked at her. "Liott and Daniel both know you didn't do it," and then she repeated, "They didn't leave because you were in prison."

"I let them down. I let everybody down."

She hated to see him like this. Quickly she began, "Liott was having trouble coping here. She's very proud, you know. She wouldn't live here with your father and me. She insisted that she and Daniel have their own place, and found work at the Airport Holiday Inn. The pay wasn't very much and so she worked a lot of hours, but she found a place for her and Daniel. We'd see them once or twice a week. Then Daniel started to have trouble in school; some kids were making fun of him because he spoke Thai, and then they started to make fun of Liott's accent. He was sent home twice for fighting. On the day after the second fight, Liott called us from the airport and said she and Daniel were leaving for Thailand. Your father and I rushed there to try and talk her out of leaving . . ." Ida began to cry. "We were too late. By the time we arrived, their flight had already left."

It was as if Cleve had been punched in the gut and the wind knocked out of him. On the bus ride from Kansas he had tried to imagine what she would look like after all this time. He tried to imagine what Daniel, as a young man, would look like.

"I have something you might like to see."

Lost in his own thoughts, he hadn't heard her. "What?"

"I have kept his letters. Daniel and I—I always manage a small gift and card at Christmas and on his birthday, too. I have no idea how they actually get to him." She smiled and chuckled. "I just send them to Daniel Spires in care of Chuk Ra Met, Thailand, and he always thanks me." With that she stood up and walked over to the table under the wall phone and opened a drawer. She removed a packet of letters tied with a red ribbon and handed it to him. He held it as if they would break.

"Go ahead, Cleveland, untie the ribbon and read them. His English has gotten better every year. Someone must be teaching him, Liott maybe, I don't know." Cleve was staring at the stack of letters in his hand. "Go ahead, open them up, read them, you'll see." They were in chronological order and the sixth letter in the stack, sent three years ago, contained a picture. As he studied it, Ida said, "You should put that in your wallet, Cleveland. Every father should have a picture of his son with him."

He took the picture out and, at her urging, returned to eating breakfast. In between mouthfuls he told his mother about Chuk Ra Met, Thailand. He knew it well, and just talking about it seemed to make him feel better. As he finished the last bite, he looked at Daniel's picture and said, "He's grown up by now."

"He looks like you, Cleveland."

He smiled at her and nodded. "They're safe there . . ." his voice trailed off and then he added, "and happy, I'm sure."

After they spent the morning catching up, his mother went to the grocery store and he read *The Cleveland Plain Dealer*. Later that evening she cooked him his favorite dinner: baked ham, sweet potatoes, and pumpkin pie. Cleve didn't tell her she could have fixed him anything and it would have been his favorite meal. He didn't have to go through a cafeteria line to get it. There were no guards at her kitchen door to keep him in there. The meal had been prepared especially for him. He was home, and as Ida fell to sleep that evening, she said a silent prayer and asked God to keep her son close to her.

Just down the hall, Cleve fell asleep in the room he'd slept in as a boy.

# 6

## COMMITTED

The driver who'd picked Paul Stanley up at the Sapporo airport couldn't speak a word of English, so the hour-and-a-half drive was spent in an awkward silence broken only by the driver's silly grin and bobbing head as he caught Stanley's eye every now and then in the rearview mirror. It was after midnight; Stanley was dog-tired as he surveyed the hotel's lobby, devoid of people except for an older Japanese gentleman dozing on one arm behind the registration desk. *"Konichiwa,"* Stanley said, almost completely exhausting his repertoire of the Japanese language and interrupting the man's cat nap.

The man started awake and responded in quite understandable English, "Ahh, General Stanley, we have been expecting you. I am sorry you caught me . . ."

"You speak English?" Stanley interrupted, not at all hiding his surprise.

"Yes, I do, sir. Welcome to Kilomanjaro. Your room is ready and I have your room card and this for you," he said, reaching under the counter and pulling out a sealed manila envelope with a key card on top.

"Thank you," Stanley said reaching for a nearby pen.

"There is no paperwork. Yamamoto-san has seen to all of that," he said with a dismissive wave of his hand and a smile. "If there is anything else you might need, I will be happy to have coffee, tea, or perhaps something stronger sent to your room."

"No. Nothing. It's been a long day."

Nodding, the man said, "Your room is the fourth one down this hallway," and he pointed to a corridor to Stanley's left. "My name is Yogi. I am here all night. Just let me know if I can be of service."

Once in his room, he opened the envelope and found a series of newspaper clippings, only some of which were in English. On top of the stack was a post-it note that read, *Stanley-san, welcome to Kilomanjaro. Breakfast is at 7:30 a.m. and you will be our first briefer starting at 9:00.* It was signed simply, *Yamamoto.* He leafed quickly through the clippings, concentrating only on the ones he could read. They were from English language newspapers from all over Asia and reported on military sales that had taken place over the last few years. It was all old news to him since he and his staff at United States Pacific Command had been the ones who had brokered the deals on behalf of the US government. In tomorrow's briefing he would go over each sale, they would ask him a lot of questions and, if tradition held true, he'd be done in about an hour to an hour and a half, depending on how many questions they had. In the past that had been it. He'd been dismissed, put on standby, and only recalled if they felt they needed him, which had been rare.

This time, however, he intended to break tradition. This time *he* was going to ask *them* some questions. Tomorrow he was going to get some answers. He showered, set the alarm for 6:30 a.m., and collapsed into bed.

The next morning, as he walked from his room to the resort's restaurant, he could see a spectacular sunrise glistening off the open fields of dazzling, unblemished snow that surrounded the hotel. In the distance he could see ski lifts, empty at this early hour, but waiting for their first passengers to arrive in the next few minutes. What struck him, however, was how empty the place seemed to be.

Seito Yamamoto was a big man by Japanese standards. Stanley stood at six feet, two inches, and he and Yamamoto could look each other squarely in the eye. Yamamoto looked fit. Slight graying at the temples of an otherwise black head of hair gave him a distinguished look. Stanley had never seen him in anything but a coat and tie. Unlike some of the others whom he knew were influential in their governments, he didn't have a clue what Yamamoto did for a living besides honcho this bunch. As Stanley approached, Yamamoto smiled charmingly and extended his hand in the western manner. "Paul, you look well. Welcome to Hokkaido."

Stanley had made it a practice to keep things formal with his employer, so while Yamamoto may have used his first name, Stanley, lacking any invitation from Yamamoto to do otherwise, stuck with the more formal greeting, "Yamamoto-san, it's good to see you again." Then, waving his hand around, he asked, jokingly, "Have you leased the entire hotel? Where is everyone?"

"The resort is ours for the next three days. There is a small housekeeping and kitchen staff here to tend to our needs. I hope you find everything to your liking."

Stanley simply shook his head, unable to comprehend the extravagance. "It's beautiful."

Inside the restaurant Yamamoto wasted no time. Speaking to the others gathered in the room, he announced, "If we could find seats, we will get breakfast started. We have much to discuss over the next few days." He turned to Stanley and said, "General Stanley, your place is here," and then motioned for him to take a seat between the men from North Korea and China, neither one of whom bothered to greet him.

English was the common language among them and all of them spoke it with accented fluency. As breakfast was being served, the North Korean seated at Stanley's left asked in a voice loud enough so that everyone at the table could hear, "So, General Stanley, what do you think my country is doing with the crude oil that has been so charitably given to us recently by your country?"

This was not a deal that Stanley had brokered. Rather it had been accomplished by a series of non-governmental relief agencies as a humanitarian necessity after reports surfaced that thousands of North Koreans were freezing to death due to a shortage of crude oil in the country. He replied, "I hope you are distilling it into fuel oil for heating and cooking."

"Come now, General Stanley. You are among friends. There is no need to be so politically correct. I didn't ask what you *hoped* we were doing with it. I asked what you *really think* we are doing with it." There was a pause and then he pushed, "So . . ."

By now the room had gone silent and all eyes were on him. Stanley knew full well what the hell they were doing with the donated crude oil, so he looked the North Korean straight in the eye and said, "You're refining it into fuel to keep your tanks, airplanes, and ships operating."

The North Korean looked at Yamamoto, smiled, and then turned back to Stanley. "You are correct, General. Our military still operates very well, while many of my countrymen starve and freeze thanks to the idiot who now holds power in my country." He spat the word "idiot" out as if it caused a bad taste in his mouth.

Stanley put down his knife and fork and looked at the North Korean. "If you were to say that in Pyongyang . . ."

"I would be publicly executed," the North Korean said, finishing the thought and laughing while the rest of the room joined in. When it died down, he continued, "The world only thinks it knows what kind of a man rules North Korea today. What it does not know is that he is a sexual deviant who dotes on young girls only twelve or thirteen years old. He smuggles them in from all over Asia using our navy's ships and our air force's planes. The fuel it takes for these missions to satisfy his lust could heat thousands of homes in my country."

Stanley wasn't quite sure how to respond, so he merely nodded.

"But it will not be long before the pervert who rules North Korea is but a bitter memory and there will be sufficient fuel for everyone in a unified Korea."

"A unified Korea . . ." Stanley practically stuttered the words, which seemed so strange to him. He looked at the North Korean, who was nodding, and it was then that he noticed every other head in the room except Yamamoto's was nodding as well. "But how . . . ?"

Yamamoto stood up. "Gentlemen, we must step back a moment from such serious discussion or we will surely ruin General Stanley's breakfast." Laughter again filled the room, but Stanley sat stone-faced. He was tired of being the only one in the room who didn't know what was so fucking funny. As the laughter died down, Yamamoto continued in a humorless voice, "General Stanley, I appeal to your patience. Your attendance at this meeting will be different from the others. We intend to fully integrate you into our association. Over the next several days you will become only the ninth person to know what it is we plan to accomplish. What is about to happen is radical yet simple. It may at first hurt certain of our countries but that hurt will be short-lived. What we will do will hurt your country, how severely I cannot predict, as I have rarely been able to predict your country's reaction to world events."

*World events?* Stanley seized on those two words.

Yamamoto continued, "Just by hearing our frank discussion this morning about North Korea, you have crossed a line and now you stand on the side of that line where we must demand your absolute loyalty. What you will learn over the next few days cannot ever be discussed with anyone that is not in this room right now. To do otherwise would make you a traitor to this brotherhood that deeply values your membership and your contributions over the years. Our existence is a secret and our plans depend on the element of surprise. If we lose that advantage, we will fail."

Stanley's mind was reeling, it was all coming at him so fast. He could feel every eye in the room squarely focused on him.

"Do you understand the line you have crossed, and can we expect your absolute loyalty?"

"Yamamoto-san, I . . . I . . ."

The edge in Yamamoto's voice was demanding, "Stanley-san, the question requires a simple *yes* or *no*."

For them it was exactly that simple, and he knew they couldn't care less why it wasn't equally as simple for him. Yamamoto's reference to world events kept flashing in and out of his mind.

"General Stanley, your answer?"

He had to decide now; there was no other way. Stanley put his hands down on the table and said, "Yes."

# 7

## BLUE NOTE

da Spires knew her son was mourning the loss of his wife and son. The sorrow she felt for him was beyond measure. Yet she was pleased when Cleve announced he was going to look for work. To her that meant he had no plans on leaving Cleveland any time soon.

THE SIGN IN the window read, *Speaks's Barber Shop,* so Cleve assumed Alonzo Speaks still cut hair there. This was where his father had gotten his hair cut and where, as a boy, his father had brought him. Stepping inside, he recognized Alonzo, grayer and heavier than Cleve remembered him. Alonzo looked up from the customer in the chair and nodded at Cleve, but the recognition was not mutual as the old man turned his attention back to the man in the chair.

Cleve sat down, observing a younger barber at work in a second chair. Between the two barbers was an empty chair and the counter behind it was empty as well, so Spires assumed if he played his cards right this morning, he could be cutting hair at that empty chair by tomorrow. He needed a haircut, so Cleve waited his turn, deferring to one customer who came in after him so that Alonzo would be the one cutting his hair. When it was his turn, Cleve got up, and as he eased into the chair, said, "How are you, Alonzo?"

The old man placed the cape around his neck and asked, "Do I know you, Mister?"

"It's been a long time. Cleve Spires."

Alonzo stopped what he was doing and then reached around and removed the cape he'd just placed over Cleve. "I think you need to find another place to get your haircut," he said, his tone flat and unequivocally final.

The younger barber started to intervene, but Alonzo cut him off. "Stay out of this, Freddie. It's none of your concern."

Cleve had not expected this. He looked over his shoulder at the old man who was glaring at him. Wordlessly, he got up out of the chair.

Alonzo unloaded on him. "You gonna walk out of here, just like you walked out on your old man."

Cleve, his back to Alonzo, clinched his fists in an almost reflexive response to the old man's bitter words.

"You come home, have you . . ."

Whatever the old man said after that was lost on Cleve as he gathered his coat and headed out the door, pulling it shut behind him. As he headed down the street, reeling at the shock, he didn't care where his feet carried him as long as it was away from here. If he stayed, he wasn't sure what might happen. One part of him wanted to cry. Another part wanted to go back in there and punch the old man in the mouth.

From behind him he heard, "Sergeant Major Spires."

Hearing his name with his former rank in front of it shot another wave of humiliation through him. He turned to see who it was and found Freddie, the younger barber, behind him. "It's not Sergeant Major anymore. It's Cleve . . . just Cleve."

"Sergeant Major," Freddie persisted, "my father doesn't understand. He's never served, but I did. I was in the 82nd Airborne. I was at Fort Bragg when they sent you . . ." his voice trailed off.

Cleve began to walk away.

"Lots of folks at Bragg said you got screwed. They said it was racial. They said it was some kind of conspiracy to keep a black man from becoming the next Sergeant Major of the Army."

Cleve didn't want to hear any of this. There was no point to it. He kept on walking away.

"I'm sorry my father made such a big deal out of a haircut."

Cleve didn't look back or say anything. He merely raised his arm and waved his hand. He walked a couple of blocks and ducked into a corner restaurant, bought *The Cleveland Plain Dealer,* and looked through the classifieds.

There might be something to the old adage that bad things happen in threes, because he was rejected for two more jobs before he gave up just after dark, sometime around 5:00 p.m. In both cases, he was sure it was because he was honest and checked *yes* in answer to the question, *Have you ever been convicted for a felony?* that appeared on each application. As he sat on the crowded bus and thought about all that had happened, he suddenly felt claustrophobic. He got up, moved to the door and got off at the next stop. Home was still quite a distance away, it was snowing and the temp was well below freezing, but he thought the walk might do him some good. He knew he needed some time before he got home. He couldn't go home to his mother until he'd climbed down off of the psychological shelf the day's events had put him on.

Down the block he saw a bright neon sign, much like other signs along his route home. This one read, *Blue Note Bar and Grill,* but what made it stand out was the blinking *e* in the word "note." *Blue Not,* he thought, *OK, don't be blue.* He hesitated before going in, but decided a cold beer might help him chill out. It was a weeknight and still early, but the Blue Note had a pretty good crowd of about twenty people inside, most sitting at tables and booths. He took a seat at the bar.

"What can I get you?"

Her nametag read, *Wanda,* and he found her quite attractive in spite of his frame of mind. He surprised himself at how pleasant his voice sounded as he answered, "A beer would be great."

"OK. Do you have a favorite or do you just want to trust me on this?" she asked with a smile.

Smiling, he said, "I'll trust you."

"OK, then! I've got a draft here that's brewed locally. People kind of like it. Let's give it a try."

As she walked to the beer taps at the end of the bar, he caught a whiff of her perfume. Then she was back with his beer, and to his surprise, more conversation. "I haven't seen you in here before. Are you new in town?"

He hesitated and then answered, "Yes." He took a drink of his beer.

"Well, what do you think so far?"

"About the beer or Cleveland?" he quipped.

She laughed. "Both."

He liked her easiness, but continued to play it close to the vest. "The beer's good and Cleveland's OK."

She broke away from him long enough to fill an order for a waitress, but once that was done she came back. "Where's home?"

He liked her. "I was born and raised here, but I left a long time ago. Came back to visit my mother."

"That's nice. Cleveland's home for me, too. Been here all my life." She paused and then added, "I'll bet you notice a lot of change if you've been gone for a while."

Without answering her question, he asked, "Worked here very long?"

"I bought this place about a year ago. Decided I wasn't cut out to be the reclusive widow for the rest of my life. It's been good for me, doesn't take a lot of training to run a bar, just some common sense. I keep busy, get to meet people and have some purpose to my life, not to mention that this place manages to turn a little profit each month."

"Sorry about your husband."

She liked that he was considerate and had listened to what she'd said. "Thanks. He was a good man. At least he didn't suffer. It was a cerebral hemorrhage. One minute he's here and the next, he's gone." She paused only momentarily and then asked, "How about you? Your family here in Cleveland with you?"

He didn't want to answer this, but he didn't want her to walk away either, so he told a half-truth. "No. Other than my mother, I have no family."

Then Wanda asked the question that cut right to the heart of the matter. "Well, you know what I do for a living, so how about you?"

*Well, I don't have a job. You see, I used to be a special forces command sergeant major, but I got put in jail for ten years for murder. Now I'm a retired private, ex-con, out-of-work barber. Wanna go steady?* Instead he said, somewhat to his surprise, "Not working right now. I'd like to stay here in Cleveland for a while. It's been a long time since I've seen my mother, and she is getting up there in years. I don't have anywhere else to go right now, so it just seems to fit. Don't suppose you have a job here . . ." He looked down at the bar and was about to apologize for putting her on the spot.

Without hesitating, Wanda answered before he could say anything else. "Well, since you asked, I need a jack-of-all-trades kind of person around here. Someone who can clear a table and reset it, and change a keg, which means hauling it up from the basement." She pointed to a door on the other side of the bar area. "Maybe tending bar occasionally or helping out in the kitchen if we get busy. It's evening work. I don't know how that might work out with your mother. I need someone to help me clean up after we close and get ready for the next day's business. It's part time, twenty, maybe twenty-five hours a week. I can't pay much more than minimum wage, but I'll give you half of any bar tips I get. You don't look like a guy that's afraid of a little hard work. So, yeah, I sure could use you around here."

He was stunned and just sat there.

She stuck her hand out. "Damn, I just offered you a job and I don't even know your name. I'm Wanda . . . Wanda Cheevers."

He took her hand, smiled, and said, "Cleveland Spires; most folks just call me Cleve."

"Nice to meet you, Cleve Spires. You named after the city?" she was smiling at him.

He chuckled, "Yeah, my father's idea. He came back here after getting out of the navy. Got a job with the department of public works. Retired from there. When I was born, he felt like he owed the city something, so he named me after it."

"Nice," she said, still smiling at him. "So how about it? Interested in the job?"

He paused for a moment and then said, "Wanda, just to be

fair, before you answer the *When do I start* question, you should probably know . . ."

She held up her hand and cut him off, "You're not a serial killer are you?" They laughed, she harder than him.

"No."

"Well, then, here's what I know. I've got an instinct about people. It never fails me. I think I can trust you to do a good day's work around here. I think I can trust you behind this bar with the cash drawer open. I think I can trust you to be courteous to our customers and polite to the others who work here. I'll trust that instinct."

He searched for the words, but all that came out was, "Thanks."

Wanda replied, "No thanks are necessary. Can you start now?"

He nodded and then said, "This may sound silly, but I should call my mother and let her know where I am." He waited for her to laugh, but she didn't.

"Cleve Spires," she said looking at him sweetly and speaking softly, "that's one of the sweetest things I've ever heard a grown man say. The phone is in the back, on the wall, just as you go through the kitchen doors. There's an apron hanging back there as well. Make your call, grab the apron, and I'll show you around before we get too busy."

CLEVE CREPT INTO his mother's home at 2:30 in the morning. He was tired, but he felt better than he had in a long time. His world was beginning to rise from the ashes. As he walked into his dark bedroom, he walked over to the window to pull the blind before undressing and looked outside at the snow that had really started to come down hard. As he stood there, he noticed a white Cavalier, the only car on the street, pull from the curb at the end of the block. He had walked home from the Blue Note and at that early hour there was hardly any traffic. A car like it had passed him, and, now, here it was again, but he couldn't be sure it was the same car, could he? It did, however, strike him as odd, and then a yawn overtook him.


AS HE PULLED from the curb near Spires's house, Tetsu Agaki's mind was elsewhere. Boredom had overtaken him about two days ago. He was nearly certain that his mark wasn't going anywhere. In fact, after today's events, it appeared to him that Spires had found work. Why else could anyone spend that much time in a bar and then walk three or four miles home in these freezing temperatures?

He hated Cleveland, Ohio. No dirtier than Tokyo and certainly no bigger, the incessant wind and snow blowing off of Lake Erie made his life miserable. And then there was Michiko, his mistress, whom he missed terribly, but whose expensive lifestyle he could more easily afford with the money Billy Driscoll was paying him.

As he closed the door to his hotel room, he reluctantly took out his cell phone and searched its address book for Driscoll's number. The phone on the other end rang no more than two or three times before Driscoll's voice boomed into his ear, "What the fuck have you found out, Agaki?"

He hated this man, this miserable American whom he secretly hoped would one day be snuffed out like a candle in a hurricane by Cato Fujiwara. But when you're getting ready to screw somebody it is often the best policy to remain deferential. "Driscoll-san, he is still in Cleveland, staying at his mother's house."

"Yeah, and . . ."

Agaki got ready and turned the screw. "It is impossible for me to tell you what he might be planning to do at this point."

"You fucking little bastard . . ."

"Driscoll-san, I will stop my surveillance and return to Tokyo if you wish, but . . ."

"Yeah, yeah, yeah, I know, you can't be sure. You little fucker."

Agaki knew he had him where he wanted him. "That is true, Driscoll-san." Agaki let that sink in for just a second and then asked, "What would you like me to do?"

Silence.

"Driscoll-san, are you still there?" Agaki knew he was. He could almost feel the steam coming out of his ears. A wry smile crossed Agaki's face.

"If, I find out you are screwing me . . ." Driscoll cut his threat short almost as if he knew it was pointless. There was more silence, and then, "You got one more week. I want updates every two days. Don't fuck with me, Agaki! You understand?"

"Hai, Driscoll-san, I understand." The wry smile had turned to a full grin.

After showering, Agaki turned on the television and was greeted with a commercial for Disneyland in Orlando. As he fell asleep, he decided that tomorrow he would make a reservation there for the last three or four days he was to be in the states. He knew Spires wasn't going anywhere, but that wasn't something that Driscoll needed to know for another week and that additional week would earn Agaki another thirty-five to forty thousand dollars. If he couldn't kill Driscoll, he could at least drain some money out of one or more of his bank accounts.

# 8

## OPERATION LIGHT SWITCH

The conversation around the breakfast table was in English, which some of the men spoke better than others. It was mostly small talk, for which Paul Stanley was not in the mood. He picked at his food. He was sure of only two things at this point. First, he was going to get his wish to know more about this odd collection of men. Second, he'd apparently crossed some kind of line, but he was unsure of what that meant and that did not sit well with him.

At precisely 9:00 a.m., Seito Yamamoto stood. The conversation immediately ceased. "Gentlemen, shall we adjourn to the conference room. General Stanley, you are our first briefer."

Stanley, standing along with the others, nodded.

While the conference room was luxuriously appointed, there was a complete lack of any technology. Stanley didn't need it. He'd been told many times that he should never carry anything with him while traveling to meetings like this one that might in any way cause anyone to ever ask any questions about his reason for travel. While he never really understood their requirement for such secrecy, he faithfully honored it.

Yamamoto was the last to enter the room, pulling the doors closed behind him. When everyone was seated, Yamamoto nodded to him. Stanley began, "Gentlemen, this morning I'd like to begin with the most recent sale of F-16 fighter jet technology to the Japanese government."

Before he could proceed any further, Yamamoto interrupted him. "Paul, I don't want to seem rude or in any way disrespectful, but could you please begin with the aviation package that was sold to the Vietnamese air force two years ago?"

He adjusted easily. "Certainly, Yamamoto-san."

Yamamoto interrupted again, "Paul, you are one of us now. Please call me Seito." Turning his attention to the others, he said, "Gentlemen, we've not ever formally introduced ourselves to our newest colleague. Now is as good a time as any. Lee, let's start with you."

This was a big step forward, Stanley thought, although he already knew that Park Son Lee was South Korea's minister of foreign trade. Park Son bowed. "It is a pleasure to finally meet you, General Stanley. My country's minister of defense, Kim Joon Nam, speaks quite highly of you."

Stanley nodded to him. One by one, they each introduced themselves. Among them was one other minister of foreign trade, two ministers of culture, one minister of defense, one minister of foreign relations, and one minister of banks and securities. That left only Yamamoto. "Paul, you and I have known one another now for what, a decade?"

"Yes."

"And in all that time, I am sure you have wondered who we are, what we are all about. We call ourselves simply The Association. I am sure you have a million questions for us, but I am going to ask you to please hold them for a while longer. Much of who we are and what we are about will become clear to you as we progress through our agenda."

Stanley realized he must have looked a bit bewildered, but decided he would trust Yamamoto, so he nodded politely.

"All right, then, with that order of business behind us, Paul, please continue."

"Well, as we all know, the sale to Vietnam was one of the most contested military sales I have been involved with. While the riff between our countries has healed itself over the decades, Congress saw the sale as a re-militarization of an old enemy. I'm afraid that mindset still exists among certain members of Congress."

Before he continued, Nguyen Van Thuy, Vietnam's minister of culture, stood and asked, "Can you arrange yet another sale to my country?"

Stanley suddenly could feel every eye in the room on him. He had not anticipated this and his instinct was to say no. It was suddenly very hot in the room. He didn't think no was an answer that they would accept. Yet, if he said yes and then couldn't deliver, what would they think? The room was so quiet he could hear his own heart beating.

Yamamoto pressed him, "Paul, this is an important question for us. We are planning what I think in the military you would call an operation. We call it Light Switch and it will commence soon. There is some concern that our reserves of ammunition in Vietnam are not sufficient to sustain our initial successes."

It was like being handed a couple of pieces to a jigsaw puzzle, but not having any idea what the overall puzzle picture looked like. *Reserves of ammunition, Operation Light Switch— what the hell are these guys up to?*

"Paul," Yamamoto continued, "I can see the wheels turning.

There is much that you do not yet understand, but you will in good time. For now, we need your answer to Thuy's question. Can you arrange another sale identical to the last one? Equally as important, we need for this new sale to be finalized before June."

It was February. The last sale had taken six months to wind its way through Congress for approval, and then it passed only by the narrowest of margins. Stanley didn't have an answer. He just stood there.

"Your assessment, General Stanley?" Yamamoto asked in a tone that left no doubt that they expected an answer now.

Nguyen Van Thuy offered, "I can have four ships standing by for loading by April, General Stanley. I simply need to know if you want them on the east coast or the west coast."

"But you . . . we . . . can't be sure that . . ." Stanley realized he was spluttering.

Yamamoto interrupted, "I will explain much of this to you later. For now, answer the question, please."

Stanley swallowed and felt a knot rise in his stomach. "Yes. It won't be easy, but I believe . . ."

Thuy prodded, "And the ships . . . where do you want them?"

*Jesus*, he thought. *I'm not even sure* . . . He caught Yamamoto glaring at him. Pressed to answer, he said, "Two on the east coast and two on the west. If you want this done by June, we will have to use both the ammo port at Sunny Point, North Carolina, and the one at Port Hueneme, California."

Stanley was almost relieved when one of the doors to the conference room swung open and every eye in the room shifted from him to a young Japanese man in kitchen whites entering the room carrying a tray full of bottled water and a bucket of ice balanced over another tray of glasses. Yamamoto immediately flew into a rage, shouting at him in Japanese. The man said something back to him, but kept moving toward a table at one end of the conference room.

Stanley understood none of it, but was thinking that a glass of cold water would taste pretty good right now. He was completely unprepared for what happened next as Yamamoto pulled a pistol from under his suit coat and shot the young man. Even though Stanley saw him pull the pistol, he jumped as the shot reverberated through the room, followed by the clamor of trays, bottles, ice, and glasses falling as the young man slumped to the floor. Coolly, calmly, Yamamoto stepped toward the already mortally wounded man and emptied the clip into him. Stanley's ears were ringing and he could not believe what he was seeing. He scanned quickly around the room only to see the others sitting rather impassively as if none of this was any surprise to them. Stanley, on the other hand, stood there realizing he had just witnessed an execution.

Yamamoto looked at Park Son Lee. "Let's adjourn for a while. I will get someone to clean up this mess." It was as if the death did not matter in the least, but the spilled bottles, ice, and broken glass were the inconvenience. "Park, will you please explain all of this to our newest member."

Lee nodded and then said, "Paul, if you will come with me." Stanley hesitated. Lee waived his hand as if he were an impatient teacher waving his student in from the playground following recess. "Come with me, please."

They exited the conference room, walked through the restaurant where they had had breakfast, and then stepped onto an outside patio. The morning sun shimmered off the unblemished blanket of snow. In the distance, Stanley could see ski lifts taking vacationers up steep slopes where they would in a few minutes begin their descents down the mountain through the fresh powder. He suddenly longed to be so carefree, until Park pulled him back to reality.

"You have no understanding of what happened just now." Park meant it as a fact. Stanley took it as a question.

"No."

The South Korean nodded and said, "Let me explain."

"That was an execution. I know an execution when I see it." Stanley, who normally kept his language fairly stilted with them, said, "What the fuck did that kid do to deserve that?"

"It was harsh . . ."

"Harsh?" Stanley was nearly shouting at Park. "That was fucking murder, plain and simple. What the hell are you guys up to? You can't just go around killing people like that."

Park paused for a second with his head down looking at the ground. He then looked up and said, "If you are finished, I will explain."

The others had joined them on the patio, but they were all just standing around in a group, smoking and talking as if this was just another smoke break. He drew a deep breath and looked at Park. "Explain . . . you're going to explain to me? How do you *explain* murder?"

"The staff here has all been told that they are not to come into that conference room when we are in session. The man broke that cardinal rule . . ."

"Did he deserve to die for it?"

The answer came quickly. "Yes." Park pointed to the others. "We have all killed for less." He gave this a moment to sink in. "Did you understand the exchange between Yamamoto and the young man?"

"No," Stanley answered curtly.

"Then, allow me to fill you in. Perhaps, that will help you to better understand why he had to die. To be honest, I am not sure why Yamamoto did not kill him as soon as he opened the door. If I had had a weapon, I might have done it myself." Park waved his hand dismissively and said, "But that is not important. What is important is that Yamamoto told him to leave immediately. If he had done so, he might just still be alive. But he didn't. Instead, he told Yamamoto that Cato Fujiwara likes to have ice water available when he meets here."

The name Cato Fujiwara meant nothing to Stanley.

"Before this meeting is over, you will understand Fujiwara's significance to our cause. If this man was so free to use Fujiwara's name, what might he say to someone about such a unique group as ours meeting here at Kilomanjaro?"

"But what could he say? He didn't hear anything, much less see anything. He likely doesn't even know that you are from different countries . . ."

Park interrupted, "It doesn't matter, Paul. This group—" and he waved his hand in the direction of the others, "what we are about to do has been a very long time in the planning, and none of us will take any chance that our plans are discovered until we are ready to show them to the rest of the world."

"And exactly what are your plans?"

Park smiled and gave a shrug. "I am not the one to disclose any more to you than I already have. Yamamoto will brief you. When that is finished, General Stanley, I think you will understand our obsession with secrecy."

Yamamoto appeared at the patio door and said, "Gentlemen, we are ready to resume." They filed back into the conference room. The body was gone. The blood-stained carpet had been cut away and removed, but otherwise it was as if nothing had ever happened. They spent the remainder of the morning talking about the ammo sale to Vietnam and by the time they broke for lunch, it was a commitment—but one that Stanley was not at all sure he could live up to. Lunch was light and at its conclusion, Yamamoto told him, "Paul, you are excused from our session this afternoon."

Stanley had a pounding headache and as much as he wanted to return to his room and forget about all of this, he still didn't know exactly what it was these guys were up to. "But, Seito . . ."

Yamamoto interrupted him holding up a dismissive hand, "Dinner is at 7:00. After that you and I will talk. Much of what you are wondering about will be answered then. Thank you, Paul." It was polite. It was also firm. Stanley had learned as much about them as he was to learn for now. Yamamoto reiterated, "I will see you at seven, then."

# 9

## HEAVYWEIGHT

Calling up the stairs, Cleve said, "Mom, I found a gym. I'm going to check it out and then head to work. See you in the morning."

Ida knew that a couple of days by no way established a routine, but she was optimistic that her son was settling into a new life in Cleveland, here in her house, and given what he'd endured over the last ten years, she would do everything she could to make his life here as comfortable as possible. "OK, son. Tell Wanda, I said hello." She didn't know Wanda Cheevers, but the job she'd given her son certainly indebted Ida to her, and she looked forward to thanking her in person at some point.

THE GYM WASN'T much to speak of, an old warehouse rather haphazardly converted by Randolph Washington, a retired teacher. Most everyone called him Uncle George. It was easy to see that he wasn't in business to make money. In fact, Uncle

George operated this place, The Neighborhood Gym, through a patchwork of grant money, donations, and a generous monthly contribution from his own teacher's retirement pension.

"How much is a membership?"

Uncle George immediately saw something in Cleve. He'd looked him up and down, and, smiling, replied, "Depends."

Cleve smiled back. "On what?"

"On if you're willing to do a little work around here."

Cleve, surprised, but enjoying the verbal sparring, replied, "Well, then, that depends on what kind of work you got in mind."

Uncle George chuckled and pointed to a group of young men who were huddled around a weight bench where all the free weights were located. Since there were only a few weight machines in the place, this area would be the focus of anyone's attention who wanted to lift weights. "See those guys over there?"

Cautiously, Cleve answered, "Yeah."

"Every afternoon for the past week they come in here and lock up that free-weight area. I've watched them literally bully younger kids right out of the place."

"So, boot them out."

"Yeah, well, look at me," he gestured with his hands and then pointed in their direction, "and look at them."

Cleve didn't judge the older man.

"They'll clear out of here about five o'clock or so, but in the meantime, school gets out at three o'clock, and that's when a lot of kids would like to come in here and catch a little workout. But they won't. Like me, they're afraid of these guys."

"Call the police."

"Yeah, well, I tried that. They wanted to know what these guys were doing that was against the law. Unfortunately, bullying isn't even a misdemeanor. The police knew it. More importantly, them guys over there," he pointed in their direction, "well, they knew it too."

Cleve looked them over. He'd handled more than a few of these types of situations in the army and in prison as well. He wasn't afraid.

Uncle George said, "Listen, I don't mind if these guys come in here, but why can't they come in earlier, while school is still in session, or after five o'clock when the school kids tend to start clearing out and going home? I hardly have any high school or middle school kids come in here anymore, and if that doesn't change, I'm going to lose some of my grant money. If I lose that, well, then . . ." his voice trailed off. He didn't need to finish his thought for Cleve to figure out the consequence. "It would be great if you'd talk to them. Tell them you work for me. I'll back you up on that. If you can get them to agree to something, then, man, I'll let you work out here as much as you want to for free."

Cleve looked at him and then at the bunch in the free-weight area. "OK, let me see what I can do. No guarantees, though."

"Thanks, man. Say, I don't even know your name. I'm Randy Washington, but everyone calls me Uncle George," he said, extending his hand.

"Cleve, Uncle George, Cleve Spires." The two shook hands and Cleve strolled off in the direction of the group of young men.

He started with a forty-pound dumbbell and did some military curls. Cleve had massive shoulders and biceps that tapered down to a narrow waist. He could see them eyeing him. When he was warmed up properly, he strode over to the weight bench where he estimated they were working with about 175 pounds. He'd watched them. Four of them had struggled mightily to lift that much free of the holder, lower it to their chest, and then raise it once before placing it back in the holder. The fifth one, however, had managed five repetitions before he put the bar back and stood to the high-fives of his buddies.

"Mind if I try?" Cleve said from behind them.

They turned. Four of them didn't say much, but after sizing Cleve up, the apparent strongest of them scoffed, "You want to match me, old man?" He laughed, and his four buddies followed him into the trap.

"No, man. I want to beat you!"

All of them were crowing different insults at Cleve's brazenness as he lowered himself onto the bench and asked one of them to spot him. Smoothly he removed the bar from the holder and proceeded to bench press 175 pounds ten times before placing the bar back on the rack. The group of five had gone silent somewhere around repetition number six. Cleve stood. "OK, I'll give you the five reps I just beat you by. How about if we add twenty-five pounds and try it again?" The question was directed to the group's obvious leader.

"OK, you're on," he replied. "But I go first."

"Sure, whatever you want." Cleve grabbed two ten-pound plates and a couple 2½ pounders.

The younger man sat down, leaned back, and lifted the bar out of its holder. Cleve watched as he performed the first three reps with relative ease, but the fourth was more tentative and by rep five, the spotter was hovering over the bar as the man struggled to set it back into the rack above his head.

"Good job, man!" Cleve said. As he eased himself onto the bench, he said, "Now let's see what I can do with this." When he finished his tenth repetition, holding the bar at arm's length above his chest, he asked, "Is that enough, or do you want me to beat you worse than this?"

Silence.

Cleve placed the bar smoothly back onto the rack and sat up. "Now, gentlemen, here's how it's going to be. I'm starting a weight-lifting class here for school kids. I'm assuming none of you are in school, so I don't want to see you here at three o'clock. You can come before that or after five o'clock, but between three and five, stay away."

"You can't tell us . . ." their leader, the mouthy one, began to object.

Cleve glared at him. "Oh, but I can." He pointed to Uncle George, who had been watching all of this from his place behind the counter. "Uncle George has hired me to teach that class, and that's the only time I can do it, so . . ." He shrugged his shoulders and held both hands out in front of him with palms up.

The group started to move away, grumbling among themselves. Cleve caught them, "Oh, and gents, there's one other thing. If Uncle George or anyone else, for that matter, tells me you guys are bullying people around here, then you will have me to answer to. That's not something Uncle George has hired me to do, but, well, let's just say that's my promise to you." Their grumbling continued, but they headed for the door. Before they got too far away, Cleve said in a voice that could be heard throughout the gym, "You guys have a nice day." He turned and winked at Uncle George, who was walking over to him.

"Did you mean it?"

"Yes, sir. If any of these guys bother you again, you just call me."

"No, I meant the part about teaching a class to school kids. Did you mean that?"

Cleve had already forgotten. "Well, now, Uncle George, I don't know if I can . . ."

"Listen, Cleve, I don't know where you came from or how you got so strong, and frankly I don't give a damn. I like you. I like your demeanor. My bet is you could really teach some of these kids around here a thing or two about conditioning, and along the way serve as a role model. And that, my brother, is every bit as important to me as anything you can teach them about strength."

"Yeah, well, you probably ought to know . . ."

The old man interrupted, "That you got so strong lifting weights while you were in prison?"

His insightfulness and bluntness stunned Cleve. "Well, yeah. Prison's not the only place I learned about strength training, but you should know I just got out. I . . ."

Uncle George held up a hand. "Cleve, I don't care what you did. I can judge a man by my own self. I judge you to be a pretty damn good one. So, how 'bout it? Teach that class?"

Cleve paused. This was the second time since returning to his home town that someone had just trusted their instincts about him. "Well, yeah, sure. When do you want me to start?"

Uncle George pointed to the door, where four boys whom Cleve estimated to be about fifteen or sixteen stood peering in. "How 'bout right now?"

By the time 4:30 p.m. rolled around, Cleve had ten kids around him listening intently to what constituted the components of a good workout. By 5:00 p.m., refreshed by his workout and shower, Cleve was feeling pretty good about himself and looking forward to seeing Wanda to tell her about his class at the gym. As he walked the last block to the Blue Note, he was momentarily distracted by the blink of the brake lights of a white Chevy Cavalier parked along the curb.

Tetsu Agaki, absorbed in a travel brochure about Orlando, Florida, had not been paying attention until he happened to glance into the rearview mirror on the passenger side of his rental car and saw Cleve Spires about to pass him. As he jerked the travel brochure over his face, his foot resting against the brake pedal moved just enough to engage the brake lights. He could feel his heart beat faster as his mark continued down the sidewalk toward the Blue Note.

Inside, Cleve found Wanda behind the bar getting ready for a busy night. "There he is. How's it going?" Wanda asked.

"Great! You aren't going to believe what I just got myself into."

CLEVE'S ROUTINE CHANGED dramatically with the addition of the weight-training class. The first night there were four youth participating, but by Thursday, only three days later, there were twelve and Cleve had to set that as the limit mostly due to equipment limitations. Everyone, including Cleve, Ida, and Wanda, liked this new routine, each for their own reason.

THE THURSDAY NIGHT football crowd at the Blue Note was robust, and somewhere around nine o'clock Wanda asked Cleve if he'd bring up another keg of Bud Light from the basement and switch out the empty. After clearing off a couple of tables and loading the dishwasher, Cleve headed toward the basement to retrieve the keg. When he returned to the top of the stairs, he heard a commotion coming from the bar area. He set the keg down and observed Wanda and a customer exchanging words. He heard Wanda calmly say, "You've already had too much. I'm not going to serve you. Coffee, tea, soda, food, but you're not getting any liquor in here."

The response was as foul as any Cleve had ever heard, and everyone in the place was now aware of the disturbance going on in front of the bar. The drunk took a step toward Wanda. As

Cleve moved to a position behind him he realized the trouble-maker was one of the bullies from the gym earlier in the week, the strong one, the one whom Cleve had beaten so badly at the weight bench. Cleve saw the drunk's left fist curl into a ball. He thought for a second that the drunk was going to lash out at Wanda. Instead, he hit the bar with such force that a couple of customers' drink glasses bounced up and down in a clatter.

"Listen you bitch, you either serve me or I'm coming behind the bar and getting it myself."

Wanda stood her ground as the man started to move to the end of the bar. Cleve stepped in front of him. "Remember me?" By now, even the customers whose tables or booths didn't have a good view had moved to see what was going on. Cleve started to say, "You don't want to . . ." The drunk swung hard at Cleve's head. Cleve stepped aside as the wild swing carried the man past him, exposing his back.

Cleve balled his right hand into a tight fist and delivered a lightening blow to that soft spot on the lower right side of the man's back. The kidney punch, illegal in the boxing ring, but very effective in hand-to-hand combat, sent the offender directly to his knees. Gasping for air that would not come, he quickly keeled over onto his face where he lay writhing in pain and twitching as if trying to find a position that would allow him to breathe again. Someone had called 911. A siren wailed.

"Are you OK?" Cleve asked Wanda.

Her eyes fixed on the man on the floor, Wanda managed a muffled, "I'm fine, but . . ." She pointed to the poor bastard, who still struggled to grab even the quickest gasp of air.

The siren, louder now, distracted Cleve, but he looked at Wanda and said, "Don't worry about him? He and I met the other day at the gym. I thought I'd taught him a lesson, but, I guess he's a slow learner."

Wanda stared at the man still twitching and writhing on the floor. "He can't breathe. Is he going to be OK?"

"In a few minutes he'll be able to get his breath back, but he's going to be sore for a few days. I probably hit him a little harder than I should have."

"Don't be silly, Cleve," Wanda said as the first police officer burst into the bar. The sight of him made Cleve immediately uncomfortable.

The officer stood over the man. "Willie Fairchild. Well, well, well. Looks like you might have met your match." Fairchild was alternately gasping and choking and showed no signs of being able to stand. There was no urgency on the officer's part to cuff him or otherwise restrain him. Apparently confident that the perp wasn't about to go anywhere, he turned his attention to Wanda. "Mind telling me what happened here?"

She explained. The officer interrupted periodically with a question or two. By the time she got to the part about Cleve, he had mysteriously disappeared into the kitchen.

# 10

## BIRTH OF A TRAITOR

Paul Stanley's head thumped from the headache that had started following the assassination he'd witnessed. He was in little mood for dinner, but his attendance was expected, according to Yamamoto's voicemail left when Stanley was showering. As he trudged down the hall towards the restaurant, he could hear all of them in there chattering as if nothing out of the ordinary had happened.

The dinner prepared for them was superb: fresh sushi, huge prawns served with a pungent cocktail sauce, filet mignon, and fresh, crisp asparagus that was so long out of season he wondered where in the world they'd found it. Yet the food held little interest for him. All he did was pick at it.

After dinner, they adjourned to the bar for cognac and cigars. Stanley took a snifter, hoping it might help his headache, but at first refused the cigar. When he noticed he was the only one not smoking, he plucked a Macanudo from the humidor and let one of them light it for him. Despite what he'd witnessed, he wanted to fit in with them and he had the feeling that they were still watching, still evaluating him. It wasn't long before the strong cognac and nicotine combination masked his headache. He'd formulated a series of questions he wanted to ask Yamamoto, but as he waited for his chance to approach his handler, a man he'd not seen before walked up to Yamamoto and whispered something. A moment later, Yamamoto announced that it was time to move to the baths.

Stanley had been in Japanese bathhouses before. He knew the rituals associated with the bath in Japan, but, again, trying to fit in, he simply followed Yamamoto's lead. Stripped naked, they hung their clothes on wooden pegs outside the shower area. As they filed past, an attendant gave each a pair of wooden sandals, a short wooden stool, and a pail containing a long-handled brush, wash cloth, and bar of soap. They proceeded into a white-tiled shower area, where each man sat on his stool in front of a low showerhead. The cloth was used to work up a good lather and the brush was to wash their backs. The social conversation from the bar followed them into the shower room. The shower's hot water and steam further helped to relieve Stanley's headache. As he scrubbed, he looked around to see where they would go next, but the only other door he saw besides the one they'd just come in was one he was sure led outside where the temperature was near zero.

Yamamoto watched the others, and when everyone had finished rinsing off, he stood. "Gentlemen, shall we?" he said and waived his hand toward the door that Stanley thought led outside. "Paul, please follow me." They entered a magnificent Japanese garden with carefully pruned evergreens lining both sides of a narrow stone path. In the summertime, it would have been beautiful, but the blast of frigid air that blew past Yamamoto and washed over Stanley took his breath away. The pine clumps on the ends of the branches were capped with six to eight inches of snow. Although the night sky was dark, the snow reflected a small amount of ambient light. The gravel path crunched under their wooden sandals as the weight of their footsteps broke the ice that bound the stones together.

*You have got to be shitting me!* Stanley thought. His wet naked ass quivered from the cold. He scuttled down the path behind Yamamoto like a schoolboy would follow his headmaster. After about fifty yards or so the path forked. Yamamoto went left and Stanley dutifully followed him. It wasn't long before he realized that the others had taken the right fork. Stanley could hear the laughter and voices of women. While seven of his colleagues were about to end their day in the pleasures of the flesh, Paul Stanley was heading to . . . *What is this? School? Christ, I'm cold.*

The water steamed in the Hokkaido night air. Mother Nature had heated it to a perfect 106 degrees Fahrenheit, and it supposedly contained just the right mix of minerals to be both soothing and healing. Yamamoto slipped into the natural stone pool easily. Stanley took a more cautious approach, sitting on the pond's edge, his ass freezing, his legs, dangling in the water, on fire. As he eased his body off the ledge, it started to snow. Stanley stood waist deep in the hot water, his nether region burning like hell while everything above the waterline was freezing. Yamamoto smiled at him from across the pool. Only his head, a neatly folded washcloth draped over it, was visible above the water. "Paul, do you have the washcloth with you?"

"Yes," Stanley chattered, and held it up.

"Good, then wring it out, fold it and drape it over your head as I have. It will help to insulate your head and prevent heat loss. I suggest dipping it in the hot water every three or four minutes; otherwise, it might freeze up there."

Stanley did as instructed and immediately his shivering was reduced as he eased himself further down into the water.

"You did not enjoy your dinner?"

"It was very good."

"But you only picked at it. I watched. I suspect the events of today are bothering you. Am I right?"

Stanley had had enough of their decade long cat-and-mouse game. "Seito, let's get down to business. You killed a man this morning. You tell me I am to know what you are planning, but you give me only small pieces of information. You ask me to do things that I am not sure I can pull off. To be frank, I am tired of being kept in the dark. I know how much I owe you and your associates, but I think, by now, I have earned the right to know what you are planning."

Yamamoto nodded. "There is no question you have earned the right to know. We have teased you with information. We have been content to watch you try to fit the pieces together. It has all been a harsh test of your loyalty, and today was an unplanned but final test of that. So let me begin by telling you about The Association. More than thirty years ago we were all students together at the University of California-Berkeley. We were sent there by our respective governments because we were each considered among the best and brightest. In the beginning of our studies, our only common ground was that we were Asian, but as we got to know each other we found out we had much, much more in common. We held similar views on politics, government, right, wrong, freedom, and subservience. Then we discovered none of us cared very much for the way our governments ran our countries. We vowed that we would do something about it. We formulated our utopia and then we made a pact that each of us would aim our lives, our ambitions, at making it happen." He waved his hand in the direction the others had gone. "Our colleagues have all risen to great levels of influence in their governments. As for me, well, let's just say I have developed certain relationships here in Japan that will serve us well going forward. But together we have all kept our eye on that utopia we dreamed of thirty years ago as students. Soon all of our work will culminate in Operation Light Switch."

"Protecting that secret is why that young man had to die this morning?"

"It is exactly why!"

Stanley shook his head. "What is Operation Light Switch?"

"There will be coups in each of our countries. I suspect you already have discerned that. What you don't know is that they will occur at precisely the same time. Some may take longer than others to succeed, but after two, perhaps three days, we expect to completely control the government offices, key businesses, media centers, airports, and seaports in each of our countries."

The scope of this boggled Stanley's mind, but he managed to ask, "When will this happen?"

"That is something that I will not disclose to you except to say that we are very close. It is, I believe you would say, only disclosed to those who have a need to know. The deadlines we have asked of you are important. We need those sales to insure our ultimate success."

"OK, then, if you won't tell me when, then, at least, tell me why. What's in it for The Association?"

"What we are about to do will change the economic face of the entire world." Yamamoto gave this a moment to sink in. He could almost hear the wheels turning in Stanley's brain. "Pay careful attention, Paul. Once we have seized control of each of our countries we will form a coalition. One might call it The United States of Asia, and once we are in control we will cease all trade, all relations with countries that are outside of ours. We will only trade among ourselves. There will be no importing, exporting, no diplomatic relations, no trade agreements; nothing will exist between us and the rest of the world."

Stanley squatted in the hot water, trying to grasp the detail of what he'd just heard. *It's ludicrous,* he thought. When he found his voice, he said, "This is crazy. It can't possibly work. You will ruin these countries. Look at how much just Japan will give up in trade with the US alone. Where will you get your oil?"

"Those of us in The Association are very aware of what Japan and, perhaps, South Korea will give up. These countries will show the others what it means to sacrifice for the good of all. But before you say it won't work, consider that the natural resources you mention are in untapped reserves in our eight countries. Now consider why they are untapped. The terrain in some of our countries where vital minerals are located is hostile. The distances within and between our countries are great. Many currently lack sufficient industrial infrastructure. Perhaps most important, the lack of cooperation between governments, much of it based on petty cultural differences, keeps us from maximizing resources available in the region. This will end with our consolidation of power.

"We will recreate the equivalent of your American Revolution and your Industrial Revolution all at once. Only now we are at a greater level of technical proficiency than your country was at the turn of the last century. We don't have to discover the power of the steam engine. We have nuclear power. Our railroads can move at over 200 miles per hour. Our ships, which are many, move thousands of containers, millions of gallons of oil, relying on powerful engines rather than the wind. Computers can simulate any number of engineering functions that a hundred years ago had to be accomplished through trial and error. Our revolution, if it helps you think of it as that, will take five years to accomplish compared to the decades it took your country to change."

"You simplify the issue of petty cultural differences," Stanley retorted. There is out-and-out hatred among many of your countries that has been going on for decades, some for centuries. Your own country of Japan is, perhaps, the most hated. You can't possibly expect these various populations to simply swallow the pill you will feed them after Operation Light Switch."

"We are prepared to handle dissenters. Reeducation will be a choice."

"And for those who chose not to be reeducated?"

"They will be eliminated."

The matter-of-factness of it stunned him, though he should have been prepared based on what he witnessed that morning. Bluntly Stanley said, "That's not reeducation, that's genocide, Seito."

Yamamoto stared hard at him. "What you are thinking is what I would expect of an American. Your country has gone around the world on various crusades claiming your desire to see other countries become less savage. What would the world do without you being its conscience? But tell me, Paul, who was the watchdog for your American Indians during the peak of your country's Industrial Revolution? Who watched out for their interests as your pioneers moved west and discovered the Indians on the best farm land, on the best mineral deposits, or in the way of your railroads?"

Stanley had no answer.

"Your silence tells me you see my point."

Stanley thought he knew the answer, but he asked anyway. "So where does your power come from?"

"In every country except mine, we have created alliances within the military."

Disdainfully, Stanley muttered, "So you will turn the military loose to kill the people they are meant to protect."

"Once again, Paul, your American is showing. How dare you condemn us. How is what we are doing any different than your American-Indian Wars?"

Stanley didn't answer. Yamamoto was leading him in circles. It wasn't hard to do. Yamamoto and his band of brothers had had three decades to rationalize their actions. Stanley was hearing all of this for the first time. He asked, thinking he'd discovered some kind of Achilles' heel, "What about Japan? You can't pull this off without her." Stanley was probably as familiar with the Japanese self-defense forces as he was with any of the other countries' militaries. He knew that since the capitulation of the Japanese at the end of World War II, the world, led primarily by the US, had purposely kept Japan's military small and ill-equipped, never wanting to risk the chance of Japanese militarization again. "Japan's self-defense forces aren't capable. You will fail in Japan and without Japan, your plan has no chance to succeed."

Without hesitation, Yamamoto shot back, "You are right. The coup in Japan must succeed. You are also correct; Japan is unique. It is the only country in The Association where the government derives its power from purely economic forces. Government and business are closely tied to one another. Have you heard the term *Zaibatsu*, Paul?"

Stanley shook his head.

"It refers to Japan's most influential business leaders. It is an open secret that these men, fewer than thirty, control Japan's government. Thirty years ago, I tried to gain influence with some of them, but I had little to offer. My competition was American wealth that drew the *Zaibatsu* to the west." He shrugged his shoulders. "These men will regret turning their backs on me. There will be no place for any of them after Operation Light Switch. None of them will survive."

Stanley was getting used to their brutality, but not their logic. "You haven't answered my question. How will you take them down? You admit you have not infiltrated the Japanese defense forces. Who will be your enforcer in Japan?"

"The Yakuza."

Stunned, Stanley snorted, "The organized crime syndicate! You're going to turn your country over to organized crime? That's fucking nuts!"

"What do you know of them?"

"They're crooks. If it's illegal, they're into it. How can you . . .?"

Impatiently, Yamamoto raised his hand above the water's surface. "Again you judge too quickly. Make no mistake about it. Cato Fujiwara is a loyal commanding general and as ruthless to the cause as I am. His organization is our army. They are well disciplined, well dispersed, and well-armed. Remember, Paul, Japan's strict gun laws leave it as a nation unprotected. The police do not even carry lethal weapons. Fujiwara's organization is composed of small teams that will simply walk in and take over on the appointed day. Any resistance will be quickly and harshly dealt with."

It was all too crazy for Stanley. He shook his head and asked, "And the world's reaction to this? How will you deal with that?"

"We will likely be condemned in the court of world opinion, but words are ineffective weapons. If you see this differently, I would very much like to hear your view."

The place fell quiet. The wind came up and rustled through the pine boughs. Finally, Stanley resignedly said, "I don't know. A lot of companies will lose a lot when you close your markets.

It just doesn't make sense to me. Isn't there a lot of money to be made by broadening markets rather than closing yourself off to them?"

"Now, my friend, you have struck upon the very reason that dictates our decision to close our markets. You think we cannot survive without you. You think we need your multinational companies to come here and pay our children next to nothing to produce goods to supply your markets, where those same goods are sold at unconscionable margins of profit. Your western companies take these profits and invest next to nothing in Asia. When you find you can produce something cheaper somewhere else, you pack up and leave, you move on to greater and greater profits and leave the workers behind to wonder where their next meal will come from. Yes, your politicians and businessmen will cry foul, but their cries will fall on deaf ears. And, if, on the unexpected chance that your government should decide to invade, where might that take place? Your military is good, but it not nearly large enough for such an invasion. So you might create a coalition. We will already have ours formed and ready to oppose you on any front."

Stanley's headache had returned. The snow fell harder.

"There is one other important thing you must know and it is perhaps our best-kept secret."

The day's revelations had rendered him shell-shocked. Resignation evident in his voice, he replied, "And what is that, Seito?"

"Only the eight of us and now, you, Paul, know about our plan to consolidate power and isolate ourselves from the rest of the world following our revolutions."

"What?" This secret within a secret blew Stanley's mind. "How have you . . ." He struggled to organize his thoughts. Yamamoto remained silent. "You know there will be some who will resent this. They will revolt against your plan once they know."

"We have already talked about how dissenters will be handled." His matter-of-factness belied their ruthlessness. There was little else to be said. The night air bristled in silence.

"And me?"

"That is up to you, Paul. You have been instrumental to our cause. You will be welcome to live among us and, if you should choose to do that, you will likely be the only westerner. That may be awkward for you, and, if it is, I will apologize in advance. We will shield you as best we can, but it is very likely that your collaboration with us will be discovered. When it is, you will be branded as a traitor."

The word "traitor" stunned Stanley, but it didn't take long for him to grasp the gravity of what he'd become a part of. The wind had died down and in the not-too-far-off distance he could hear the laughs of their colleagues and their female companions. Finally, Stanley asked, even though he was fairly certain he knew the answer, "This morning you asked if I was prepared to cross a line. What would you have done if I had been unwilling to take that step?"

Yamamoto stood up and moved toward the edge of the pool. "Paul, as a military professional you surely recognize surprise is the essence of Operation Light Switch. You witnessed the measures we will take to preserve our advantage." Reaching the edge of the pool, he raised himself onto the ledge. He stood in the freezing night air and turned to look down at Stanley. His entire body was shrouded in a cloud of steam as the cold collided with the heat coming off his body. He looked supernatural. "Had you not crossed the line, Paul, there would have been two deaths here today." He headed for the adjacent pool. Over his shoulder, he said, "Come, there is someone over here who is looking forward to meeting you."

# 11

## HIGH IMPACT

"Here you are," Wanda said, walking up behind him in the kitchen as he stood stacking dishes into the dishwasher. "Officer Nunoz has a few questions."

Cleve dried his hands on a towel slung over his shoulder and turned to face them. Nunoz offered his hand. "That punk has been on our radar for a while now. Looks like tonight he finally got what he was asking for."

Wanda thought she detected some reluctance on Cleve's part, but watched the two men shake hands and then walked away.

The Blue Note closed early that night. Police cars parked for an hour or more in front of a bar tend to discourage business. Wanda was behind the bar when Cleve finally emerged from the kitchen. Nunoz had been gone for over an hour. Looking around at the empty room, Cleve said, "See you tomorrow."

"Whoa, whoa, whoa, there, hero, not so fast. Before you get out of here, you gotta tell me where you learned to fight like that." For Wanda, it was a purely innocent question borne out of curiosity. For Cleve, it was something he'd prefer not to discuss any more after having hashed through the details of his army career with the equally curious Officer Nunoz. "So, what can I get you? Want a beer? Something stronger?"

"Wanda, I'd rather not . . ."

Picking up on his reluctance, she said, "Well, OK. Cleve, I didn't mean to . . ." she paused. "Are you sure I can't get you something? We don't have to talk about it, but I'm going to have a drink. Nothing like that has ever happened in here since I've owned the place. I've dealt with drunks before, but they've always left on their own after I refused to serve them. This guy wasn't going to leave, and if you hadn't been here . . . well, I don't know what might have happened, but it would have been a lot worse than a little broken glass on the floor."

He looked at her and smiled.

"C'mon, Cleve, let me buy you a beer or something."

He liked her. "OK, how about a cup of coffee. I just shut the coffee maker down in the kitchen. It's still hot." He fetched a cup and when he returned to the bar area, Wanda was sitting at a table nursing a beer. He sat down. She smiled at him, but didn't say anything.

"The army . . ."

She looked at him. "Excuse me?"

"I learned that in the army. Hand-to-hand combat training. Never really had to use it until tonight. Works pretty well, doesn't it?"

She laughed and nodded.

Cleve knew what was going to happen, probably by tomorrow. He realized that it would be better if it came directly from him rather than the cops, so he began, "Wanda, remember the night

I started to work here, I wanted to tell you something, but you said you didn't need to know. You said you were a pretty good judge of character."

"Sure, I remember."

"Yeah, well, let me fill you in tonight, before the police do it tomorrow. No surprises, OK?"

Wanda nodded.

He told her everything about his time in the army, his court-martial and his imprisonment. He concluded, "So when I got out, I really had no other place to go except to come back home." It was getting late, but he saw she was crying.

"Cleve, I'm so sorry. I don't know what to say. It all seems so unfair. Your family. How devastating to them. Are you going to go see them? You have to, you know. They're waiting to see you."

Although he knew his mother had wanted to ask the *are you going to go see them* question, Ida hadn't. Wanda was the first. He'd been working on the answer. "As soon as I build up a little money in the bank, I'm going to Thailand. I don't know what will happen. I really don't have any expectations at this point, but you're right. I have to see them."

They sat in silence for a while and then Cleve said, "It's late. I'd better let you get on home. Tough night, huh?"

"Yeah. Let me drive you."

"No, it's OK, I don't live far."

"I insist." She got up and went to the back to gather her coat, boots, and gloves.

As they walked to her car, Cleve noticed the white Chevy Cavalier, the only other car parked on the nearly deserted street, a hundred or so yards behind Wanda's. As she drove off, he noticed the car's lights come on and as she dropped him off in front of Ida's house, he noticed the same car pull to the curb a few hundred yards behind them.

"Cleve, thanks. I don't know what I would have done if you hadn't been there tonight." She leaned over and kissed him on the cheek. "See you tomorrow."

The peck had surprised him, but he recovered nicely. "Same time, same place." He flashed her a smile and got out of the car, glancing down the street at the white Cavalier, still parked at the curb, its exhaust billowing into the night air.

Cleve unlocked the front door and entered, locking the door behind him, but instead of heading up the stairs to his room, he proceeded down the hall to the kitchen and exited through the back door. He trudged through the foot of snow on the ground in the small back yard until he reached the alley. After negotiating a mound of snow pushed to the side by a plow truck, he dashed down the alley for a couple of blocks before cutting back over to the street. As he rounded the corner, he could see the car, half of a block in front of him, still pulled to the curb, its engine still running.

Tetsu Agaki was reviewing his airline ticket for Orlando. He was to depart Cleveland at 10:00 a.m., about ten hours from now. Agaki did not see Cleve approach the car from the rear, but when Cleve tapped on the passenger-side window, he could see the instant recognition in Cleve's eyes.

*It's the Japanese guy from the Leavenworth bus station. What the hell?* Cleve tapped the window again, louder this time.

Agaki panicked. He floored the gas pedal and the four-cylinder engine suddenly screamed like two tomcats fighting in the early morning quiet. He struggled with the automatic gear selector and then remembered the safety feature that had confounded him several other times. Keeping one foot down on the gas pedal, he jammed the other against the brake pedal and snatched the car into gear. He pulled his foot off the brake and the little car leapt from the curb.

Instinctively, Cleve jumped back. He yelled, but Agaki couldn't hear him over the tinny scream of the car's engine. What happened next took only a split second.

VIC CELLES WAS finishing six hours behind the wheel of a Cleveland Metropolitan Transit Authority bus. He was tired, hungry, and ready for his day to end. The bus's sign board read, *Out of Service.* For a change, it wasn't snowing, the streets were clear, and, at this early hour, traffic was nonexistent. There was, in fact, only one other car in sight, parked along the curb with its engine running about a hundred yards in front of him. There was some guy on the sidewalk bent over as if talking to the driver of the car. Celles figured it was a drug sale. He remembered looking at the speedometer. He was cruising at about forty-five miles per hour, ten miles over the posted speed limit, when the car lurched from the curb and sprang directly into his path.

He jerked the wheel left and tromped the brakes, but the distance between him and the car was insufficient for his evasive action to work. The right front half of the bus impacted the Cavalier at about forty miles per hour, enough speed to carry the bus on top of the little car. Agaki never knew what hit him. As the driver's side door caved in, he was mercifully knocked unconscious and could not feel what happened next. The right front wheel of the bus rolled onto the car's roof and crushed the driver like squashing a bug. None of this took more than a second.

Celles, who, a few minutes earlier, had unfastened his seat belt to reach a bottle of water, was thrown forward, smashing his head on the windshield of the bus.

From his vantage point on the curb, Cleve could see the bus

driver draped unconscious over the steering wheel and dashboard. While he could not see Agaki, he could not imagine how he could have survived the terrible collision. He pushed the carnage in front of him out of his mind. *Get to the guy in the car. Move the bus. Get it off the car.*

The bus's front door was jammed closed. Quickly he rushed to the back door, but the hydraulic piston holding it in the closed position did not yield to his best efforts. Looking around for anything he could find, Cleve grabbed a piece of cement block and finished breaking out the front windshield, already shattered from the collision's impact. He climbed in over the crumpled bumper, pulled the driver from his seat, and laid him in the aisle. It was then that the crackle of the radio caught his attention. He keyed the switch on the side of the mike and said, "Anyone on this frequency, do you read me? Over."

"This is Cleveland Metro Dispatch. Who is this?"

"There's been an accident in the 900 block of Marcus Avenue. Two people hurt, including your driver. Please send an ambulance now. We need help. Do you copy? Over."

"Roger."

Thankful there was no further debate, Cleve set about getting the bus off of the little car. Once that was done, he pulled the door handle but only the rear door responded. He slammed the bus into park and raced back to the open door, jumped to the ground, and ran back to the crumpled heap that once was Agaki's car. "Damn," he spoke the oath to no one in particular; it was a one-word summation of a hopeless chance to save the life of the man he'd wanted to confront. Agaki's head and upper torso were visible through the opening that used to be the driver's-side window. His eyes were open, but unseeing. Cleve reckoned that his death had been nearly instantaneous. *Who is he?*

Cleve cleared the broken glass from around the window opening and reached in trying to feel something that might yield some identification. He found a billfold. It contained some US dollars, some Japanese yen, an American Express card, and an international driver's license. The name on the credit card and the license identified the man as Tetsu Agaki. The name meant nothing to Cleve. *OK, so why were you following me?*

It was then that he noticed a small, pocket-size notebook lying amidst the shards of broken glass on the seat next to the dead man. Cleve reached for it and began to thumb through the pages. Much of the information was written in hieroglyphic-like Japanese Kanji. But there were a few names recorded in English. There was a *Steve Armstrong* with a San Francisco address. A *Frank Brooks* lived in Los Angeles. Cleve could now begin to hear the sirens of approaching emergency vehicles. He thumbed quicker through the pages. There was a *Steve Cowper* from Honolulu. And then he found the name *Billy Driscoll* with the notation, *Windsor Hotel, Bangkok.* Cleve's eyes froze on that page. The name brought back stark memories of the courtroom at Fort Lewis, Washington. Driscoll had been a government witness and had testified that he had been the one who delivered the pallet of equipment to the airport at U-Tapao, Thailand. He certified to the court-martial board, as he had to Thai customs officers at U-Tapao, that the pallet contained only harmless personal military equipment, no weapons or dangerous cargo. Driscoll testified under oath that he had no idea how the contraband weapons and ammunition had gotten buried in the center of that pallet. Yes, he knew who Command Sergeant Major Cleveland Spires was. No, he had never met him, but he had been careful to add that he knew Spires had visited Okinawa. Driscoll's testimony placed Cleve at the First Special Forces Battalion headquarters at the time the murder weapon had disappeared from the arms room, and added that he thought the

command sergeant major was there when the security policeman had been killed on Kadena Air Base.

*What the hell?* The ambulance pulled up, its siren now silent
but its emergency lights lighting up the deserted street. Cleve
tucked the notebook in his hip pocket. Seconds later, a fire truck
and a police cruiser pulled in alongside the ambulance. For the
second time that evening, Cleve was talking to the police. He
explained to them that he was heading home from work and
witnessed the accident as the car suddenly pulled from the curb
directly into the path of the bus. He made a mental note that
he would need to square this lie with Wanda before the police
revisited her tomorrow, as he was sure they would.

# 12

## ARMS DEAL

**N**avy Captain Jay Chance stood in the doorway of his boss's office. "Welcome back, sir, but you ain't gonna like this." He held up a couple of pieces of paper in his right hand.

Paul Stanley smiled and said, "What you got, Jay?"

"The Vietnamese want another aviation package."

Stanley feigned complete surprise. "You can't be serious."

"As a heart attack, boss. They claim they expended most of the ammo training their pilots. Of course, all that flight time ate up most of their repair parts. Now that they are so well equipped and trained, they want more ammo and repair parts to keep things that way."

"What's the latest intel say on their scrap with China over the Spratly Islands?" Stanley knew what The Association had planned, but this was just a way that he could confirm that the intelligence agencies had no idea what was coming. One of the last briefings he'd just sat through on Hokkaido was from the

Chinese representative. There was oil under the Spratlys and The Association had great designs upon it.

"No change there. Vietnam, China, Malaysia, and the Philippines are all laying claim to them. None of them really give a dam about the islands. It's all about the oil, boss." Chance paused and then added, "China's navy has been more active in the area in the last five or six years. That's why Vietnam wants their air force trained up and ready to go. I dunno, it's the old argument: air power versus sea power. I personally think Vietnam doesn't stand a snowball's chance in hell if they get into a scrap with China, but if Vietnam thinks they are right . . . We sure learned how tenacious they can be, didn't we?"

Stanley shrugged, "I don't know the answer either, but Vietnam versus China does seem a bit like David versus Goliath," he said with a sly smile.

"Yes, sir. Here's a little wrinkle I'll bet you weren't expecting. I know it sure as hell caught me by surprise. Look at this." He stepped to the desk and laid the two pieces of paper down. "This is Vietnam's letter to us requesting another sale. Take a look down here." He pointed to the bottom of the second page. The letter was also sent to the CEOs of both BP and Exxon Mobil. "BP and Exxon both know that if China gets the Spratlys and there's oil there like everyone thinks there is, then China will keep the oil for themselves. Admiral McKeever had me in his office yesterday after he got a call from both of the CEOs asking him to approve the sale and move it on through Congress. Neither one wants to see the Chinese get their hands on that oil."

Stanley knew the point was moot once The Association launched their plan. No western oil company was going to get their hands on that oil. "Any idea what the boss is thinking at this point?"

"No, sir. He was pretty noncommittal yesterday when he called me to his office. He's also a little pissed off. He doesn't like being pushed around by these two oil companies." Chance smiled at Stanley, "Guess that's why you get the big bucks, boss. He said he wanted to see you about this as soon as you got back to the office."

"I'm assuming we've got the shit they are asking for?"

"I did a quick check yesterday on that because I knew you'd want to know before you go see the ol' man. Short answer is yes. The logistics challenge is that the stuff is strung out over a dozen or more depots. Collecting it and getting it ready for shipment will be a nightmare." Chance laughed, "More to the point, they want the stuff delivered in June, if you can fucking believe it."

He feigned surprise and asked, "Can we do it?"

"Won't be easy, boss, but the experts tell me it's worth the effort. Here's why. All this shit we're selling to them is obsolete and it's just taking up space in a warehouse somewhere. If we don't unload it, sooner or later we're going to have to dispose of it and that might cost more than the money we'll make selling it. I don't know, sir, but I think if it's pitched to Congress that way, they'll tell us to sell it rather than wait to have to spend the money to dispose of it. Just seems like good business to me."

*Perfect,* Stanley thought, but said, "Well, it wasn't easy the last time. That sale barely snuck through the Senate Armed Services Committee."

Chance thought for a second and then said, "Yeah, but this time there's a couple of big-time oil company CEOs behind it. If these guys turn their lobbyists loose in Washington . . ."

Stanley nodded, picked up the phone on his desk, and punched in the extension for Admiral Chet McKeever's executive officer. "Burt, it's Paul Stanley here. Got word the admiral wants to see me ASAP about selling some shit to the Vietnamese. What's his calendar look like today?"


IT WAS THE first week of March when the press got wind of another possible sale of obsolete weaponry to the Vietnamese, the second such sale in less than a year. Admiral McKeever was the guy the Department of Defense looked to for a recommendation and he advised the secretary of defense that the sale made good business sense. The press, however, politicized and moralized it. In editorials across the country, the Department of Defense came off as an arms dealer without a bit of moral or ethical conscience. The secretary of defense downplayed the ethical implication by trying to say that arming Vietnam helped to make China less of a military threat to the US. It was all Washington-speak, however, from a man under a lot of pressure from the oil lobby to "get on board" and keep the Spratly Islands out of the hands of the Chinese. BP and Exxon Mobil had even gone so far as to sign agreements with the Vietnamese government to develop the Spratly oil fields. If the yield was even half as good as the geologists were predicting, this deal would yield the oil companies and the Vietnamese government billions of dollars.

The secretary of defense took little time in passing the sale on to the Senate Armed Services Committee with the recommendation to approve it. Now it was up to them to give the thumbs up or thumbs down. The rules for foreign military sales and grants were different. If the committee approved the sale, it was a done deal. This was not something that the full Senate would vote on. If everything went by strict party lines, the Republicans on the committee, who were expected to favor the sale, held an eight-to-seven majority. A simple majority vote by the committee was all that was needed for approval. This would have, in fact been a done deal except that one Republican senator's conscience got in the way.

SENATOR ROBERT JOHN Boyett (R-New Mexico) was a decorated Vietnam War veteran and the newest member of the Senate Armed Services Committee. In 1968, as a young army captain, he'd called artillery in on his own company's position as a battalion of North Vietnamese army regulars were about to overrun them. In the ensuing chaos, the artillery barrage dispersed the numerically superior enemy. None of Boyett's soldiers were killed in the attack, though a few were wounded by the friendly fire including Boyett himself, suffering a serious injury to his right shoulder. To this day he was limited in what he could do with his right arm. For his courageous and life-saving decision he was awarded the Silver Star.

Boyette had not been a member of the Senate Armed Services Committee when it had approved the first sale to the Vietnamese. Now, however, he had just held a press conference and vowed that he would not vote for this second sale on ethical grounds. His "upset" vote was all over the news that evening.

PAUL STANLEY SAT in his home in Honolulu and watched the evening news with a sinking feeling in the pit of his stomach. He realized that without Boyett, the committee vote on the sale would fail by a margin of one vote. He'd done everything that he could do up to this point to push this sale through, but it was now out of his hands.

# 13

## LIE FOR ME

Ida Spires met Cleve as he unlocked the front door and stepped into the house. "My goodness, Cleveland, what is going on down there? Are you OK? Tell me you weren't involved." She was looking him up and down as if expecting to see some visible signs of harm.

"I'm just fine, Mom. But I was involved. I'm the one that called it in." He paused. Ida knew he had more to tell her. "How about we go in the kitchen and I'll put on a pot of coffee. I need to tell you some things."

He sat her down at the kitchen table. "The driver of that car was killed."

"Oh, my," murmured Ida.

"He was following me, Mom." She looked at him incredulously. "I saw this guy in line behind me when I bought my bus ticket in Leavenworth. I'm sure it's the same guy. He must have waited just long enough to find out where I was headed and then took off. Since I've been home, I've seen that car before on a couple of occasions, but didn't think much about it until tonight." He filled Ida in on the happenings earlier in the evening at the Blue Note. "So, when Wanda and I get in her car, I notice this guy follows us here to the house. After Wanda dropped me off, I came in the house and left through the back door. When I saw who it was in the car, I tapped on the window. He panicked and pulled in front of the bus. Poor bastard never had a chance."

Ida took a sip of her coffee. "So who is he, Cleveland?"

"Name's Agaki, Tetsu Agaki. He's apparently from Tokyo."

"Why is he following you?"

Cleve produced the notebook from his pocket and opened it to the page with Billy Driscoll's name on it. "I don't know, but I found this on him," and he pointed to Driscoll's name. "This guy, Billy Driscoll, was a witness in my court-martial. He's the one that delivered the pallet of equipment to the airport that had the contraband in it; the stuff that triggered the whole mess that sent me to prison. It looks like he's in Bangkok."

"What do you think it means?"

"Good question. I don't know, but I'd sure like to ask this Billy Driscoll some questions."

Ida hung her head and asked the question, "So, you are going to go . . .?"

He nodded and said, "I have to."

Tears were welling up in her eyes. "And so . . ."

"We both knew I was going to go at some point, didn't we?"

Crying now, she couldn't speak.

"But there's something else that I need your help with. I need you to lie for me, Mom." There was no more delicate way of putting it. "I told the cops that I was walking home from work tonight. I don't want them knowing I was out there trying to talk to this guy. I don't want them to know anything about this notebook," he held it up. "And I sure as hell don't want them to know anything about Billy Driscoll."

"But Cleveland . . ."

He shook his head. "Mom, trust me, the cops will twist all of this around and I will somehow be implicated in that guy's death. I don't need that again. You've got to cover for me so I can get to the bottom of this."

Lying was not something Ida took lightly, but this was her son, who'd been wrongly convicted once before. She was not going to let that happen again. "OK, Cleveland, I understand."

"Thanks, Mom. Now I need another favor."

"What is it, Son?"

"I'm going to call Wanda and ask her to lie for me as well. I know how this all works. The cops are going to be at her doorstep in the morning asking her if she knows the kind of man she has working for her. I've already told her about the court-martial and my time in prison, but she doesn't know what happened after she dropped me off here at home tonight. It might help if you could talk to her as well. I need someone to vouch for me. Would you do that?"

Ida nodded. "Give me just a minute to collect myself, Cleveland. Then call her."

# 14

## THE YAKUZA

Cato Fujiwara was not a patient man. He'd left two messages for Tetsu Agaki in less than twenty-four hours, and that was one more message and about twenty-three hours more than he had expected before a response. The two were old friends who had grown up together on the tough streets of post-war Tokyo. From petty thievery, they graduated to becoming vice kingpins, controlling most of Tokyo's gambling, prostitution and extortion. Then, about thirty years ago, Agaki had gotten caught with a kilo of heroin and sent to prison for fifteen years, while Fujiwara continued to grow his crime kingdom. Today, he ran organized crime throughout Japan. The Yakuza, Japan's Mafia, was a true enigma. On the surface, everything about it reeked of legitimacy, but the organization had an ugly under-belly, and there was no one in the organization more ruthless or revengeful than Cato Fujiwara.

In order to maintain his appearance of legitimacy, he avoided associating with the likes of Agaki, a convicted drug peddler.

But through the years he'd maintained a private friendship. Because Agaki had been a loyal soldier, keeping his mouth shut even when facing a long prison sentence, Fujiwara took care of his wife and two children when he was in prison and now tossed easy jobs his way, mostly surveillance work. Such was the case now as Fujiwara had a manager whom he suspected was skimming money off of the club he ran in Tokyo's glitzy Roppongi district. Fujiwara wanted Agaki to shadow the guy and report back. Impatiently he pushed the button on the phone and waited for his chief counsel to answer.

"Yes, Fujiwara-san." His chief counsel was young, well-educated, and ambitious, but what Fujiwara really liked about him was a ruthless streak he'd observed. The chief counsel had paid most of his way through the prestigious Tokyo University by gambling. A great head for numbers, he knew the odds of winning weren't in his favor, so he cheated. During his senior year, he'd cheated in a game at one of Fujiwara's clubs and gotten caught. He now owed the Yakuza, but Fujiwara cut him a deal of sorts. He'd won nearly one hundred thousand dollars before he'd been caught, and for this Fujiwara blamed the club's manager. Fujiwara had both men brought to a deserted warehouse where he told them that their debts were to be settled by a duel. He handed each of the men a pistol, put them back to back, told them to take five steps, turn and fire. The survivor would have all debts forgiven. Fujiwara himself counted the paces. "One . . . two . . ." The young college student turned and fired three shots into his opponent's back. The club manager slumped to his knees and then fell on his face, lifeless. Fujiwara gave the survivor his card and said, "This is my private number. Give it to anybody else and I will have you killed. Tell anyone about what happened here today and you will die. When you have graduated, call me." That was ten years ago. In that time, the young man had graduated, gone on to complete his law degree at Fujiwara's expense, and was now the chief legal counsel for the Yakuza. Fujiwara trusted few others as he did this man.

"Find Agaki. Have him call me. I have an urgent job for him."

The young attorney bit his tongue. He'd met Agaki. He knew who he was and he was aware of his boss's affinity for him, but he took very seriously the part of his job that required him to shield his boss from the likes of men like Agaki. He also knew that part of the price one pays for accessibility to power is to have to perform tasks that are below one's station. "Yes, sir."

When calls to half a dozen underlings who should have known where Agaki was hanging out these days produced no results, the chief counsel swallowed his pride and called Agaki's wife, whom he found a tearful, sobbing mess. "Tetsu is dead."

"What?" He feigned concern because he knew his boss would want details. "How is that possible? Just a month or so ago, I saw him. He looked well. He and Fujiwara-san dined together in his office."

Crying lengthened the time it took her to answer and tested his patience. "An auto accident."

This seemed odd to him. There were thousands of auto accidents daily in Tokyo, but seldom were any of them fatal. Tokyo traffic is so jammed up that seldom are fatal speeds reached and when fatal accidents occurred, they usually made the news. "Where and when?"

"I am not exactly sure if it was three or four days ago. He was in the United States following somebody."

"Who?" Again it was a question his boss would want to know.

"I don't know. They have told me he pulled in front of a bus."

With polite sympathy, he offered his condolences, ended the call, and headed for Fujiwara's office. "Fujiwara-san, Tetsu Agaki is dead."

Fujiwara hung his head. "How can that be? When? Where?"

"I spoke to his wife. She was notified by authorities in Cleveland, Ohio."

"Cleveland? In the United States? What the hell was he doing there?"

"She told me he was following someone. She did not know more than that."

Fujiwara, not even attempting to conceal his rage, slammed his fist down on the desk top so hard that the receiver fell from the phone. "I want to know who he was working for and I want to know who he was following. Find out. You have until tomorrow morning."

"Tomorrow? Fujiwara-san, I am working on . . ."

Again, the fist slammed the desktop. "You have nothing more important than this to work on. Find out and let me know by tomorrow morning."

# 15

## GUILTY UNTIL PROVEN INNOCENT

Cleve walked in the kitchen entrance at the back of the Blue Note at 4:00 p.m., greeted by Wanda's concerned look. "There's a detective out front. He's already questioned me. I went over what happened here last night, but that isn't what he wants to talk about, Cleve."

His shoulders drooped. "Let me guess. He wants to talk about what I was doing last night at the accident."

"I told him I didn't know anything about that, that you had left here about 11:30 last night and walked home. He knows all about the court-martial, the prison sentence. I don't like it, Cleve. He acts like you're guilty of something."

He shrugged, "Yeah. I've been here before. Innocent until proven guilty isn't the premise that the cops work on."

"What can I do?"

He smiled at her, "Nothing, Wanda. You've already done it. Thanks for covering for me about the walking home thing."

"You bet." It caught him by surprise when she leaned into him and gave him a hug. "Well, come on and I'll introduce you to Detective Bergstrom."

"I WANT TO ask you a few questions about the accident you witnessed last night." Cleve judged Bergstrom to be in his mid-thirties, certainly not older than forty. He was tall, fit, and no nonsense.

"OK, but I gave the officers last night as much as I know about it."

"Um, yeah. I've read their report. But I talked to the bus driver this morning."

"So he's OK?"

"Bad bump on the head. They kept him overnight at the hospital as part of a concussion protocol, but, yeah, he'll be OK."

"That's good."

"When I talked to him this morning, he told me he saw someone on the sidewalk, bent over as if they were talking to the car's driver. Was that you, Mr. Spires?"

Cleve was ready for this question. "I was on the sidewalk next to the car when all of a sudden the driver stomps the accelerator. In fact, it kind of scared me. I wasn't expecting it. I don't know, maybe he caught sight of me in the rearview mirror and it scared him. Then before I knew it, he pulled from the curb directly in front of that bus. I watched the bus roll on top of the car. The driver didn't have a chance of surviving the impact. The bus driver is lucky he wasn't thrown out of the bus. He wasn't wearing a seat belt."

"Mr. Spires, we recovered the deceased's cell phone."

Cleve responded with cautious puzzlement. "And . . ."

"And it seems that the deceased had placed several international phone calls to the Windsor Hotel in Bangkok, Thailand."

Cleve didn't like the direction the questions were going, but found this bit of information useful, "And . . ."

"Let's stop beating around the bush, shall we, Mr. Spires." You and I both know that you have a history in Thailand. Now we have a dead man that you may or may not have been talking to just before his death who was communicating with somebody there . . ."

Cleve interrupted, "I told you I was not talking to the guy in the car. I was simply alongside the car when it pulled . . ."

Bergstrom held up his hand, "So you've said. But you must admit it's all a bit curious, isn't it, Mr. Spires?"

"Look, Detective, I've told you everything I know about the accident. You are trying to piece things together to prove something, and I don't particularly like it."

"Your wife and son are in Thailand, aren't they, Mr. Spires?"

*Shit! How the hell does he know that?* "Umm, yes. What does that have to do with anything?"

"Are you planning on leaving town to go visit them anytime soon?"

*Where's he getting his information?* Cleve looked over at Wanda and immediately knew the answer. "I have no definite plans at this time."

"Good. Until I tell you differently, please don't leave town. The death of the car's driver remains an open investigation, and it is likely that I will have further questions, Mr. Spires." Bergstrom closed his notebook, placed it in his inside jacket pocket, and said, "Do you understand?"

Cleve nodded, but was pissed. The supercilious son of a bitch that was walking away from him reminded him of the Criminal Investigation Division agents that had arrested him a decade ago. They knew they had their man and they were going to prove it no matter what. He was also angry at Wanda for giving this bastard more ammunition than he should have had.

"CLEVE, I . . . I'm so sorry."

He didn't say anything to her. Shaking his head, he walked back in the kitchen, grabbed his apron, and went to work. The remainder of the evening he stayed as far away from her as possible, fearing that if he said anything at all, it would be rude and offensive. By evening's end, Wanda, herself, was getting angry. She'd been wrong to give Bergstrom such personal information about Cleve's family, but she'd only been trying to help. So after the front door was locked, she found him in the kitchen. "Are you ever going to talk to me again?"

"Why would you give him . . ."

"I know. I'm sorry. I don't have a lot of experience talking to police detectives. I was just trying to make the point that you are a good man . . ."

"Wanda, he doesn't think so. And as much as I hate to say it, it isn't his job to think I'm a *good man*. It's his job to investigate, and, guess what, yours truly is his prime suspect . . ." Cleve paused, his confusion apparent, "and I don't even know what the sonuvabitch thinks I did. But I know he isn't going to relent until he thinks he can prove something."

"OK, Cleve, I screwed up. I'm sorry. What can I do to make it up to you?"

He sensed her remorse was genuine and smiled at her. He could see the relief on her face. "Don't know any good lawyers, do you?" It was meant to be a joke.

She wanted to slap her forehead and mutter, *that's it, that's what I can do to help,* but she didn't. The fact was that she did know a lawyer, a very good one, that was both a family friend and her lawyer. He'd been her husband's college roommate and proven his friendship time and time again as her husband's will wound its way through Ohio's probate court system. Wanda decided that tomorrow she would give Lee Shaw a call and see what advice he might be able to offer.

# 16

## CATO FUJIWARA

The Yakuza's chief counsel had been up all night trying to determine who the hell Tetsu Agaki had been following in, of all places, Cleveland, Ohio, and who had hired him to do that. A dozen phone calls to well-placed colleagues in the organization had yielded nothing except one name, a friend of Agaki's, that might possibly know something. In the opinion of the chief counsel, the guy was a nobody, just like Tetsu Agaki. He'd never even heard of this guy until Fujiwara had sent him on this wild goose chase, but his name had come up in a couple of conversations. The difficulty was that no one he'd talked to knew for sure how to get in touch with this guy. One, however, had suggested a pachinko parlor in a particularly seedy part of Tokyo might be a good place to start.

In his college days, pachinko parlors had been the place where the chief counsel found his hookup to high stakes card games. On the surface, these places appeared as harmless as an arcade. In fact, there was no age limit for entrance, so many of them were occupied by bored Tokyo teenagers looking for a place to congregate. But every pachinko parlor had that guy in them. Find that guy and, for a fee, he could hook you up with anything and everything, most of it illegal and all of it illicit. Tonight, the chief counsel had shown up at this particular parlor in his thousand-dollar suit and tie, flashed a 5,000 yen note at the bouncer at the entrance and asked him for the name of that guy and to point him out. That guy told him the man he was looking for wasn't there, but had been earlier. He'd left with a woman, a whore. That guy, for 50,000 yen, not only gave him the address where she practiced the oldest profession, but took him there to boot.

In his time working for the Yakuza, he'd been in some pretty seedy places, but the hotel gave him the heebie-jeebies. The hallways were littered with all kinds of trash, including used condoms, drug paraphernalia, and discarded food boxes that now swarmed with all sorts of insects. He caught sight of several rats as he walked down the hallway to the room he was looking for. Knocking once, he got no answer. He knocked again harder. He tried the knob, but the door was locked. He reared back and kicked the flimsy door open with his right foot and, as he stepped into the dingy, little room, he pulled a pistol from a shoulder holster under his suit coat. He watched the man roll off the woman in the direction of a table next to the bed. He could see, in the low light, a pistol lying there. The woman was screaming her head off. Skillfully, he fired one round, the noise muffled by the best-that-money-could-buy silencer affixed to the pistol's muzzle. The screaming stopped. The next round hit the pistol, blowing it far out of the man's reach. "Another move and the next round goes through your head."

Both hands went in the air. "Who are you? What do you want?"

"You know Tetsu Agaki," the chief counsel said, not as if asking a question.

Scared and puzzled, the man answered with a nod.

"I want to know why he was in the United States and who hired him."

"I . . . I don't know . . ."

"You have one more chance to answer before you end up like her," and the chief counsel nudged the barrel of the pistol in the direction of the woman.

"OK . . . OK . . . he told me he'd been hired by an American soldier. His name is . . ." there was a pause while the man choked down his panic and tried to recall the name. "Tetsu said his name is Driscoll. This Driscoll was paying him a lot of money to follow somebody."

"Who? Who was he following?"

"I don't know. Tetsu never said who." There was a pause as he tried to dredge up more information stimulated by the muzzle of the gun pointed at his head. "All he told me was the man he was to follow was about to be released from prison." He raised his hands higher in the air and shrugged his shoulders, "That's all I know."

Blood splatter covered the wall. The bed was soaked in the woman's blood from the gaping hole in the back of her head. The chief counsel put the gun against the man's head and said, "The only reason I am not going to kill you right here and now is that I might need to speak to you again." Returning the pistol to its holster, he reached in his pocket and produced a roll of bills. Peeling off 100,000 yen, he said, "I will get this place cleaned up. Get dressed and get out of here. You and I never spoke. If you tell anyone about tonight, I will find you and kill you. Do you understand?"

The chief counsel thought it was comical to watch the naked

man bowing up and down like a robin pulling a worm out of the dirt. He kept repeating, "Hai . . . Hai . . . Hai, we never spoke. Yes, I understand. Thank you, sir. Hai . . . Hai . . . Hai."


IT WAS 8:00 a.m. by the time the lawyer made arrangements for the flop house to be sanitized. Back in his office at 8:30, he already had a message from his boss wanting to know what he'd found out. The urgency confounded him. Taking the time to shave, wash up, comb his hair, and don a fresh shirt and tie in the bathroom that adjoined his office, he felt somewhat refreshed as he headed down the corridor toward Fujiwara's office.

"You are late. I had expected an answer by the time I walked in."

The chief counsel was not used to this kind of surliness. "I apologize. It was not as easy a task as I . . ."

Impatiently Fujiwara waved his hand. "So what did you find out?"

"He was in the United States to follow a man, I don't know his name, but he apparently has just been released from prison. Driscoll is the name of the man who hired Agaki. I am told he is an American soldier."

Fujiwara lowered his head and shook it. "Dammit!"

"Do you know this Driscoll?"

Fujiwara did not answer. Instead he waved his hand dismissively toward the door. "You are not to mention this to anyone. I will handle the matter from here."

The matter perplexed the chief counsel. None of this amounted to a small hill of beans as far as he was concerned. He merely nodded at his boss, who had turned his back and was staring out the window of his penthouse office overlooking the vast surroundings of Tokyo.

"Close the door behind you."

"Of course, Fujiwara-san." The chief counsel left, hoping that he would never hear the name Tetsu Agaki again.

As the door closed, Fujiwara turned to the phone on his desk and punched in a number. In a few seconds a man answered, "Hello."

"It's Fujiwara . . ."

The voice on the other end took on a courteous, almost deferential tone. "Uh . . . yes . . . Fujiwara-san, how may I help you?"

"I need to know if and when a certain person might book an airline flight, most likely from Cleveland, Ohio, to Bangkok. Can you tell me if that happens?"

The man, a well-placed executive with Japan Air Lines, had done many favors for the Yakuza over the years, principally assisting in smuggling weapons and drugs into Japan.

"Yes, we can easily see that in our computers, Fujiwara-san. What is the traveler's name?"

"Cleveland Spires."

"I have it, Fujiwara-san. I will let you know if anyone by that name books passage."

"This must be done with the utmost discretion. You have my private number. Call that. Do not leave a message if I should not answer. Instead keep calling until we are able to talk in person. Is that clear?"

"Hai, Fujiwara-san, perfectly clear."

He disconnected and then punched in another number. Before the person on the other end could say anything, Fujiwara blurted, "Are you in Bangkok?"

"Hai, Fujiwara-san, I am."

"Good. You know Billy Driscoll?"

"He is one of our suppliers."

"I want you to personally watch his every move."

"Is there some sort of problem, Fujiwara-san?"

Fujiwara was in no mood to answer questions. "Just do as you are told, dammit!"

"Hai, Fujiwara-san. I am sorry. I did not mean to offend . . ." The line went dead.

Ten years ago, Fujiwara had toyed with the idea of eliminating Driscoll after he'd botched the smuggling operation from Thailand to Okinawa and killed the air force security policeman. Driscoll knew too much. If he'd been caught, he could have led the authorities all the way back to Fujiwara himself. But ten years ago, the same man he'd just directed to keep tabs on Driscoll had convinced him that Driscoll was reliable. Fujiwara had to admit that the way he'd framed Spires was masterful even though he didn't like the way Driscoll had done this without thinking of any possible ramifications had it gone wrong. But, now, here he was again, acting on his own. And this time he'd gotten Agaki, an old and dear friend, killed. His patience with Driscoll was exhausted.

# 17

## TRAMPLING ON RIGHTS

It had been almost a week since the confrontation in the bar and the accident that killed Tetsu Agaki. In that time, Cleve had not heard another word from the police and neither had Wanda. He entered the Blue Note through the kitchen door, put on an apron, and walked into the main dining room to find Wanda sitting at a table talking to a gentleman he did not recognize. As she motioned him over, he hoped it wasn't another cop.

"Cleve, I want you to meet Lee Shaw." The lawyer extended his hand. Cleve accepted the handshake, but must have had a skeptical look on his face, "Don't worry. He's an old friend of the family, not a cop. Sit down. Lee's a lawyer."

"Wanda, I can't . . ."

She stopped him. "This is free advice, Cleve. Lee agrees that at this point his services aren't required," the lawyer was nodding, "but he's prepared to help if we should need him."

Cleve looked over at the lawyer and then back to Wanda. "OK."

Shaw, noting a hint of apprehension in Cleve's voice, asked, "Do you have a passport?"

"No. I used a no-fee passport when I was in the army, but that's expired, and I couldn't use it anyway now that I'm a civilian."

"Have you applied yet?"

"I completed the application at the post office this morning."

"The detective you talked to, Wanda thought his name was Bergstrom. Is that right?"

"Yes."

"Ummm . . ."

Cleve thought that a rather ominous response.

"Bergstrom is a tough cookie. Wanda tells me he told you not to leave town."

"That's right, but that was a week ago. I haven't heard anything else from the police in that time." He looked at Wanda. "They haven't contacted you, have they?"

She shook her head, "No, not a word."

Shaw looked at Cleve. "Booked a flight yet?"

"No."

"Okay. When are you thinking about heading to Thailand?"

"Post office said that the passport would take a month if every-thing is in order, so I was looking about mid-March, sometime in that timeframe."

Shaw thought for a moment, "All right, Cleve, let's do an experiment. Sometime in the next several days, go ahead and book your flight. Let's see what happens. If the cops are watch-ing you, we'll know it shortly after that."


IDA ANSWERED THE knock on the door.

The man at the door produced a shield and said, "I'm Detective Bergstrom with the Cleveland police department. Is Cleveland Spires here?"

Ida was not normally judgmental, but she didn't like this man. She motioned for him to step in, turned, and called up the stairs, "Cleveland, there's a detective here to see you." She mumbled something under her breath and walked away from Bergstrom toward the kitchen, shaking her head.

Cleve descended the stairs. "How can I help you, Detective?"

"Mr. Spires, I thought I told you not to leave town." His tone was superior, intimidating.

Cleve wasn't intimidated. "You did, and the fact that we are standing here talking to one another should indicate to you that I haven't."

"You have applied for a passport?"

"Yes. Is that a problem?"

Bergstrom didn't answer the question, instead asking another, "You booked a flight from Cleveland to Bangkok, Thailand two days ago?"

"I did, but I don't fly until March 15."

"Yeah, well, just so you know, I've placed a hold on your passport request with the State Department."

Cleve glared at him, "You can't do that . . ."

"I not only can do that, I have."

Cleve could feel the anger rising, but he knew that was just what Bergstrom was hoping for. "Listen, you can't do this." Bergstrom was really getting to him. "I . . . I have an attorney."

"That's probably a wise move, Mr. Spires, but in the meantime, don't plan on leaving town anytime soon. We are still investigating the death of Tetsu Agaki and you continue to be a person of interest. So, stick around."

CATO FUJIWARA'S PRIVATE line rang. He looked up from the paperwork in front of him and answered it, "Hai."

"Fujiwara-san, Cleveland Spires has booked a flight on Delta Airlines flying from Cleveland, Ohio, through Chicago to Bangkok. He departs Cleveland on March 15 and arrives in Bangkok on March 17. I can give you the flight numbers if you'd like."

"No that isn't necessary. Thank you for letting me know. I will see that your courtesy is rewarded."

"Thank you, Fujiwara-san."

The line had no sooner disconnected than Fujiwara punched in another number. "Are you still in Bangkok?"

"Hai, Fujiwara-san." Hyate Inamine, the Yakuza's principal operative in Thailand, anticipated his boss's next question, "Billy Driscoll is still here as well. As you requested, I keep regular tabs on his whereabouts."

"Excellent. Do you have paper and pencil?" Fujiwara could hear him rustling around. "Listen carefully. This is what I want you to do. This is the precise order in which it is to happen. It can be no other way. I am counting on you. Do not fail."


CLEVE WAS STILL fuming from Detective Bergstrom's visit when he went to work that evening. He went straight to Wanda. "How much do you think Lee Shaw will charge to handle my case?" He explained to her what had transpired at his home earlier.

She could see the anger in his eyes. "Lee told me he suspected the police might be watching you. Computers . . . everything is so interconnected today. He's an old friend, Cleve, and he told me that any friend of mine is a friend of his. So, whatever it is, it won't be much. Take over here at the bar for me and I'll give him a call."

BERGSTROM WAS AT his desk working when Lee Shaw approached. "Detective Bergstrom, I'm Lee Shaw, and I'm Cleve Spires's attorney. I'm here to tell you . . ."

"*Tell* me . . ." Bergstrom disliked lawyers in general, but he particularly chaffed when one tried to tell him anything. "You don't tell me anything, mister. Now do you want to try that again?"

Shaw was unfazed. "No, I don't. I'm telling you that you have exactly 48 hours to either charge my client with whatever you are going to charge him with or lift the hold you have on his passport application. If you don't do one or the other, I will file an injunction with the district court, and we can fight this out in the courtroom and in the papers as well. You have no right to detain him like this, not after all of this time. It's been almost two weeks since that accident. It's time, Detective, to either shit or get off the pot, as the old saying goes."

Shaw walked away, leaving Bergstrom with smoke coming out of his ears, but he knew the attorney was right. He had thought Spires was bluffing when he said he had a lawyer. Obviously, he had one, and it looked like a pretty good one at that. Since Vic Celles's release from the hospital, Bergstrom had spoken twice to the bus driver. Each time his story had been the same. "This guy was bent down as if talking to the driver of that car. That's a tough part of town. I thought it was probably a drug deal. I don't know what they were talking about, but it sure looked like they were talking to one another."

Bergstrom could have simply given up. He'd already been told by the district attorney that there wasn't sufficient evidence to indict. Suspicion wasn't enough; he didn't want to be bothered unless there was a sure-fire charge. Bergstrom wasn't the kind of guy that would just cave in. There were too many things that didn't add up. Spires was an ex-con. He'd murdered a kid on Okinawa who'd botched a smuggling operation out of Thailand. If he believed Vic Celles, and he did, Spires was out there talking to Agaki just before he pulled in front of a bus. And Agaki had been talking to someone in Bangkok, Thailand just before his death. No, Spires was guilty of something, here. He just had to get a handle on exactly what that was.

# 18

## UNSAVORY

The Senate Armed Services Committee convened on March 15 amid a flurry of reporters and cameras. Senator Robert John Boyett literally attacked Admiral McKeever, the secretary of defense, and the CEOs of both BP and Exxon, all of whom had been called to testify, when it was his turn to ask questions. He was so aggressive that he had to be warned multiple times by the committee chair that this was a hearing, not a trial. The fact of the matter was that he really didn't need to be so tough. He was the swing vote, and his vote would kill this ridiculous sale to Vietnam. Boyett, however, wanted to make a moral point. What propelled him was the absolute conviction that the United States should not fuel conflict anywhere in the world by peddling its obsolete arms and munitions to third world countries, or any country for that matter. What Boyett did not know is that there were some dark forces at work against him.

SENATOR WILLIAM MATUCH (D-New Hampshire) was a married man with three children between the ages of thirteen and twenty. His wife detested Washington, D.C., so she stayed at home and maintained their residence in Manchester. He was serving his second term in Congress, but was facing some tough opposition for reelection from within his own party. Representing a very left-leaning district, his Democratic opponent was having some success in arguing that Matuch was way too chummy with the Republican opposition. His no vote on this arms sale, he thought, would serve as proof that his Democratic opponent had it wrong. It would prove that Matuch was a strong liberal voice in the Senate.

As he pulled from the Senate parking garage, he couldn't help but notice her. Quite attractive and stylishly dressed, he surmised she was likely some staffer from right here on Capital Hill. He was tired. The hearings earlier in the day had sapped him, but he couldn't just ignore her as she attempted to flag him down. The night was cool and a light rain had just begun to fall. He pulled to a stop, lowered the passenger side window, and said, "Need help?"

"I've locked my key inside. I feel so stupid . . ."

"Hey, we've all done it. Do you have a roadside service?"

Sheepishly she smiled at him. "No. I declined that coverage on my insurance. Bad idea, huh?"

He felt sorry for her, but didn't know what he could do to help.

Plaintively she said, "Listen, I don't live very far from here. Do you think you could give me a ride home? I have a spare key there."

He unlocked the doors. "Sure. Get in. Happy to do it." They introduced themselves to one another. As soon as he told her he was a US senator, she became quite deferential and apologetic. "Senator . . ."

"Bill . . . call me Bill, please."

"Uh, OK, Bill, I am so sorry to be bothering you like this, but I . . ."

"Nonsense. It's really no bother. In fact, it's a nice diversion to a rather long day."

The trip to her apartment took fifteen minutes. They seemed to hit it off. When he pulled to the curb in front of her building, he offered, "I'll wait here for you. Go get the key and I'll take you back to your car."

"No, you don't have to do that. I'll call a taxi . . ."

"Karen, I insist. It's no big deal. It would be my pleasure."

"Well, OK. If you're sure." She paused before getting out. "Listen, Bill, the least I can do is make you a drink. I'm not exactly sure where that damned key is, so it may take me a few minutes to find it. Come in and let me fix you a drink. Small payment for the inconvenience I've caused you."

"No . . ."

"I insist," she interrupted and flashed him a smile.

THE NEXT DAY, the day before the committee vote on the Vietnam arms sale, was a beautiful spring day. He didn't have any appointments until 2:00 p.m., so Matuch decided that he'd take his brown-bag lunch to the Capitol steps and enjoy the sunshine. As he sat down, a man approached, handed him a large manila envelope marked, SENATOR WILLIAM MATUCH— EYES ONLY. "What's this?"

Without a word the man scuttled off.

"Hey, wait. What the hell is this?" The man didn't look back, kept moving, and was soon lost in the crowd on the sidewalk below the steps.

Matuch opened the envelope, even though he'd been warned

about doing that with unscreened mail. His curiosity was aroused. Inside he found a dozen pictures, each one a pornographic portrait of what he and Karen had done the evening before in her apartment. There was also a note:

*Senator Matuch,*
*These are only a sample of the pictures we have. Everything will be destroyed if you will either abstain or vote in favor of the arms sale to Vietnam. If, however, you vote against the sale, these will be provided to every major news outlet and to your wife.*

A hollow feeling welled up in the pit of his stomach. He reached for his cell phone and called Karen. The hollow feeling deepened as the voice on the other end said, *Your call cannot be completed as dialed. Please check your listing and call again.* He tried the number again, with the same result.

He got up, threw his half-eaten lunch in the trash, returned to his office, told his secretary that he wasn't feeling well, and directed her to cancel all appointments for the remainder of the day.

ON THE SAME day Matuch's extortion was unfolding, another senator on the Armed Services Committee was having his own difficulties.

Tommy Chan, the son of a Chinese immigrant, was a graduate of Georgetown University's prestigious law school. He'd made a fortune representing interests of the Yakuza in the United States, but not always in the formal setting of a court room. He smiled broadly as he held the cell phone to his ear. "We have him exactly where we want him, Fujiwara-san. I understand there is no limit, but I think half a million dollars will be sufficient. I will contact the senator immediately."

*There is no limit* was exactly the root of the problem for Senator Theodore Truax (D-Michigan). Playing in no-limit poker games, he'd amassed about a quarter million dollars in markers that some rather unsavory characters were now calling due.

Chan had been his hook-up for these games, but a week or so ago, Chan had delivered an ultimatum, "Pay what you owe Ted, or I can't be responsible for what might happen to you. If you don't pay . . . well, these are not nice people."

Truax had the money, but he also had two sons, twins, both in their second year at the University of Michigan. The money was in their college fund. His wife kept careful track of it. He'd never be able to explain a withdrawal of that size.

Sitting behind his desk in his office, he pondered his options, none of which were very appealing. His cell phone was turned down, but he could feel it vibrating in his pocket. Looking at the caller ID, he didn't want to answer, but knew he couldn't dodge the caller much longer.

"Ted, it's Tommy."

Truax felt a sense of panic begin to overtake him, but managed to stammer out, "Uh, yeah . . . uh, Tommy . . . listen, I know . . ."

"No, Ted, you listen. I'm getting calls about you. They say you haven't paid. This is not good. You said you had the money. So why haven't you paid?"

"I . . . I just need a little more time . . ."

"Ted, I'm afraid that is something that you do not have. They want their money now." He gave that a moment to sink in. "Listen, meet me for a drink at DeLonegan's in Georgetown. Do you know where it is?" There was a long pause. Chan thought he'd either dropped the call or Truax had disconnected. "Ted, you there?"

"Uh, yeah, uh, I know the place."

"Meet me there in half an hour."

From a vantage point across the street from DeLonegan's, Chan watched him walk in the front door. He walked across the street, entered and found the senator at the bar. That would not be sufficiently private for the conversation Chan was about to have with him. He tapped him on the shoulder. "Grab your drink and let's sit back here." He pointed to a table in a dark corner of the bar. Once they'd settled in, Chan laid it out for him. "Ted, you are in some real trouble here. These people will hurt you and I'm not just talking about politically. They will *hurt* you."

"I know, Tommy, but . . ."

"There are no *buts,* my friend. The vig last week was almost twenty-five thousand dollars." He paused again for effect. "I have been authorized to make you an offer and given your current circumstances, I think it is one you can't refuse."

"What is it?"

"I have some friends, who prefer to remain nameless, but they are prepared to give you five hundred thousand dollars. By my calculation that would allow you to liquidate your gambling debt and have some left over for yourself."

Truax was desperate, but he was no fool. "What do I have to do for that kind of money?"

"It's pretty simple, Ted, if you ask me. All you have to do is vote yes or abstain tomorrow on the Vietnam aviation package."

"I can't . . ."

Chan shrugged. "What other choice do you have, my friend?"

Truax looked at him and nearly vomited.

The smile on Chan's face was insidious.

Angrily, Truax said, "You set me up for this, didn't you?"

"At this point, what does it matter, Ted? You have a way out.

The money will be deposited in an offshore account with your name on it as soon as you cast the right vote. Cast the wrong vote and . . . well, you want to see those two boys of yours graduate from college, don't you?"


MATUCH'S ABSTENTION CAUSED a ruckus within the hearing room, but when Truax abstained as well, the surprised reaction spilled out into the antechamber and, then, into the hallways of the Capitol Building. *C-SPAN* cameras caught all of it. Senators Matuch and Truax hurried out the back door of the hearing room, leaving their staffers to answer the questions of their colleagues and the press. Senator Boyett sat in his seat for the longest period of time, trying to comprehend what had just happened. For him it was the most stunning political upset he'd ever encountered.


PAUL STANLEY WAS behind his desk when Jay Chance came in his office and announced, "Boss, you ain't going to friggin' believe this. The Vietnam sale made it through."

"What?" Stanley said in disbelief. "How in the hell . . .?"

"Matuch and Truax abstained. Can you believe it? Vote passed, seven yeas, six nays, two abstentions. I caught it on *C-SPAN*. I thought the Republican committee chair was going to shit his pants. He didn't know whether to go kiss Matuch and Truax or scold them."

A broad smile covered Stanley's face, "OK, Jay, let's get this shit moving then."


STANLEY HAD NO idea how, but he could see the fingerprints

of The Association all over this. At home that night, he sat down and composed a letter to Seito Yamamoto, who'd given him an address in Tokyo and told him to write when he'd made a decision about where he might want to live in the aftermath of Operation Light Switch.

When he'd finished, Stanley held the letter in one hand and tapped it on the other. He had until October first to retire and, though he had no idea when Operation Light Switch was going to happen, he was curious to see the US reaction. *Don't be too hasty.* He laid the letter aside, and would not mail it until April first, from the post office in Pearl City, Hawaii, on his way to work.

SENATOR BOYETT WAS on record as promising to resign if this sale of arms to Vietnam was approved. He made good on his promise. Returning to private law practice in New Mexico, he tried to investigate Senators Matuch and Truax, but when both of them failed to be reelected, it became harder and harder for him to uncover any details about them. As senators they were public figures. As private citizens, scoundrels though they might be, they merely faded into oblivion. News outlets moved on to more current stories. Boyett's voice faded to silence. Washington moved on.

# 19

## DÉJÀ VU

The flight from Chicago to Japan took an excruciating thirteen hours stuffed into coach-class aboard a fully loaded Boeing 787. As the mammoth jetliner touched down at Narita, Cleve was welcoming the four-hour layover for his flight to Bangkok. It would give him a chance to stretch his legs and maybe find a more comfortable spot to catch a few winks. The terminal, however, was packed solid with travelers from all over the world. He bought a bowl of noodles and stood at the counter to eat. He walked a little bit, but airport security restrictions limited how much of that he could do. Though it felt good to escape the confinement of the aircraft, after an hour he was ready to get on with the rest of his trip.

By the time he arrived in Bangkok at noon on March 18, he was feeling the effects of traveling across multiple time zones, one of which was the international dateline. Climbing into a cab outside Don Muang Airport's international terminal, he had his first chance in a long time to use his Thai language skills. He negotiated a fair rate for the ride when he noticed the cab was unmetered. He was familiar with the route, having made the trip many times when he was in the army. But what had changed was the intensity of Bangkok's traffic. The trip was like a roller coaster ride. The cab's driver would find an open spot in traffic and speed up to sixty or seventy miles per hour, but only for a minute or two and then they'd find themselves in the middle of an unexplainable snarl of cars, buses, and noisy, smoky tuk-tuks. They'd crawl through this jumble for fifteen or twenty minutes and then blast ahead for a minute or two more. The trip, covering a distance of less than twenty miles, took over two hours in a cab, which, the driver had explained to him after they'd left the airport, "has a touchy air conditioner." It had conked out in the middle of their first traffic snarl.

He was tired, sweaty, and not in a good mood as he stood in the lobby of the Windsor Hotel and surveyed things. He remembered what Driscoll looked like, but that memory was ten years old. He wasn't sure he'd remember him now. At the desk, he asked if Driscoll was staying there. The man at the desk advised him that it was against hotel policy to provide that information. Spires walked away and tried a different approach. He found a house phone, picked it up and asked to be connected to Billy Driscoll's room. The operator promptly connected him, but there was no answer. He could wait. That was one option. But as he looked out the hotel's front doors, he saw the line-up of cabs that were constantly waiting on fares at the doors of most of Bangkok's larger hotels. He suspected one of them might be able to help him find Driscoll.

THE JAPAN AIR Lines executive dialed the number and waited

for him to answer. "Fujiwara-san, Spires has cleared immigration and customs in Bangkok."

"Thank you." Fujiwara disconnected and punched in another number. It rang only once before it was answered. "He has arrived in Bangkok. Do you have Driscoll in sight?"

"Yes, Fujiwara-san. We have been tracking him for the last twenty-four hours as you have directed."

"We? Your colleague is with you?"

"Yes, Fujiwara-san."

"And he knows exactly what is expected?"

"Yes, Fujiwara-san."

"Good. Then I will expect a call from you when it is done."

"Hai."


THE FIRST THREE cab drivers Cleve spoke with outside the Windsor Hotel indicated that they did not know Driscoll. Two of them acted fidgety when he asked. Cleve thought they probably knew him, but they didn't know Cleve, and they weren't going to cross Driscoll. He was about to return to the lobby and just wait, when another cab driver approached him. "You look for Beelee?"

Cleve, speaking in Thai, confirmed that he was.

The driver pointed back and forth between them, "We speak English. I no want other drivers to understand. OK?"

Cleve nodded, "OK."

"Beelee is your friend?"

Cleve hesitated and then said, "An acquaintance. One that I have not seen in some time. I'd like to surprise him. Do you know where he is?"

"No. But I take you someplace. If he not there, you wait. He come every night. Others," he pointed to the line of cabs, "no help you. They afraid. Beelee bad man. How much you pay?"

"How much do you charge?"

The driver thought for a minute. "You pay US dollar?

"If that is what you'd like."

"One hundred US, I will take you to place he be . . . for sure." He flashed Cleve a toothless grin.

"How far away is this place?

"Not far, but it take time to get there." He shrugged his shoulders "You know how fucked up traffic is in Bangkok."

Cleve laughed, acknowledged the fact, and got in the back seat. The fare was exorbitant, but he knew it was more for what the driver knew than about the distance they had to cover.

Forty minutes later he pulled to a stop at an intersection, pointed down an adjacent street and said, "This place, Soi Cowboy. Down there," he said, pointing down the narrow street, "Club Exotica. Beelee might be there now, but if not, ask one of the girls, they will tell you when he comes."

Cleve could see the garish neon sign, nodded, and gave the driver a crisp one-hundred-dollar bill. "Thanks."

THE ASSASSIN WAS an Amerasian man, a boy really, only sixteen. He'd come to Bangkok from Chunburri, a city about sixty kilometers south, because there was more opportunity in Bangkok for someone like him. His Thai mother died of AIDS when he was thirteen. His father, a westerner, had no idea the boy existed. His mixed blood made him an outcast in Thailand, but the hardscrabble life he'd led since birth made him a survivor. He'd found something he could do after coming to Bangkok; kill people, and he'd made good money at it. His victim tonight was his twenty-fifth contract. He could sense that the time for the kill was getting close. As he sat at the bar he reached behind him and felt for the 9 mm pistol he had tucked in the waistband of his jeans.

CLEVE FELT A little light-headed as he stepped through the open door of Club Exotica. It was the pure adrenaline rush he'd experienced plenty of times in combat. It would subside. He took a deep breath and that helped.

The only lights in the place were over a stage that sat in the middle of the circular bar. On stage a half-dozen naked dancers gyrated to an American country-western tune. The music was cranked up to headache level and the place smelled of stale beer and smoke. Cleve's eyes were still adjusting as he took a few steps further in. Two customers sat at the bar. Girls, topless, in bikini bottoms sat in groups of three or four at tables along a wall behind the bar. To his left, along the wall that ran parallel to the street, were booths, and there, sitting in one of them, not twenty feet away from him, was Billy Driscoll.

In the booth closest to the door, Hayate Inamine, the man Fujiwara had tasked with pulling off this murder saw Cleve walk in. He reached over and fondled one of the two girls sitting with him. She giggled and nuzzled his neck while her hand reached for his groin. The plan, was coming together perfectly. He braced himself for what was to come next, while the girl continued to play.

The assassin, who had fixed on Cleve from the moment he walked in, waited. Timing was important. Cleve began to move toward Driscoll and when he had closed about half the distance between them, the assassin made his move. Standing up from the bar stool, he lithely pulled the gun from behind him, took two or three steps toward his target, aimed the pistol and fired three quick shots. The first two bullets, though they hit the target, probably wouldn't have been lethal. It was the third one, however, that sealed Driscoll's fate. That bullet entered his neck traveling on a downward trajectory, severing his spinal cord and tearing out the right side of his heart before exiting through his groin.

Club Exotica was thrown into utter chaos. The assassin fled out the back door and faded into the back alley. Fujiwara's man got up from his booth and, smiling, left the bar looking for a policeman.

Cleve's ears rang from the gunshots and he was briefly paralyzed by the completely unexpected chain of events that had just unfolded in front of him. Driscoll was slumped over the table. Cleve grabbed him by the shoulders, pulled him from the booth, and laid him on the floor. Blood was everywhere, but he was able to detect a faint pulse. Driscoll's eyes were open and he was gasping for air and mouthing something. Cleve had seen soldiers fighting off death before, but he also knew when the battle was about to be lost. This was Driscoll's last battle, but maybe before the final breath was gone, he could get the truth out of him. "Driscoll, you sonuvabitch, do you know who I am?"

There was no answer. His eyes were open, but Cleve suspected he couldn't see. He hoped he could hear, maybe even talk, but there was a lot of blood pouring out onto the bar's floor.

"Driscoll, it's Cleve Spires."

No reaction.

Then it came. Driscoll's last-gasp effort to communicate with a world he was about to leave. Cleve put his ear close to his mouth and heard faintly, but clearly, "Fujiwara" and then, "Yakuza." He kept his ear close, hoping for more, but that was it. Driscoll was dead.

The name Fujiwara meant nothing to Cleve, but he knew from

his time in the Far East about the Yakuza. Remembering his luck with Agaki, he searched Driscoll's body. In a pocket of his pants Cleve found a roll of bills, US dollars.

As he stood up, a bottle crashed over his left shoulder. It hurt, but clearly it had missed its mark. He wheeled around into the screaming madam who controlled the prostitution end of the bar's business. In her best English, she was screaming at him,

"You kill Beelee! You kill Beelee!"

Cleve responded in Thai, "I didn't do this."

She looked at the roll of dollars in his hand and screamed at him, "You kill Beelee!"

Cleve headed for the door he'd come in, not sure what he should do next. He didn't like the way this was shaping up. As he stepped outside, he saw a policeman walking with another man toward Club Exotica. As soon as they saw Cleve, they broke into a run. Inamine shouted in Thai, "There he is! That's the man!"

Cleve saw it all clearly now. It was happening to him all over again. He turned, reentered Club Exotica, and dashed out the back door. He headed down the alley looking for the darkest cranny he could find. He could hear them behind him, shouting and running, but he couldn't see them. Fifty meters further down the alley, he found what he was looking for: a small passageway between two buildings, not two feet wide. It was pitch black as he felt his way along. He thought he'd gone about fifty feet when he hit a wall blocking his way. Essentially, he was trapped now. If they randomly happened to check down here, they would have him. He breathed a sigh of relief when he saw them run past the opening. The Thai cop was on the radio calling for reinforcements. Cleve knew he had to get as far away from there as he could. He waited for their voices and footsteps to fade, and then he headed in the opposite direction from them, avoiding Soi Cowboy and then retraced the route the taxi driver had used. As he walked along Sukumvit Road on his way back to the Windsor Hotel, he became aware of the roll of bills still grasped in his hand. *Great! Now they can add robbery to the list of charges! What have you gotten yourself into?*

Sukumvit Road was a busy thoroughfare and the sidewalk was lined on one side with shops and on the other side with carts of all different sizes selling all kinds of wares. He slowed his pace and stayed on the sidewalk between the shops and the carts trying to blend in as best he could as a tall, black man amongst throngs of smaller, more light-skinned Thais.

*OK. Think! Think! What are your options? Go to the airport. Get on a plane back to the US.* He quickly dropped this idea. Driscoll was a US citizen, a soldier no less. *I can be tried in the US for his murder. C'mon, Cleve, think!*

A police car passed him with lights flashing and sirens blaring. *Think about this now. They knew I was coming here tonight. This whole thing is a set up. How did they know? Why hit Driscoll? Whoever this guy Fujiwara is, he must have the answers. If I can get to Fujiwara, maybe I can get myself out of this fix. Get to the airport. Get to Japan. If he's Yakuza, that's where he'll be.*

AT CLUB EXOTICA, the madam was spilling her guts to the police about what she'd seen. The one hundred US dollars Inamine had given her earlier that night was tucked neatly away in her bra. It didn't really matter that it wasn't the black American that had killed Beelee. She would sing any song that he wanted for that kind of money.

Inamine, however, was more than a little distressed that these bumbling jackboots had not yet taken Cleve into custody. He had been right there under their noses and, somehow, they'd let him slip through their fingers. He pulled the detective aside who'd just arrived at the crime scene and discreetly slipped him a ten-thousand baht note. "Catch this guy tonight and there will be fifty-thousand more for you." The incentive started a flurry of frantic radio calls, one of which ordered that the airports be blanketed with cops looking for a black man, American, according to witnesses, about six feet, three inches tall.

AT THE WINDSOR Hotel, Cleve found the driver that had taken him to Club Exotica. "I need you to get me to the airport . . . fast. Can do?"

Two hours later, the driver pulled his taxi onto the ramp leading to the departing passenger's unloading zone at Don Muang International Airport. Halfway up the ramp, the cab driver was forced to pull to the curb by a police car approaching from the rear. Cleve slouched down in the rear seat and breathed a sigh of relief as it whizzed past them.

"Something happening," the driver said, looking in the rearview mirror at Cleve.

By the time they got to the area where departing passengers could be dropped off, there were at least a dozen police cars pulled haphazardly to the curb. Through the open window, Cleve could hear them shouting back and forth to one another. They were organizing themselves to search arriving vehicles and the airport. The driver had noticed that Cleve was slouching low in the backseat and put two and two together. "They look for you?"

Cleve caught the driver's eyes in the rearview mirror, "I know what you are thinking, but it's a big mistake. I'll pay you one hundred dollars if you get me out of here." He held up the roll of money to prove that he had the cash. "That's more than any of these cops will give you."

"Two hundred?"

Cleve was in no position to barter. "OK."

"Lay down on the backseat. You trust me. If they see you, it be bad for both of us."

As the driver began to move away from the curb lane into the faster-moving outside lane, a passenger on the sidewalk, not seeing a fare in the cab, motioned for him to pull over. A cop standing next to the man was baffled by the driver's lack of response. Suspecting something, he motioned for the cab to pull over, but was apparently diverted by a call on his radio. He motioned for the cab to proceed and then ran in the opposite direction. "That was close," the cab driver muttered.

"What was?"

"Nothing," he said. "It's OK. Trust me."

What choice did Cleve have at this point? When they were clear of the airport, he sat up on the backseat. "What's your name?"

"Tradip."

"Well, Tradip, how much to take me to the village of Chuk Ra Met?"

"Where is it?"

"Just north of Korat, maybe ten kilometers."

Looking at Cleve in the rearview mirror, the driver said, "Korat is maybe two or three hundred kilometers away. That is long way."

"I know. I'll make it worth your while, Tradip."

The cab driver knew he had the money. He was actually beginning to like this American who spoke his language better than any American he'd ever encountered, except for maybe Beelee Driscoll. But business is business. "You know my risk is great. If we are caught, we will both go to jail. Do you know what a Thai jail is like? I will need five hundred dollars."

Cleve thought for a moment and then said, "I will give you six hundred dollars if you can have me there by the morning."

FOUR HOURS AFTER Driscoll's assassination, it was painfully obvious to Fujiwara's man in Bangkok that Spires was, for the moment, at least, in the wind. It was also obvious from the harsh voicemails and missed calls from Fujiwara that a report was overdue. The phone on Fujiwara's desk rang once before he answered it.

"Why have you not called?" The voice was perturbed, caustic.

"Fujiwara-san, I am sorry to report the task is only half completed. Driscoll is dead, but Spires has not yet been caught."

"Then you have failed."

"That is so, but only for the moment. The police have launched a thorough search. I guarantee he will be captured by this time tomorrow."

"I know you guarantee it," came the cold reply. "You guarantee it with your life." The connection went dead.

# 20

## NO HONOR AMONG THIEVES

The driver swung the black Mercedes into the driveway, pulled to a stop, and punched a code into the security box. The gates swung open and he proceeded to the estate's main entrance. Standing at the door, Seito Yamamoto stepped forward, and the two men bowed deeply in the traditional Japanese fashion. "Your people did a superb job in Washington. Thank you, Cato." Yamamoto hadn't wanted to ask for Fujiwara's help in turning those two senators, but when Boyett became such a resistant force against the sale to Vietnam, he had no choice except to seek his assistance.

Stepping aside, Yamamoto motioned him inside the house, where they were met by Fukora, Yamamoto's manservant, who took Fujiwara's coat and hurried off to gather up a tea service. Fujiwara sat down while Yamamoto retrieved a bag from a nearby table. "I believe you will find this to be sufficient."

Fujiwara did not open the bag, and replied, "I am sure you have been most generous, my friend. I hope this sale of US arms to Vietnam is as important as you have told me. I understand that Japan can use the oil from the South China Sea, but I am not sure Vietnam can persevere against China's armed forces. And even if they do, I am not sure they will sell us the oil any cheaper than China."

"It is a bit of a risk," Yamamoto responded, glad that Fujiwara did not seem to want to pursue his interest in this sale to Vietnam any further.

"So, our success in Washington makes me ask, do you have a date for me?"

Yamamoto smiled but did not answer

The lack of response rankled Fujiwara, who, in his own opinion, had been more than patient with Yamamoto. "Seito, we have spent the last six months identifying targets, planning who will hit them, how they will be hit, but you must know that I will need time to communicate all of this to my men."

Fujiwara's growing impatience was a concern. It bothered him. Yamamoto took another sip of his tea. *You knew this was coming. You know how impatient he is. Throw him a bone.* "I understand that you need time." He paused to reconsider, but then turned the secret loose. "July 4."

Fujiwara smiled and then began to laugh, "How perfect. On the great American Independence Day, Japan will become mine. The irony of it appeals to me, Seito."

His use of the word "mine" stuck in Yamamoto's craw, but he had no one to blame for this but himself. Knowing full well what kind of narcissist he was dealing with, he'd told Fujiwara that in the aftermath of the coup, he would become the ruler of Japan. Yet he needed this narcissist if he was to persevere in Japan. "Cato, now that you know the date, I must ask that you do not do anything with that bit of information until we both determine it is time for you to let your men know what we are going to do. Surprise is our only advantage, and if one word of this slips out, we fail."

Fujiwara was still chuckling over the irony of the date, but his impatience was, for the moment, satisfied. "My lips are sealed. Together we will decide. Perhaps today we could discuss my living arrangements after the coup. Afterwards, I am planning on occupying the Imperial Palace here in Tokyo. Since you are to be my chief advisor, I am hoping I can convince you to move there with me."

Seito Yamamoto stroked his chin. *You will not live long enough to make that move,* he thought. But what came out of his mouth was something much different. "Cato, I think that is an excellent idea." He stood, took a bell from a nearby table, and rang it, summoning Fukora. "Bring us glasses and that single-malt scotch that Fujiwara-san enjoys so much. We have a toast to make."

# 21

## A CLOUDY REUNION

Cleve fought off sleep, not sure he could fully trust the cab driver, but he was exhausted. Eight hours later, on the outskirts of Korat, Tradip woke him to ask for directions to Chuk Ra Met. It had been nearly twenty-five years ago that he'd worked as a military advisor in this area, but, fortunately, nothing in rural Thailand had changed very much. An hour later, right at first light, the driver stopped the cab on a two-rut dirt path next to a rice paddy. As Spires peeled off the money, he asked, "This pays for your service and your silence, right? No cops, Tradip."

The driver turned and gave him a pained look. "My American friend, you hurt me. On the way, while you were asleep, we passed at least four national police cars. It would have been easy to betray you. Instead, I have delivered you here as you asked."

Cleve nodded, "I'm sorry." He peeled $800 from the roll of bills he'd pulled from his pocket.

"It is too much."

That convinced Cleve that he had worried needlessly. In the beginning, he'd thought of this man as just another hustler. He looked at him and said, "You've earned it. Thank you. I hope we meet again someday under more pleasant circumstances." They shook hands and Cleve got out of the cab.

From where he was, he thought it would be about two miles to Chuk Ra Met, and as he walked along the top of the narrow dikes that separated one rice paddy from another, he could smell the mustiness of the wetlands in the stillness of the morning's humid air. Ahead of him he heard a roster crow. Closer to the village, he saw the corral where the villagers kept their water buffalo, exactly where it had been twenty-five years ago. The pungent smell of ammonia and manure assaulted him. He caught his first glimpse of the villagers as they worked in the banana grove on the village's edge. They stopped what they were doing and stared at him. He didn't notice them fall in behind him at a distance as he headed into the village. In the village's center, women were huddled about the well, talking and filling jugs of water. As he approached, they fell silent. Ahead of him he could see the hut of Liott's father, and a pang of conscience swept over him. He took a deep breath and looked around, noticing for the first time the villagers following him. It was as if they were there to block any retreat he might have considered.

As he proceeded to Liott's father's hut, the procession grew larger, but stayed a respectable distance behind him. Then he was there, at her doorway. Her back was to him as she prepared breakfast at a low table in the hut's center. Her father saw him first, stretched out a thin arm and bony index finger and began to wail unintelligible things. Liott spun around to see him standing there.

In perfect English, she screamed, "My darling," and ran into his arms. Throwing her arms around his neck, she pulled his face to hers, smothering him in a deep, long kiss. When their lips broke apart, she whispered in his ear, "I have missed you so much." Behind her, her father continued to wail.

"What's happened to your father?"

Still embracing him, she said, "A stroke . . . two years ago . . . he has some paralysis and cannot speak, but I know he is glad to see you."

Cleve kissed her again on the cheek, stepped around her, and walked over to the old man, whose eyes sparkled behind a veil of tears. The stroke had contorted his face, but Cleve could discern a smile smeared across it. Putting his arms around him, he whispered, in perfect Thai, "Thuripp, it's good to see you again. Thanks for taking such good care of my family." The old man's head rested against Cleve's cheek and he could feel the old man patting him on the back with his left hand, the side of his body not impacted by the stroke.

Liott stood there looking at her husband and her father and had just begun to cry herself when applause and shouts of joy broke out from behind them. When all three turned to see, they found the entire village huddled around the hut's doorway sharing in the joy of this long-awaited reunion.

Cleve was overwhelmed as he whispered to Liott, "I'm so sorry."

She placed a gentle finger over his lips, "There's no need to be. It's all right now. We are back together. Daniel will be home for breakfast soon. He won't believe you are here. He's kept a calendar. This last year has been very long for him. He's counted the days since your release from . . ." She stopped short. She didn't want to talk about prison; she didn't even want to say the word. "He's been asking about you every day since your release." Then changing the subject, she asked, "I hope your mother isn't angry with me."

"No, she's not . . . she understands why . . ."

Daniel burst through the crowd and into the hut. "Papa."

Papa, the sound of it—what Daniel had always called his father—fell on Cleve's ears like a song. Turning, he saw the man his boy had become. Much taller than the average Thai, he towered above the other villagers. Cleve guessed he was six feet, two or three inches tall. Broad, muscular shoulders tapered to a narrow waist. It was obvious that the life Liott had carved out here for them agreed with him. The two men hugged.

"Papa, welcome home."

Cleve looked at Liott and beamed with pride.

# 22

## THE COMPLAINT

**B**illy Driscoll had been dead for forty-eight hours. Hayate Inamine had turned down the volume on his cell phone, but it still vibrated and it was dancing lightly now across the glass table top where he'd laid it. He looked at the caller ID and would have given anything to avoid answering, but knew better. "Hai, Fujiwara-san."

"Have they caught him?"

"He is in the wind. There is a nationwide . . ."

Fujiwara slammed the receiver down onto its cradle, stared angrily at the phone for a second or two, and then picked up the receiver again and punched in a four-digit extension.

The phone on the chief counsel's desk rang twice before he answered it.

"My office, immediately."

"May I . . . hello? Fujiwara-san, are you there?"

He was not.

THE OFFICE OF THE DEPARTMENT OF DEFENSE Inspector General (DODIG) operated a hotline that received calls from military installations, defense contractors, or anyone, for that matter, who had a beef with the department. Thousands of calls were received monthly. This call, however, spiked some interest because it pertained to a member of the US army that had just been murdered overseas. The wife of a special forces staff sergeant stationed with the First Special Forces Battalion on Okinawa, Japan, left the following message on the voicemail recorder:

*My name is Nicole Alexander. I am the wife of Staff Sergeant James Alexander. He is assigned to the First Special Forces Battalion at Torii Station, Okinawa, Japan. I am being treated for gonorrhea which was given to me by my husband after he returned from a recent deployment to Thailand. I am very angry at him, but I am even more angry at the army. My husband says he got it from a Thai woman, a whore, pardon my French, whom he met at a bar in Bangkok that is apparently owned by the First Battalion's Command Sergeant Major Billy Driscoll. I know Sergeant Major Driscoll has been killed; that is why I can now let someone know. I was afraid to say anything before because of what might happen to my husband's career, but Sergeant Major Driscoll's involvement with some whorehouses in Bangkok is an open secret within the battalion. I still love my husband and can forgive him for what he's done. But I just don't think it's right for a battalion command sergeant major to own a whorehouse in Thailand or anywhere else for that matter. Is there something you can do to make sure that this is investigated and . . . I don't know . . . maybe this Club Exotica . . . that is the name my husband gave me . . . is placed off limits or something? There are a lot of soldiers from this battalion that go to Thailand on temporary duty.*

*They shouldn't be bringing diseases like this back home with them. Please help me make sure this doesn't happen to more soldiers and their wives.*

On March 21, the DODIG reduced the voice mail to a written transcript and forwarded it to the Department of the Army Inspector General (DAIG) with a suspense date of March 25, to respond to the allegations. The DAIG forwarded the message to the commander of the First Special Forces Group at Fort Lewis, Washington, who was asked to respond by March 24.

STANDING IN FRONT of his boss's desk, the chief counsel said, "Fujiwara-san, I am working on . . ."

"Shut up and listen carefully."

The chief counsel was not used to being talked to like this. It brought him up short, but there was no mistake he was there to listen, not talk. Deferentially, he replied, "Hai, Fujiwara-san."

"There is a mess in Bangkok that requires your immediate attention."

The chief counsel knew of no issues there impacting their organization. "I . . . I know of noth— . . ."

"Billy Driscoll has been killed. Spires has been accused of the crime."

Drawing a blank, the chief counsel furrowed his brow and asked, "Who?"

"The bastard that killed Agaki has killed again."

Two and two came together. "Oh, yes. The man with the same name as the city."

Fujiwara glared at him. "I had it all arranged. Somehow Inamine managed to screw it up. Spires is still on the loose. Go there. Insure that the authorities find him."

"But Fujiwara-san . . ."

"But—*but* what?"

The snarl in his boss's voice told the chief counsel it was point-less to argue. Not wishing to anger him any further, he bowed, said, "As you wish," and started to leave.

"I also want Inamine eliminated."

The chief counsel stopped, turned, and tried to reason with his boss. Inamine controlled the Yakuza's interests in Thailand, which were many. He was a valuable asset. "Fujiwara, I must advise . . ."

The fist came up and slammed down on the desktop with a fury. "Do not ever argue over an order I give you."


AT THE HEADQUARTERS of the First Special Forces Group, Command Sergeant Major Dave Goodmon stood in front of his boss's desk. "Sir, we probably need to get on this complaint about Driscoll. I've talked to a couple of sergeants I know in the First Battalion. They didn't know about Driscoll owning a whorehouse, but they did say he spent a lot of time in Bangkok and they'd seen him more than once on Soi Cowby."

Colonel Roger Howard, commander of the First Special Forces Group, had a nickname. It was Bull. He got it based on an action in Afghanistan ten years earlier when he'd carried three wounded soldiers to shelter through a withering hail of bullets. The Silver Star's narrative read, "He mustered up the strength of a bull." Bull Howard had a connection to Driscoll few others knew about. During that same tour of duty in Afghanistan, it had been Driscoll that drilled a Taliban insurgent who was about to put a bullet in the middle of Howard's back. "OK, Ser-geant Major. Leave the message with me. I'll respond."

Goodmon, who knew of the connection between his boss and Driscoll, cautioned, "I know you think you owe him your life, but . . ." Howard dropped his eyes to a stack of papers in front of him. He wasn't paying attention. Goodmon stopped talking. He'd done his duty to advise his boss on matters like this.

"I'll take care of it, Sergeant Major."

"Yes, sir." Goodmon had a hunch his boss was going to white-wash this. He wasn't sure it would work, but he was sure it wasn't the right thing to do."

# 23

## SARAVEET

Cleve was a jumble inside. He'd made it through his homecoming and breakfast, but he knew he had to come clean, and soon. *How can I tell her? Every minute I am here I am putting her, Daniel, this entire village at risk.*

Breakfast was finished and Daniel announced, "Papa, I have to go back to the paddies. It's planting time. There is much to do. Maybe you and Mama can bring lunch to me."

Cleve smiled at the boy. "I'd like that, Son. See you then." After Daniel left, he turned to Liott. "His English . . . it's perfect. Yours is better than it was before I went to . . ." He couldn't say the word either. "How have you managed . . .?"

"Pram," was all she said.

"Saraveet? He's here?"

"He is a colonel now and commands the Tiger Brigade in Korat. He asks about you often. While you were gone, he was like a father to Daniel. He paid for him to go to private school in Korat. He graduated from there. His teachers wanted him to go on to the university." Sheepishly, she looked at him. "I did, too. But he didn't want to do that. He didn't want to be away when it was time for you to come home. Maybe now that you are back, he can go."

Pramrashorn Saraveet had been a brand-spanking new lieutenant in the Royal Thai Army when Staff Sergeant Cleve Spires had been assigned to his platoon as a military advisor. In the two years spent together, they had become fast friends. He had vouched for Cleve to Liott's father and assured him his daughter was marrying a good man. He had attended Cleve and Liott's wedding. Now he commanded the Tiger Brigade, one of the most renowned units in the Royal Thai Army. Cleve, however, wasn't sure if this was good or bad.

"Liott, there is something . . ." He paused, not at all sure how to unload this burden upon her.

"What is it, my darling? I thought there might be something bothering you during breakfast, so tell me what it is."

Apparently he hadn't been as good at hiding his emotions as he'd thought. "Do you remember Billy Driscoll? He was a witness at the court-martial?"

She nodded, already fearful of where this was going.

Cleve explained what had happened, all of it. "So, now I stand accused again of something I did not do. I came here . . ." He didn't want to hurt her, but he also knew this was going to sting. "I came here because I didn't have anywhere else I could go. They are searching for me in Bangkok. When they don't find me, they will expand the search. As long as I am here, I am a threat to you, to Daniel, and to this village. I cannot stay here."

Liott was crying. She pulled him close to her. "I cannot lose you again." Outside of the hut, they could hear voices greeting someone. A minute later, Saraveet stepped through the hut's door, offered a quick hello to Liott and then embraced Cleve.

"You have some troubles, my old friend," he whispered to him.

"So, already the news has traveled all the way to Korat?" Cleve asked.

"I'm afraid so. There is a nationwide manhunt for you. I received a message this morning. I came as soon as I saw it. Tell me what happened. Then we can see how I can help."

For the second time in fifteen minutes Cleve explained what had happened, in Cleveland and then in Bangkok.

Liott, crying, wailed, "He didn't do it, Pram. He didn't do it."

"Yes, yes, I know he didn't do it, any more than he killed that man on Okinawa. But he cannot stay here. Sooner or later they will connect you to him and they will come, or they will direct me to come to Chuk Ra Met and search for him." Cleve could only nod as he understood the truth in what his friend was saying. Saraveet turned to Cleve, "Do you have any idea who actually killed Driscoll?"

Cleve shook his head. "It all happened so fast. A man . . . three shots . . . he ran out the back of the building. Right there in front of my eyes, like it was all planned to happen just as I got there. All I could get out of Driscoll were two words."

"What did he say?"

"*Fujiwara* and *Yakuza.*"

"You are sure that is what he said?"

"Yes."

"Well, that is something. Do you know who Cato Fujiwara is?" Again, Cleve shook his head.

"He runs the biggest organized crime syndicate in this part of the world, the Yakuza."

Cleve thought for a minute and said, "None of it makes any sense. I have nothing to do with any of that."

"There's got to be a connection. We just don't know what it is," Saraveet said.

"Cleve, show Pram the notebook," Liott said.

Cleve produced the notebook and explained how he'd come by it. "Driscoll's name is in here. This notebook is what led me to Bangkok and the Windsor Hotel."

Saraveet took it from him and began thumbing through. He stopped on a page and said, "Well, that's interesting."

Cleve queried, "What?"

"Did you know Fujiwara's name is in here?"

"No. You've got to be kidding me. I didn't ever think to look . . ."

"Do you read Kanji?" Saraveet asked.

"No. Can you?"

"I have studied it some. It's not easy, so there's no way you could have known. His name is written in Japanese. But there's our connection. This guy Tetsu Agaki, Driscoll, and Fujiwara are all linked somehow."

The hut fell silent for a long minute while they all tried to think of what their next move should be. Finally, Saraveet offered, "We've got to get you to Japan and see if you can get anything out of Fujiwara. And that will not be easy, my friend. He is devilishly smart and equally as ruthless."

Cleve cautioned, "First things, first. How am I going to get to Japan? The net is tightening, Pram. I can't stay here without putting Liott, Daniel, and this entire village in danger."

Saraveet smiled slyly. "I think I can help on both counts. I must get back to Korat and make a few calls, but be ready to go tonight as soon as it's dark."

Liott, tears brimming over her eyes, grabbed Cleve, "No . . . No, you can't take him away again, not after all of these years apart."

Cleve, his arms wrapped tight around her, said, "We both know that I can't stay here. If I do I will only be caught, convicted, and sent away again and you and Daniel will be considered accomplices. As long as I am free, I can work to prove my innocence . . . If I can do that, then I can return to you and Daniel."

That afternoon, Cleve went to the paddies alone. He explained everything to his son. "I want to come with you, Papa."

"Absolutely not. If this goes badly, I don't want you anywhere around me."

"But . . ."

"Daniel, listen to me. Your mother is already beside herself with despair and fear. If you were to go with me now, that would leave her completely alone. Neither of us should do that to her, but I must. Besides, there is something that is very important you must do for me."

"What is that, Papa?"

"The villagers must be told. They cannot talk about my ever having been here. If they were to disclose that to the wrong person, the entire village falls under suspicion. All of you could be held as accomplices to my escape. It could even reach back to Pram. He could go to prison for helping me to escape. So it's important that everyone understands never to mention my coming here. I'm sorry to have to put that burden on you. Will you do that for me, Daniel? Will you make sure the villagers know to say nothing to anyone about my having been here? It's really important, son."

Reluctantly, Daniel agreed. "But you will come back won't you, Papa?"

"They will have to kill me to keep me away, Daniel."

CLEVE AND PRAM traveled under the cover of darkness that night to the docks in Bangkok. They were waved through several roadside checks set up by the national police because they were in Saraveet's official Royal Thai Army sedan. The ship's captain met them at the bottom of the gangway with his hand extended toward Saraveet, not in greeting, but rather looking for money. As he peeled off the bills, Saraveet said to him, "This is to get him into Japan. If you fail this, don't ever try to come back to Thailand again. Your reception will not be a warm one."

The captain nodded and motioned for Cleve to board, but before he did, Saraveet caught his arm, "Do you have money?"

"Cleve nodded and said, "About five thousand dollars. I took it off Driscoll. The sonuvabitch is worth more dead than he was alive."

Saraveet chuckled, "OK, then take this," and handed him a folded piece of paper. "This is the name and cell phone number of a good friend of mine in Japan, Yoshi Nagatamura. He helped me learn to read Kanji. He is a colonel of infantry in the Japanese Ground Self-Defense Force. He and I met at the Industrial College of the Armed Forces. We were in the same class. His English is better than mine. I have called him and explained your circumstances. You will need his help in Japan."

Tears came to Cleve's eyes. "How can I thank you, Pram?"

The two embraced and Saraveet said, "Come back to see us when this is all over. Take care, my old friend."

# 24

## MAN HUNT

"**S**o you are telling me that all they know after four days is that he is a black man, American, about six feet, three inches tall and about forty-five years old?" The chief counsel's voice was incredulous. "You did not even provide them his name or a picture?"

Hayate Inamine threw up his hands, "How was I supposed to do that? My cover story was that I was sitting in a bar, enjoying a drink with a couple of girls, when a man walks in and suddenly shoots another man in the same bar. How was I to know that these bumbling idiots couldn't even catch a criminal when they were nearly handed one."

The chief counsel quickly reconsidered his earlier opinion of Inamine's competence. He turned and headed for the office door.

"I will take care of this from now on. You have no further responsibility."

"Gladly. It is yours. Tell Fujiwara-san I am sorry."

On the street outside the office building the chief counsel met two men, both of them Japanese, that he had brought to Thailand with him. "He is upstairs in his office. He is alone. Now would be a good time. You have made the necessary arrangements?"

"Hai," the older of the two men said. "We have a boat waiting in Sattahip. As you have requested, he will simply disappear. They will never find his body."

"Good, then see to it. When it is done, you may return home. I have some other work to do before I leave."

They parted ways. The chief counsel went back to his hotel room to think through his next move. Of course, Inamine's point about his cover story made sense, but the chief counsel knew that certain situations required improvisation. *So why wouldn't Inamine just provide them what they needed to know? He had a file containing more than enough information about Spires that an amateur could track him down. And when the questions were asked about how he happened to know so much, simply pay them off? This was Thailand, for crying out loud. Everything was for sale. Anything or anybody could be bought.* It was unfortunate that such lack of foresight cost Inamine his life, but that was Inamine's problem. The chief counsel punched in a number on his cell phone. "Can you meet me in an hour at my hotel? I have some information I think you could use."

The voice on the other end, that of a captain in the Thai national police force and well-placed within their national headquarters, replied, "I will be there."

Over drinks, the captain perused the file. "Do I need to know how you have acquired all of this information on a man that we only have a physical description of?"

"You do not, just as I do not need to know how you will feed it into your system." He passed an envelope across the table to him, "This should adequately compensate you for your discretion. I must admit I do not know why this man is so important. I simply know that he is. It doesn't matter to us if he is taken dead or alive, all I know is that my boss wants him captured and put in prison or killed; it does not matter which."

The captain chuckled, "He is better off dead than in a Thai prison. We don't spend much on our prisoners."

The chief counsel merely shrugged his shoulders. "Please let me know when it is done. The sooner, the better. And, of course, you understand that this conversation never took place. Right?"

"I understand."

ON THE MORNING of March 28, the breakfast routines of the villagers of Chuck Ra Met were interrupted by a cordon of armed police sweeping into the village from the southern edge. No search warrants were provided. There was no concern for individual rights. The nationwide search for Cleveland A. Spires had turned up nothing, and it was the considered opinion of the chief of the national police that he had to be somewhere in the village or somebody here had to know where he was. Every villager was questioned intensively. Liott and Daniel were taken to the main police station, detained for two days, fed little, deprived of sleep, and questioned nearly around the clock by various groups of policemen.

Saraveet held his breath through all of this. It wasn't his personal safety that he was concerned about. If any one of them broke, there would be hell to pay. Likely, the village of Chuk Ra Met would cease to exist.

Finally, after dark on the evening of March 31, he parked his private car about two miles away from the village in the center of a stand of palm trees. Unless one knew it was there, it would be difficult to see from the road. From there he walked, under the cover of darkness, to Liott's hut. "Are the two of you all right?"

"Pram, you shouldn't have come. They might be watching," Liott warned.

"I took precautions. Are you both OK?"

"The bastards . . ." Daniel muttered.

"Yeah, I know. They can be brutal."

"They misjudged the loyalty of the people in this village," Daniel said.

Saraveet smiled at him, "I think you are right. I am not privy to all that they are doing, but late this afternoon a large number of them boarded helicopters. I think the worst may be behind us, but tell the villagers they still must be very closed-mouthed and vigilant. There may be some police left back to watch and listen."

Liott asked him, "How do you think they found out about us? How did they know?"

"I can't be sure, but I overheard several of them talking. They believe it was an anonymous tip. My guess is that the Yakuza is involved somehow. I don't know how, and I surely don't know why they are doing this to Cleve. But it was just a little too easy for the police to go from a sketchy physical description to now having a picture of him and details about his personal life."

"They have his picture?"

"I am afraid so, but remember he is no longer in Thailand. We got him out of here in the nick of time."

# 25

## NAGATAMURA

The voyage to Japan took two miserable weeks. The small container ship stopped at a dozen ports between Bangkok and Yokohama. Upon arrival at each of these ports, Cleve was put in a locker in the engine room and the door was locked. He could only trust that they would come and let him out after the ship had cleared customs and immigration. In some places, he'd been in that box for over eight hours in stifling hot conditions, unable to sit down, unable to relieve himself. Though he had never really considered leaving, the captain had warned him not to leave the ship. They wouldn't wait on him. When their business in a particular port of call was complete, they would leave, with or without him. In the busy port of Yokohama, Japan, they had laid at an outer anchorage without customs and immigration clearance until a berth finally opened up. Somewhere after midnight on April 1, the captain came to him and said, "It is safe now for you to go ashore."

The captain was not a friend. He had been paid to deliver

Cleve to Japan. Now that the ship was tied up at its berth, the captain believed he'd fulfilled his end of the contract. Everything from this point on was on Cleve. He put on the darkest clothing he had and stepped down the gangway, stayed in the shadows as he fumbled his way to the port's main gate, and waited there trying to decide how he would get past the security that checked everything coming and going. He watched what went on for over an hour until he thought he understood the routine of the three guards that were there, and then he caught a break. A lineup of six trucks pulled to a stop and the three guards became occupied checking the papers of each driver. While they were busy, he quickly exited the gate and was absorbed into the dark streets of Yokohama.

He must have walked nearly a mile, not knowing at all where he was going or even where he'd been, before he decided to hail a cab. The driver spoke no English and Cleve spoke no Japanese, but Cleve had the notebook. He pulled it out, turned to the page, and gave the driver the address Agaki had listed under Fujiwara's name. The driver shook his head. He held his hand up and rubbed his thumb and first two fingers together.

*He wants me to pay?* Cleve didn't know what to do, but he reached in his pocket, pulled the roll of bills out of his pocket and held it up. The head shake turned to a nod and they sped off into the night. At some point in the trip the driver said, "US dollar," and shook his head. "Japanese yen," and then he nodded. He pulled in front of a small store front with a plate glass window with a slide-through and pointed to it. Then he made a motion for Cleve to go. The driver got out of the cab and accompanied him to the window. A woman appeared, and the driver said something to her in Japanese. In broken English, the woman looked at Cleve and said, "I change dollar to yen. You give me dollar."

Cleve peeled off a thousand dollars. She worked an abacus and give him back Japanese yen. He only hoped he wasn't getting ripped off. He had no idea what the current exchange rate was, and there was nothing posted at the storefront that would tell him. They got back in the cab and two hours later the driver dropped him in front of a huge skyscraper somewhere in the heart of Tokyo. Then the shocker came. The cab ride cost him almost a third of the money he'd just changed, somewhere over three hundred US dollars. *Welcome to Tokyo,* Cleve thought.

It was nearly 5:00 a.m. and, by Tokyo standards, the street was quiet. He walked up to an entrance of the skyscraper and found the door open. He entered into a large lobby at the other end of which was a security checkpoint blocking access to the elevators. On the wall were two large directories, one in Japanese Kanji, the other in English. He scanned the English version, but found nothing that even came close to Fujiwara's name. He noticed one of the security guards giving him the eye, so he decided it was time to retreat. He left the building and navigated his way across eight lanes of sparse traffic to a small park, where he took a seat. The temperature was quite mild for early April. He wanted to call the contact Saraveet had given him, but not at this early hour. He was exhausted and laid down on the bench.

Two hours later he was awakened by a Tokyo cop tapping him on the sole of his shoe with his nightstick. Cleve felt the adrenaline rifle through him. The cop said something in Japanese. Cleve replied in English that he didn't understand. The cop motioned for him to get up and move on. Spires was only too happy to comply. The streets were now a jumble of cars and buses and the sidewalks were crowded with pedestrians who, he assumed, were on their way to work. From a vantage point just down the street, he watched people crowd into the skyscraper by the hundreds. A couple of blocks further down the street he came to an entrance to the Tokyo subway, walked down the steps, and found a men's restroom where he could freshen up.

At 8:00 a.m. sharp, Cleve found a pay phone and called Yoshii Nagatamura.

"Hai, Nagatamura."

"Colonel Nagatamura, this is Cleveland Spires, a friend of Pramrashorn Saraveet's. I believe he called you about me."

"Ah, yes, Mr. Spires. Are you in Japan?"

"Yes, sir, I am." Cleve told him where he was by referencing the address he thought was Fujiwara's.

Nagatamura immediately became cautious, "You must get out of there. They have security cameras everywhere."

Cleve knew he'd screwed up. He explained to Nagatamura that he was now away from the building by more than a block and then added, "But, Colonel Nagatamura, I went into the building early this morning to see if I could find Fujiwara."

"Ummm," was his ominous reply. "Who saw you there?"

"One security guard was looking my way, but didn't approach."

"OK. We cannot undo what has been done. We do have the advantage that everyone thinks you are still in Thailand. Let's hope they have no reason to check the security camera footage from last night. I am close by, but must attend a daily briefing in half an hour. It usually lasts only thirty minutes. I will meet you in the park across from the office building. Do you know it?"

"Yes, I do."

"Good, I will see you around 9:30 a.m."

Cleve was easy to find. There just weren't many tall, black men in that particular park in Tokyo. Yoshii Nagatamura introduced himself, and Cleve almost immediately liked him. Small in stature, he was trim, fit, and, most important, ready to help Cleve.

"We must get you off the street. I have a good friend who has an apartment not far from here . . ."

"Colonel Nagatamura . . ."

Please call me Yoshii. May I call you Cleve?"

Cleve nodded, but warned, "I don't think it's a good idea to put your friend at risk."

The colonel waved a dismissive hand, "Not to worry. He is not here. He is in the United States, attending the Industrial College of the Armed Forces (ICAF), just as Pram and I did several years ago. He did not want to give up his apartment in Tokyo. Such places are very hard to come by. He pays rent on it, even though he does not live there. His father is very wealthy. For him, I think, the saying you Americans use is, *it is no big deal.*"

Cleve nodded, "Right, then, 'no big deal.'" Getting down to business, Cleve asked, "How much do you know about this guy Fujiwara?"

"Very little more than you, to be honest, but I have heard the stories about him. He controls the Yakuza. Exactly what all that entails, I can only imagine. He is very wealthy. The building you were in last night belongs to a management company that is, supposedly, owned by the Yakuza. He has tentacles everywhere. Some are legitimate, most are not. Pram explained that you believe Fujiwara is somehow linked to the murder that sent you to prison and to the one that you are accused of in Thailand."

"That's right."

"Cleve, I must tell you, it will be difficult to get to Fujiwara. A man like that will have an army of security around him. Do you have a plan?"

"A plan?" Cleve scoffed. "I don't even know what this sonuvabitch looks like."

Yoshii smiled, "Well, then there is something I can help you with. A picture of him will not be a problem. He is in the news often. Sometimes it is good news and sometimes it is bad."

"Great. Once I get the picture, I can stake myself out here." He paused, thinking, and then asked, "Do you think this park has surveillance cameras?"

Yoshii thought for a moment. "Ummm, I doubt it." Then he pointed to the skyscraper across the street, "But that building and the sidewalks around it will have them, as will the subways. Stay away from these."

"So, then, my first step is to lay eyes on this guy. He has to go in or come out of that building sometime. I'll just keep an eye out."

"OK, Cleve, but be very careful. He has been around for a lot of years. To survive in his business, he has to be crafty."

THEY WALKED TO the apartment so Cleve could get a feel for the area. Once they got there, Yoshii left, but returned shortly with pictures of Cleve's target and some food. They ate noodle soup together and discussed Cleve's plan to surveil Fujiwara's building.

At 2:00 p.m. he was on his way back to the park, but stopped in a department store and purchased a pair of binoculars, small enough to fit into his jacket pocket. By 3:00 he was sitting on a park bench two hundred meters away from the entrance he'd used earlier that morning. It was about 5:00 when a black Lexus pulled to the curb in front of the entrance. The driver got out, walked around the car and opened a rear passenger door on the curb side. Cleve grabbed his binoculars and focused them just in time to see the passenger face him for the briefest of moments before turning to head into the building. "Got you, you sonuvabitch."

# 26

## EVERYONE'S LOOKING

Lucas Johnson's secretary showed up at his door with a furrowed brow and a high-pitched urgency in her voice. "Colonel Johnson, it's General Richardson on line one for you. I mean it's really him, not his secretary . . . it's him." Lieutenant General William F. Richardson, commanding general of the United States' Army Combined Arms Center at Fort Leavenworth, Kansas, rarely placed his own calls, and when he did it was to other generals. Lucas snatched the phone from the cradle, punched line one, and said, "Colonel Johnson, sir."

"Lucas, I've have just finished talking with the chief of staff of the army . . ."

*What the hell?*

"Something has happened that is going to require you to assume command of the First Special Forces Group sooner than you expected . . ."

*Bull Howard must have popped on the brigadier general's list.*

"The chief has relieved Colonel Howard of his command . . ."

*Oh, shit!*

"He has asked me to pass a couple of things on to you. First, he wants you out there yesterday. You will assume command as soon as you get there and, as I said, that needs to be pronto. There will be no change of command ceremony. Second, he has an investigation he wants you to conduct . . ."

*Not good!*

"Remember the death of the First Battalion's command sergeant major in Bangkok a while ago?"

"Yes, sir. I saw the article in *The Army Times*."

"Well, on the heels of that, a spouse of a soldier in the First Battalion filed a complaint with the DODIG alleging that the dead sergeant major was involved in some rather suspicious activities in Thailand. Howard was supposed to investigate, but, apparently, didn't. He blew it off and when the chief found out, it pissed him off so bad, he fired Howard. He wants you to find out what was going on with this sergeant major. Sorry I don't have any more details than that."

It was a shitty way to have to begin a command, but Lucas also knew it needed to be taken on, investigated, and dealt with. He'd learned a long time ago that bad news isn't like wine. Bad news will never get better with age. "Ummm, well, sir, this isn't the way I'd hoped to begin command, but . . ."

"I understand, Lucas, but you know why this is important . . ."

"I do, sir. I absolutely do."

"Lucas, I know the chief has confidence in you. Told me that, himself."

"I appreciate it, sir."

"Listen, Lucas, I know this isn't going to sit well at home. It looks like this move will be squarely on your wife. You've got to get out to Fort Lewis, ASAP. I will alert the transportation office. They will be prepared to help in any way they can. Your

Permanent Change of Station orders are being cut as we speak. You can pick them up at personnel within the hour. You can use my plane to get to Fort Lewis. Just let me know when you want to fly, but remember it needs to be soon."

"Got it, sir. The chief of staff wants me there yesterday."

Richardson chuckled, "You got it, Lucas. Good luck. Call my office if there are any problems at all."

"Roger that, sir."


EARLY ON THE morning of April 3, Lucas Johnson, his wife, and two little girls stood next to an Army C-12 at Fort Leavenworth's Army Airfield. "Sorry about this, honey," he whispered to her.

She kissed him gently on the cheek and whispered back, "I love you, Lucas Johnson, but you owe me for this one." They both chuckled and Lucas bent down to say goodbye to his daughters. "OK, girls, see you in Fort Lewis in a few weeks. Tell your Grammy and Grampy that we can't wait to see them at Christmas." Both girls hugged their father good bye. From the VIP waiting area, they watched the C-12 depart.

Four hours later, he sat behind his new desk at the First Special Forces Group headquarters in Fort Lewis, Washington. Across the desk from him sat Command Sergeant Major Dave Goodmon and the group's executive officer, Lieutenant Colonel Sam Ellerson. He signed his assumption of command order and handed it back to Ellerson and then shifted his attention to Command Sergeant Major Goodmon. "OK, Sergeant Major, tell me what you know."

"Colonel Howard didn't investigate the complaint. He didn't talk to anyone on Okinawa about it . . . not the battalion commander, the exec, or the acting command sergeant major. He just said he'd investigated and found the charges baseless. I warned him, sir . . ."

"I know you did, Sergeant Major. I talked to Colonel Howard. He told me he didn't listen to you. I think he regrets his misplaced loyalty."

"Did he explain why, sir? I mean did he tell you about Driscoll and him?"

"Yeah, he did, Sergeant Major."

"I told him. 'Where there's smoke, there's fire.' He wouldn't listen."

"Not your fault, Sergeant Major." Lucas turned his attention to Ellerson looking for some background information. Lucas had been almost always assigned to Special Forces units, but had never been assigned to the First Special Forces Group or any of its subordinate units. It was one of the reasons he was so excited to get this command opportunity. He would have to learn their mission from the ground up, new faces, new units, and a new part of the world to work in. Given the chief of staff of the army's direction, he knew exactly where he had to begin learning. "Sam, tell me about the First Battalion."

"Sure, sir. They cover a huge geographic area, nearly all of Southeast Asia. The battalion commander, Lieutenant Colonel Greene, is an experienced operator, but is new to the command . . . only been there about three months. I talked to him. Apparently he and Driscoll agreed that they needed to divide and conquer. Thailand is one of their heaviest commitments, so Driscoll was supposed to be keeping an eye on things there while Greene handled all the other countries. Greene told me Driscoll told him that this was the way he'd worked with the old battalion commander, so Greene thought 'if it ain't broke, don't fix it'. He said he ran it by his exec, who agreed. Both admit, though, that Driscoll didn't get much supervision.

"So what do you think? Was Driscoll dirty?"

Goodmon answered first, "Could be, sir. Since all of this came to light, I've talked to quite a few non-commissioned officers (NCOs) assigned to the battalion. They told me that they rarely saw Driscoll in the field, but when they would get back to Bangkok, they would run into him on the street."

"What street?"

Goodmon gave his new boss a sheepish look, "Soi Cowboy, Sir."

Lucas had not been to Thailand, but he'd heard about the place, especially Bangkok. He shook his head, "Let me guess. Sex district?"

Both Ellerson and Goodmon nodded.

The room fell silent for a few minutes while Lucas digested all of this, then he looked at Goodmon and asked, "Sergeant Major, I see in your file that you speak Thai."

Goodmon responded in Thai, "I speak it fluently, but reading it is more difficult. I can read it, but it takes me some time to decipher." Then he added, in English, "I can get by speaking, but reading takes longer."

Lucas smiled at his sergeant major and then looked at Ellerson. "OK. Sam, can you handle things here for a few days? I think the sergeant major and I are going to take a trip to Bangkok and talk to some folks about our man, Driscoll."

ON APRIL 5, *USA Today* ran a story containing all the sordid details of Driscoll's death. The reporter had done a splendid job of research. It told the story of a highly-respected army officer, one Colonel Roger Howard, relieved of his command for 'inaccurately' reporting the details of an army special forces command sergeant major killed in a sleazy Bangkok bar, one in which he may have had some business interest. The suspected killer was Cleveland A. Spires, a former command sergeant major, who was disgraced some ten years earlier for killing an airman on Okinawa. The reporter then speculated that there may have been a revenge motive at work here because Driscoll had been a witness in Spires's court-martial.

The *USA Today* story was picked up by *Stars and Stripes* and run in their April 7 edition and distributed throughout the Pacific Rim.

LUCAS JOHNSON AND Dave Goodmon arrived in Bangkok on April 7 and decided they would start their quest for answers at the Windsor Hotel. When the young lady at the front desk summoned the hotel's manager, he feigned an inability to understand as an excuse not to answer questions about Driscoll. That excuse fell apart as Goodmon said to him in perfect Thai, "In that case we can speak in your language, and I will be happy to translate for Colonel Johnson." The manager told them that Driscoll had stayed at the Windsor every time he came to Thailand. He refused to give them an exact accounting for how many nights that might have been in the last year, nor did he want to disclose what Driscoll had paid for the rooms he'd occupied. Goodmon went to work again. In Thai, he said, "OK, listen, we were hoping for your cooperation, but if you refuse, we will have no option but to go to the police and ask for their cooperation. We will lead them here, to your hotel." Goodmon paused for effect and when he was sure he had the manager's attention, he proceeded. "We will tell them you refused to cooperate. What do you think they will do then?" Again, he paused before offering a more attractive alternative. "Or you could just cooperate with us and we could leave the police out of it. What's it going to be, pal?"

While the manager collected the data, Johnson and Goodmon were given the key to Driscoll's old room. "He always stayed in the Lotus Suite," the manager volunteered.

"Have the police been through the room?"

"No, not yet."

Lucas looked at Goodmon, "Do you suppose they don't know he was staying here? How is that possible?"

"I don't know, sir." Goodmon laughed. "Sometimes the Thai police can be so efficient that they get in their own way. The uniformed cops likely think the detectives have done that and the detectives don't want to get their hands dirty, so they would leave a detail like taking a look at Driscoll's hotel room to the uniformed guys. So, let's get up there and take a look before they wise up."

The room contained many more civilian clothes than military uniforms, indicating that when Driscoll was here, he dressed as a civilian most of the time. This was later confirmed by the manager. "I rarely saw him in uniform." There were also hundreds of pornographic photos of Driscoll with different Thai women performing all manner of sex acts. Again, the hotel manager proved useful. "The girls all call him Beelee. He employs many of them at three bars; two on Soi Cowboy and one in the Patpong district. Often he would bring some of them here." And the final thing they found in Driscoll's room was a notebook, alphabetically divided. In it, they found the names of three banks: one in Costa Rica, one in Panama, and a third in Switzerland. With the name of each bank appeared what looked to be an account number.

It was approaching dark by the time they finished with the room and followed up with the manager. They decided to catch a bite of dinner before heading to Club Exotica. As Johnson and Goodmon headed for the hotel's restaurant, a US soldier came in and recognized Goodmon. "Sergeant Major, what are you doing here?"

Goodmon made up some story that sounded good and kept their true mission confidential. The two exchanged pleasantries, and as they were parting the soldier offered Goodmon a copy of today's *Stars and Stripes*. "There's a story on page two," the soldier said and then added, "Pretty ugly, Sergeant Major."

As they sat down for dinner, Goodmon opened the paper to page two, groaned, and passed the paper to Johnson, "Take a look at this, boss."

Lucas read the story with interest, but when he got to the part about Cleveland Spires being the suspect in the assassination and the subject of a manhunt in Asia, his stomach tightened up and he ate little.


FOR THE MOST part, their trip to Club Exotica was a useless effort. The hotel's manager had alerted all three bars. He had a vested interest in doing this. As a *ferang*, which is Thai for foreigner, Driscoll was prohibited from owning a business. So the official paperwork showed three Thai men, each as a bar owner. For this deception, Driscoll had paid them a small percentage of each bar's profits. However, now that the American was no longer on the scene, their percentage of profits would rise dramatically. The hotel manager knew they would appreciate his loyalty in some way which he hoped would be monetary.

The next day Goodmon and Johnson returned to the US and Lucas filed his report.

THE US DEPARTMENT of Defense, working through the US State Department, petitioned the governments of Costa Rica, Panama, and Switzerland to disclose the contents of the three bank accounts. The results floored everyone. Billy Driscoll had nearly five million dollars disbursed among the three banks.

The same *USA Today* reporter that had initially broken the story petitioned the Department of Defense with a Freedom of Information Act request and was given a copy of the investigation's results, which broke in a story published on April 15. The story was slanted in such a way that the murder looked more and more like it was an act of revenge by Cleveland Spires. This story was more broadly reported and found its way into papers throughout the US and much of Asia.

IN TOKYO, CATO Fujiwara called his chief counsel into his office. "You have seen the newspaper reports?"

"Yes, Fujiwara-san."

"Yet Spires remains free?"

"Yes, Fujiwara-san."

"How many days has it been?"

"Fifteen, I believe."

Fujiwara didn't like that he did not have the exact number at his command. "Do you think he has managed to escape from Thailand?"

"It is possible, I suppose . . ."

The fist slammed the desk top, "You suppose?"

"Fujiwara-san . . . perhaps if I knew why this man is so important . . ."

Again, the fist came down, harder this time than the last. His patience exhausted, Fujiwara screamed at him, "It is important because I say it is. Now get out of here and make sure that the manhunt for Spires becomes an international one. The Thai police have botched this. Spires could be anywhere. I want him found."

SEVERAL HOURS LATER, both Fujiwara and his chief counsel got the surprise of their lives. The building's alert security manager had just put two and two together. He'd been told by a night security guard about a black man who'd come into the building earlier, very early in the morning. At the time the security manager thought little of it, but had taken the time to go back and review the camera footage. Now, however, the picture in the newspaper was the same man, he was sure of it. After reviewing the security camera footage again and confirming the man in the lobby that morning was Spires, he prepared a notice to all building occupants that if they saw this man in the building they should report it to security immediately. The notice warned that they should not approach the man, as he might be armed and dangerous. It contained the same picture of Spires that had appeared in newspapers, a picture that was ten years old, taken as he was leaving his court-martial on his way to Fort Leavenworth.

The chief counsel grabbed his copy of the notice and scrambled to his boss's office.

"Fujiwara-san, have you seen . . ."

Fujiwara held the same notice in his hand. "He is here, in Tokyo. He was even in this building. You will lead the search for this man. I want every one of our people on the lookout for him. Do not fail, or you will wind up like Inamine."

IT WAS DUSK. Ida Spires stopped what she was doing in the kitchen to switch on the lights when she heard the knock at the front door. Opening it, she found Detective Bergstrom standing there with two papers under his arm.

"May I come in?"

Wordlessly, Ida backed away from the doorway.

Once inside, Bergstrom took the newspapers from under his arm and unfolded them. "Mrs. Spires, have you seen these?" He spread out *USA Today* and *The Cleveland Plain Dealer* in front of her.

Ida's heart was racing, but she refused to let Bergstrom see her distress.

"Have you heard from him?"

"No."

"Mrs. Spires . . ."

"I said I haven't heard from my son," she repeated. *But even if I had, I wouldn't tell you,* she thought.

"I have reopened the Tetsu Agaki case."

"Who?" She knew who he was talking about, but she wasn't going to give Bergstrom anything.

"The Japanese man that was killed just down the street. We think your son . . ."

This detective was persecuting her son. He made her skin crawl. She hated him. She practically snarled at him, "That man was following my son. Cleveland went out that night to find out . . ." She stopped, but it was too late, she'd already said too much in her anger, and Bergstrom jumped on it.

"So, he didn't just happen upon Mr. Agaki on his way home from work?"

Ida said nothing.

"Look, Mrs. Spires, I need to talk to your son. If he contacts you, tell him that he needs to . . ."

"To what? Turn himself in? Expect that he'll receive fair treatment? He did that once, Detective. I don't think he'll trust that again."

"I want you to think about something. The Thai police want him for the murder in Bangkok. Interpol wants him. They are all looking for him. If he's caught out in that part of the world, he will be turned over to the Thais and they will put him in one of their cesspool prisons. At least back here in the US he'll get humane treatment. We won't extradite. Driscoll was a US citizen and a soldier, so the US will handle it here. But we will try him for the murder of Driscoll and, if I can prove it, for having some role in the death of Agaki as well. But at least he'll be in the US. Think about it, Mrs. Spires. Where would you rather your son be incarcerated?"

"Get out of my house, Detective. Don't come back here."

"OK, Mrs. Spires, but if you withhold information from me, then you become an accomplice and we *will* prosecute you for that crime. Don't make me do that."

# 27

## FORGIVE US OUR TRESPASSES

Yoshii Nagatamura sat down next to Cleve on the park bench. He placed a paper bag between them and said, "Open it."

Cleve opened the bag and peered in. It contained a black, hooded sweatshirt, size XXL, and a pair of Douglas McArthur sunglasses. "What's this?"

"Put them on, now. Your picture is in every newspaper in Tokyo and the *Stars and Stripes* as well. They believe you killed Driscoll out of revenge. Interpol is involved, which means that Japanese authorities have been notified. If you are captured, it is all over. The bad guys win."

Cleve pulled the sweatshirt over his head.

"Pull the hood up and put on the sunglasses. Let's go back to the apartment. You are not safe on the street."

"OK . . . OK . . . I'll go to the apartment, but I need you to sit here for a few minutes and tell me what happens."

"I don't understand."

"I've been looking for a routine in his life, something that Fujiwara does frequently, like a habit. I think I've found something, but you can confirm it for me. Every other day Fujiwara comes down to the street, gets in his car, and is driven somewhere. He leaves precisely at 1:00 p.m. and returns between 6:00 and 6:15 p.m."

"Where does he go?"

"I have no idea. That's the next step." Cleve glanced at his watch. "It's 12:30 now. My bet is you will see Cato Fujiwara come out that door right there," Cleve pointed to it, "and get into a black Lexus sedan at 1:00 p.m. sharp. Come to the apartment and tell me if I'm right or wrong."

AT 1:25 P.M., Yoshii entered the apartment and said, "You are right. He departed promptly at one o'clock."

"Can you check on his return for me?"

"I will."

YOSHII WALKED INTO the apartment at 6:45 that evening with some food and a smile on his face. "He was back at 6:10 p.m. You say he does this every other day?"

"Yes."

"So, on Wednesday, I will meet you in front of the apartment in my car. We will follow him and see where he goes. Does that sound like a good plan?"

"Exactly what I was hoping you'd suggest."

FOLLOWING ANOTHER CAR in Tokyo traffic was not an easy task. It required getting close and staying there and, hopefully, not being spotted. As they eased their way out of down-town's congestion, Yoshii was able to back off a little, and by the time they reached the western edges of Tokyo's sprawling sub-urbia, he was able to give Fujiwara's driver a good quarter mile. "Where the hell is he going?"

Cleve shrugged. He had absolutely no idea where the hell he was. "Do you know where we are now?"

"Vaguely. But if we go much farther we will be in the country-side. I can't imagine . . ." He shut up as the black Lexus turned right into what appeared to be a driveway, came to a momentary stop, and then proceeded in. Everything after that was blocked from their sight by a high concrete wall. Yoshii slowed as he approached the driveway. They saw the unmanned gate swing-ing closed. As they eased past the driveway they could catch only a glimpse of the estate's main house, some one hundred meters from the entrance gate. The two men followed the wall as it turned right at the next intersection and then right again and, finally, right again. Yoshii commented, "The damn place occupies the entire block. I know we are far from the city center, but, still, this much land, this close to Tokyo, only comes at a premium price. I mean, just take a look at the other homes around here. They are nothing like this." He pointed to the gate again as they drove by for a second time.

"Any idea how we can find out who lives here?" Cleve asked. He jotted down the numbers on the wall next to the gate. "Any idea what street this is?"

At the next intersection, Yoshii looked at the street signs, all in Kanji. "It translates to Cherry Blossom Road. I have never heard of it, but I don't get out this way much. Do you think this is where he comes every time?"

"Good question. I guess the only way we will know is to wait until Friday and do this again. Can you do that, Yoshii? I know I am taking you away from your work."

"It's OK, Cleve. I am due some leave. I will put in for a week off tomorrow. There should not be a problem with General Ishikawa approving it."

Thursday was one of the longest days he'd ever endured, cooped up in the small apartment waiting on Friday to come so they could test their theory about Fujiwara's routine. Yoshii had brought him some back copies of *Stars and Stripes* and Cleve had pored through them. In one he'd read about the change of command at First Special Forces Group. The article did not include any of the sordid details about Colonel Roger Howard's relief from command, but, instead, focused on the record of its new commander, Colonel Lucas Johnson. Cleve recognized him from the accompanying picture. He thought Johnson had not changed much in the decade that had intervened since the court-martial.

When Friday afternoon finally came around, it didn't take very long for them to determine that Fujiwara was headed to exactly the same place as the last time. They broke off the tail. Though it was risky, they stopped at a small out-of-the-way coffee shop to decide what they should do next. As they sat down, Yoshii offered, "I googled that address. Got nothing but some real estate information. Nothing specific to that property, just the surrounding environs. From what I could tell, that place has been there for some time . . . twenty, maybe thirty years . . . and the neighborhood has grown up around it. I could not determine who the owner is. Maybe I could ask around the neighborhood. Someone must know something."

"That's a good idea. What do you think about me relocating? I noticed a small hotel just across from the estate the other day when we circled the block. It's a lot less populated out here. Less likely that somebody might recognize me and, if we get the right room, I could surveil the place without leaving the hotel. I've got money." He pulled the roll of bills from his pocket. "You might need to change this into yen for me, but there should be enough here to cover the hotel room for a few days at least."

YOSHII RENTED THE room for a week, requesting one overlooking the street, offering some lame excuse about wanting to see what traffic was like before heading out each day. From their fourth-floor perch, they could see down into the estate, but the view yielded little information except that the main house was huge and the surrounding grounds were well maintained. The next morning, the pair watched a landscaping truck pull up to the gate, punch in a code, and drive in. Four men and a bevy of equipment spent the morning manicuring the lawn and beds.

Yoshii ventured out to see what he might learn from the neighbors while Cleve maintained his vigil at the window overlooking the estate. Somewhere around two o'clock he noticed a postman place some mail in a recessed box in the wall next to the gate. It sparked an idea. Impatient to wait for Yoshii's return, Cleve focused his binoculars on the gate area and its surrounding area. He was looking for security cameras. If there were any, he couldn't see them. Cautiously, he walked out of the hotel and across the street to the mailbox looking for any signs of security. Once there, he opened it and quickly thumbed through the mail it contained. It was then that he realized the fatal flaw in his plan. All of the envelopes were addressed in Kanji. He could not read any of it.

Yoshii's plan hadn't worked either. "It's unbelievable. I must have talked to a dozen people. All of them said they live around here. None of them knew a thing about who lives inside those walls. I don't even know if it is a man, a woman, a couple, nothing. One man told me he has heard that she is a wealthy widow who won't go out in public because she is still grieving her husband's death twenty years ago. Another man told me that it's two men who live there. He said he thought they might be gay and that is why they don't ever go out."

As they talked, Cleve observed a provisioner's truck pull to the gate, punch in a code, and enter. "That must be how they get their food." He pointed to the truck and then changed the subject. "I took a risk today."

"How?"

"I watched the postman put some mail in a box next to the gate. So I went over . . ."

"Cleve, there have to be security cameras . . ."

Anticipating this response, Cleve held up his hand, "Relax, Yoshii. I looked before I went over and then, again, as I was heading that way. If there are any there, I couldn't see them. I was only there for a minute or less, then I got out of there. I thought I might find out something about the people that live there, by looking through their mail. There was a problem, however."

"What's that?"

I can't read Kanji."

Yoshii laughed but added, "You took a huge risk. Security cameras these days are quite small. Are you sure they didn't take your picture?"

"Well, it's been a couple of hours. I've watched. No police, nothing. Don't you think that if someone saw me picking through their mail, they would have called the cops by now?"

Yoshii shrugged, "I suppose you are correct. He paused and then asked, "So what's next.?"

"I think we need to keep checking the mail."

"But you can't . . ."

Cleve quickly nodded and said, "But, you can." They both smiled at one another.

THE NEXT DAY the postman arrived at the estate promptly at 2:00 p.m., just as he had the day before. The two watched him reach the end of the block before Yoshii headed down the hotel's steps and over to the mailbox. Cleve watched him and kept an eye on the estate. Yoshii thumbed through the newly delivered mail. Suddenly he looked in Cleve's direction, held up an envelope, and pointed to it.

*What the hell?* Cleve thought. He watched Yoshii replace the mail except for the envelope he had held up for Cleve to see and then scurry back to the hotel.

"Jackpot!" Yoshii exclaimed with a smile on his face, as he closed the room door behind him. "Look at this." He held the envelope out.

Cleve took it. It was addressed to a *Seito Yamamoto*. But it was the return address that stunned him. It was one of those pre-pasted return address labels that often come in the mail when a charity is asking for a donation. This one read, *Major General Paul Stanley, 1894 Kaanipii Road, Pearl City, Hawaii.* "What the hell is this?" Cleve pointed to the estate. "The guy inside there is penpals with a major general in Hawaii?" It was purely rhetorical. Cleve didn't expect an answer and Yoshii offered none. There was silence as both men wrestled with the question, *What should we do now?"* Finally, Cleve said, "I'm going to open it."

Yoshii cautioned, "What we have done is against the law here in Japan, just as I am certain it is illegal in the United States as well."

Cleve looked at him and then said, "Yoshii, I'm already suspected of murder. It seems to me that a little mail tampering at this point is rather incidental." He tore the envelope open and pulled out the letter:

*Dear Seito,*

*The sale to Vietnam has been approved. Though I am not sure how you and your colleagues managed to pull this off, I must congratulate you. I did not think it would survive the hearings. Rest assured that I will work personally to get the shipments moving. I anticipate we will be ready to load ships by mid-April and all ships will have sailed by the first of June. I hope that this meets your operational timeline.*

*There is some news regarding me personally. The chief of staff of the army has requested my retirement on or before the first of October. Per your advice, I have decided that I will take up residence in Tokyo following retirement. I will remain in the army as long as possible. I hope that I can continue in some way to serve The Association. I look forward to hearing from you.*

*Best personal regards,*

*Paul*

Cleve handed the letter to Yoshii. He said nothing until Yoshii looked up. "I don't know what the fuck we've stepped in," Cleve said, "but it doesn't smell very good to me. The sale I think the letter is referencing is an aviation package to Vietnam. I read about it in the papers before I left the states. The idea wasn't very well liked . . . got a lot of bad press. But, why would an active duty US army major general be sending a letter to this guy?" He jerked his thumb toward the estate. "Why is he telling this Yamamoto-person he will do everything he can to expedite the shipments and that he hopes it meets his operational timeline?"

Yoshii shrugged his shoulders, as puzzled as Cleve. A couple of minutes passed in silence as the two men wrestled with what they'd just uncovered. Then Yoshii offered, "What if this guy Yamamoto," he pointed to the estate, "and Fujiwara are planning on hijacking these shipments? I mean it seems so outlandish even for a scoundrel like Fujiwara, but maybe he's trying to corner the market on arms sales in this part of the world these days. He controls everything else that's illegal out here."

The quiet between them fell again as both men considered Yoshii's speculation. Then Cleve broke the silence. "I'm going to sneak inside that wall tonight. I want to see if there's more to it than we can see from up here."

"That's a bad idea, my friend. There's bound to be security someplace in there."

"Maybe, but I don't think so. I watched a landscaping crew work four hours in there. I would have seen them avoiding sensors, cameras, whatever. There are no guards patrolling the place. I think that they believe that they are safe being this far out from the city center. But, I will be cautious. I will need for you to purchase a few things for me. Can you get me an all-black pair of pants, a black long-sleeve T-shirt and some black shoe polish?"


THERE WAS A full moon, the streets surrounding the estate were well lit, and he had no idea what type of security might be in place, but he tried not to think about these things. Every inch of exposed skin was coated with black shoe polish to help him blend into the night. They went to a point along the eastern side of the estate that looked to be as far away from the main house as possible. Yoshii give him a leg up, he pulled himself up to the top of the wall, rolled over, and dropped to the ground. From where he was he could see light coming from several windows on the ground level. He stayed in the cover of the well cared-for shrubbery for as long as he could, but knew that at some point he was going to have to cross an open lawn that was at least fifty meters long. On the other side was another row of shrubbery that would be his next hiding point. He took a deep breath and sprinted across the open area. He was getting near the main house now. He knelt and used his binoculars to look for anything that might look like a security camera. Seeing nothing, he moved closer. At the end of the shrubbery he stopped, shocked at what he saw.

The satellite dishes were all at least eight feet in diameter, seven of them, each one of them oriented in a different direction. *What the hell?* They were directly behind the main house, almost in its shadow, which explained why they hadn't been able to see them from their room in the hotel. *Who is this guy communicating with? More important, what are they talking about?* Cleve took out a paper and pencil and began to make a sketch of the dish farm. Locked in to what he was doing, he nearly jumped out of his skin when he felt the nudge against his right leg. He froze. Looking down, he saw a beautiful doberman pinscher staring up at him. He immediately tightened up, expecting the big dog to sink its teeth into him, but instead it whimpered softly and nudged his leg again. He reached down with his hand and stroked the dog's ears. "Good boy." It nuzzled his hand. "Some attack dog," he whispered. Its stubby tail wagged. Cleve knelt down while the dog licked his face. It sat there beside him while he hastily finished the sketch.

The whistle was loud and shrill. Then in Japanese, he heard words he could not understand, but the dog turned in the direction of the voice and perked its ears.

Cleve looked at the dog. "You better go or we're both going to be in trouble."

The whistle came again along with the same call. The dog bolted off toward the main house. His heart in his throat, Cleve made his way back to the east wall and a large tree. He climbed to a branch that hung just over the wall and lowered himself down on top. Yoshii was waiting on him. "Find anything interesting?"

"This guy must have one hell of a Direct TV bill."

"What?"

"Let's get out of here. I'll explain when we get back to the hotel."

FUKORA, SEITO YAMAMOTO'S manservant, tried to sound upset. "What have you gotten yourself into. What is this black stuff on your ears?" The dog attempted to lick him. "And on your tongue as well. What is it? Smells like shoe polish. Where did you get this?" he asked as he took a slightly wet towel and gently rubbed its ears. "Tomorrow you will have to show me what you got into tonight." When he was satisfied that he'd gotten it off the dog, Fukora switched off the porch light and the dog followed him out of the room.

"THIS GUY HAS got a network of satellite dishes behind that house that some major corporations would kill to have." He showed Yoshii the sketch. "These things are massive, each aimed in a different direction. I can't imagine what household needs a network like this. There's something going on here, Yoshii."

Yoshii had gotten a bottle of scotch to celebrate their breakthrough with the letter. He poured each of them a generous glassful. "So what's our next move, Cleve?"

Cleve didn't answer. He sipped the scotch and walked back to the window overlooking the estate. Finally, he turned and asked, "Yoshii, can you get me to Okinawa?"

"What?"

"Can you get me to Okinawa? The First Special Forces Battalion is there. I need to get this information to them so they can get it back to their higher headquarters."

"But, Cleve, you will be taken into custody . . ."

Cleve walked over to the desk and picked up Stanley's letter. "Yeah, I know, but with this letter," he snapped his middle finger against the letter's edge, "and some luck, this Major General Stanley, Fujiwara, and this guy Yamamoto will be investigated, maybe even taken into custody as well. Then I can get a chance to ask them some questions. I think it's somehow all related."

"I don't know . . ."

"No, I don't know either, but please don't try and talk me out of this. You might just succeed."

Yoshii laughed, stroked his chin, and then said, "There is a ferry. It's risky. I will need to see how it all works."

"What about customs and immigration?"

"I will check. But Okinawa is a prefecture of Japan. Since the ferry is traveling from one prefecture to another, I don't think customs or immigration will be an issue. Let me make a few calls."

Spires watched the estate as Yoshii called the ferry line.

When the call was finished, he looked at Cleve and said, "We have some luck on our side. There is no customs or immigration required for either departure or arrival. I was also able to get the last remaining private cabin for you. You sail tomorrow at noon.

I will pick up the ticket and give it to you. Keep the hood up on your sweatshirt and wear the sunglasses. Get to the cabin as soon as you can and don't come out. Your picture is everywhere and your size and color make you conspicuous. But maybe we have some luck left, my friend. We will need it."

# 28

## DOUBT

Ida Spires was beside herself. Bergstrom's cockiness had both unnerved and angered her. Not knowing what else to do, she decided to take a walk. Perhaps it was subconscious, but she wound up at The Blue Note Bar and Grill.

The place was busy, but no more than usual. Wanda saw the elderly black woman come in. She looked out of place. She'd never seen her before. Walking over to her, Wanda asked, "Would you like a table?"

Ida noticed her name tag and broke down in tears.

Wanda stepped closer, "Now, now, dear. What's the matter?" She put her arm around Ida and maneuvered her to the nearest empty table.

When they'd sat down, Ida looked at her and sputtered, "Wanda, I'm so sorry. I don't usually behave . . ."

Wanda liked that Ida had called her by name, even though she knew she'd gotten it from her name tag.

"I'm Ida Spires, Cleveland's mother."

A surprised look covered Wanda's face.

"Have you seen the papers?"

Wanda nodded. "Yes."

The abbreviated, yet tentative response immediately riled her. "You don't think he did it, do you?"

"Well, I don't . . ."

"He didn't," Ida snapped. "Cleveland isn't like that. He didn't kill that man . . . what's his name . . . Driscoll. There's a Cleveland police detective, name of Bergstrom. He keeps coming around. He's trying to prove that Cleveland had something to do with that man that was killed in the bus accident. It isn't fair. It just isn't fair," she repeated.

Wanda sat back in her chair. Some customers wandered in, and she motioned for another waitress. "I'm going to be here for a few minutes. Cover for me, OK?"

"Look, Mrs. Spires, I must admit, after getting to know your son, none of this seems in character."

Ida looked at her. "He went to Thailand to confront this Driscoll person. He was sure that he knew something. He even thought Driscoll might be the real murderer of that man on Okinawa." Ida wiped the tears from her eyes and looked at Wanda.

"Have you heard from him?" Wanda asked.

The question made Ida cautious. "You're the second person to ask me that today. The other was that detective."

Wanda leaned forward, patted her arm, and said reassuringly, "I know, Ida . . . may I call you Ida? He was by here earlier today. I told him I hadn't heard from Cleveland since he left for Thailand."

Ida apologized, "I'm sorry, Wanda. I'm just not sure who to trust, but Cleveland trusted you, so I do too. So, to answer to your question, I honestly have no idea where he is, if he is OK, I don't even know if he is still alive." The sobbing began again. "I just had to get out of the house. I don't know why I came here . . . maybe I thought . . ."

Despite any lingering doubt she may have had about this woman's son, Wanda felt genuinely sorry for the old lady. "I know, Ida, I know. This must be very hard on you."

Ida had been alone in the world for a long time. Then Cleve came home. She was more fearful now of losing him forever than she had ever been before. The two women sat and talked over coffee for an hour before Wanda said, "I want to help, Ida. But I don't know what to do. How can I help?"

Ida shook her head. "You have helped, Wanda. You gave him a job when no one else would. You gave him back some of his self-confidence. I can't thank you enough for that. I'll let you know when I hear from him."

Wanda liked Ida, but she was also a realist. The deck was stacked against Cleve Spires, and there was a dark side to her thoughts. She thought the odds that either of them would ever see him again were a long shot.


HALFWAY AROUND THE world, Cato Fujiwara sat at his desk and fumed. Cleve Spires was in Japan. He was a loose end and Fujiwara didn't like loose ends. He was beginning to question the trust and confidence he had in his chief counsel. He could not understand how Spires had not been captured or killed. It was nearly midnight. He sensed a complacency in his chief counsel, who had long ago gone home to his wife and three children. *Why isn't he working?* Incompetence, complacency, and failure to achieve results were the three deadly sins in Fujiwara's rulebook. The chief counsel, like Inamine before him, was guilty of all three. *Perhaps,* thought Fujiwara, *I should find someone else.*

# 29

## REUNION

The three-day voyage between Yokohama, Japan and Naha, Okinawa, seemed interminably long. He'd spent most of the time in a cramped interior stateroom with no view to the outside. It made his jail cell seem spacious. The few times he ventured out in search of something to eat, he felt like everyone was watching him, as if they recognized him from some picture they'd seen somewhere and they were searching their memories trying to remember the details. All it would take is one person to notify the captain. If they suspected he was on board, they would have the port locked down tight. Escape this time would be impossible.

The announcement to disembark was in Japanese, but he could hear people shuffling down the passage in front of his cabin as they made their way to the gangway. Pulling the hood on his sweatshirt up and slouching so he didn't stick out quite as much, he maneuvered himself into the middle of the crowd and tried to stay there. From the top of the gangway he looked around and saw nothing that appeared out of the ordinary. He walked down the gangway, across the tarmac, and past the front gate until he came to a que of taxis. The line was long, but it moved quickly. When it was his turn, he threw his backpack into the backseat and told the driver, "Torii Station."

The driver turned around and looked at him. In broken English he said, "Very far. You pay now."

After his experience in Tokyo, this didn't surprise him. He pulled a wad of yen notes from his pocket. "How much?"

When he saw the bills the driver smiled broadly. "Five thousand yen . . . very far . . . very far."

Cleve forked over the money and an hour later the driver deposited him at the front gate of the US Army Garrison, Okinawa at Torii Station. He pulled his retired ID and showed it to the Japanese security guard who waved him through. Ten minutes later he stood in front of the gate to the First Special Forces Battalion Headquarters. It had changed dramatically since he'd been here last, just before his incarceration. The place looked like a prison. Twelve-foot high chain link fencing surrounded the compound, and on top of that was triple-strand concertina wire, these measures all in response to terrorists, most of them Muslim Jihadists looking for targets wherever they believed they might find a soft spot. Gate access required a magnetic-strip pass card. Lacking that, there were instructions for visitors to press the intercom button and state their business. Cleve took a brief moment to rethink what he was doing and then pressed it.

A crackly voice responded, "First Special Forces Battalion. Can I help you?"

Cleve leaned toward the voice, "I'd like to see the command sergeant major."

There was a long pause, then, "Do you have an appointment?"

"No, but it's important."

Another long pause, as if the person on the other end might be checking directly with the sergeant major. Then, "May I have your name and what it is you need to see him about?"

He was prepared for it to come down to this. It inevitably had to at some point. "Cleveland Spires. I need to talk to him about the death of Command Sergeant Major Billy Driscoll."

Another long pause. When the voice came back on, it wasn't the same one. Whoever this was was much more authoritative, more directive. "Enter the building through the door directly in front of you." The gate buzzed and he proceeded the twenty-five yards or so to the building's front doors. As soon as he'd entered, he was confronted by the deceased Billy Driscoll's temporary replacement, Acting Command Sergeant Major James Featherstone, who stood in front of him. Two burly NCOs stepped in on either side of Cleve, while another moved to a position directly behind him. All three had 9 mm pistols leveled at him. Featherstone said, "You've got a lot of guts coming here like this. I've called the military police (MPs). They will be here in a minute. In the meantime, don't try anything funny."

Cleve put his hands in the air, "I won't, Sergeant Major, but before you let the MPs take me, I have something to show you. It's important."

"What is it?"

Cleve handed him the letter from Major General Stanley.

Featherstone looked it over quickly and said, "What do you want me to do with this?"

"Well, I'm not exactly sure, but I don't think either of us can just ignore it. I took this out of a mailbox at an estate in Tokyo. The owner of the estate is involved with the Yakuza in some way and this General Stanley, whoever he is, is somehow connected to all of it. Doesn't it seem a little strange to you, Sergeant Major?"

A young soldier, a specialist 4th class whom Cleve suspected was probably the battalion admin clerk, walked over to Featherstone. "The MPs are here."

He looked at the letter and then back at Cleve. Featherstone told the specialist, "Have them wait in my office." Then he said to Cleve, "I'm going to see if the battalion commander will see you. In the meantime, if you try anything . . ."

Cleve shook his head. "I'm not going to try anything." He paused. "Thanks, Sergeant Major."

LIEUTENANT COLONEL DARRELL Greene's office was quite spacious. At one end, in front of two large windows, was a huge mahogany desk. On one side, along an interior wall, was a long rosewood conference table with a dozen chairs neatly arranged around it. The wall was covered with photographs of some of the more dramatic geographic landmarks throughout the battalion's area of operation. As they entered, Featherstone said to Cleve, "Your lucky day, Spires. The boss is gone more than he's here."

Cleve shrugged his shoulders and said, "I've been called a lot of things lately. Lucky hasn't been one of them." Cleve, Featherstone, and Lieutenant Colonel Greene chuckled.

Greene had already read the letter, but was curious as to how Cleve had come by it.

Cleve explained as Greene appeared to be reading the letter again. When Cleve was finished, Greene looked up from the letter and said, "Your record doesn't inspire confidence. How do I know you haven't just fabricated all of this, including this letter." He held it up.

Cleve reached in his pocket, at which point the three NCOs who had followed him into Greene's office and were guarding him took a step in his direction. Cleve backed off. "OK . . . OK . . . I'm reaching for a piece of paper. It's a phone number. OK?"

Greene nodded, "It's OK, gents. Let him get it."

Cleve pulled out a folded sheet of paper. "This is the phone number for Colonel Yoshii Nagatamura in Tokyo. He'll vouch for me and the authenticity of that letter."

Greene took the slip of paper and, pointing to a chair in front of his desk, said, "Have a seat."

Greene punched the number, introduced himself, and then put Nagatamura through a series of questions. When Nagatamura disclosed that he was a graduate of ICAF, it gave Greene some definitive questions he could ask. Once convinced that he was legit, Greene asked him to explain his relationship to Cleve Spires.

Nagatamura replied, "A mutual friend of ours in Thailand, a classmate of mine from ICAF, asked me to help him here in Japan. We discovered that there is something going on with your country's foreign military sale to Vietnam. He should have shown you a letter from a Major General Paul Stanley. We were together when we discovered that letter. Neither of us is exactly sure what it means, and Cleve thought you might be able to help. I am assuming this call is prompted by his arrival at your headquarters."

Greene acknowledged that he was, in fact, there, thanked Nagatamura for the information, and said goodbye. His next call was to his boss, Colonel Lucas Johnson.

Cleve watched, listened, and was stunned when he heard Greene ask to speak to Colonel Johnson. After Greene hung up, Cleve asked, "Was that Colonel Lucas Johnson?" He put special emphasis on the name Lucas, just to confirm what he thought he already knew.

"It was. Do you know him?"

Cleve could only shake his head at the irony of it all. "Uh . . . yeah . . . we've crossed paths before."

AT FORT LEWIS, Lucas Johnson sat behind his desk and tried to come to grips with what Greene had just told him. Not only had Cleveland Spires surrendered himself on Okinawa, but he was offering some conspiracy theory involving an army two-star general, the Yakuza, and the controversial sale of arms to Vietnam. He could have interrogated Spires by secure video conference, but he'd been planning a visit to the First Battalion anyway. This phone call just moved that up to first place on his priority list. And he would finally have the chance to have an honest talk with Spires to ask the questions that had bothered him since the court-martial. That afternoon, he boarded a US Air Force C-17 at Joint Base Lewis-McChord for the ten-hour flight to Okinawa.

AWKWARD WAS THE only word to describe their eye-ball-to-eyeball encounter in Greene's office. Johnson started off on the wrong foot immediately, "Sergeant Maj— . . ." For Spires, it stung. For Johnson, it was an unforgiveable gaffe. "Uh . . . uh, Spires." Even to Lucas his correction sounded overly officious. "Colonel Greene has briefed me, but I'm interested in your take. What do you think all of this means?"

"I don't know exactly, Sir. But what I do know is this. I didn't kill Driscoll. Cato Fujiwara . . . you know who he is?" Lucas nodded. Spires continued, "Fujiwara and Driscoll are somehow connected."

Johnson held up a hand. "How do you know that?"

"Dying men don't lie, Sir. Yes, I was there when Driscoll was shot, but I didn't pull the trigger. Some Thai kid did that and then ran away. I tried to help Driscoll, but there wasn't anything I could do. The last two words out of his mouth were *Fujiwara* and *Yakuza*. I think he was telling me who had him killed."

Johnson nodded and said, "OK. Go on."

"So, I manage to get out of Thailand and to Japan. I want to confront Fujiwara and in the process, he leads me to Seito Yamamoto. Then I find the letter from a Major General Stanley in Hawaii to Yamamoto. It's all somehow connected and I think they are planning on doing something with that arms shipment to Vietnam." There was a pause. Spires and Johnson looked directly at one another and then Spires said something he'd been holding in since Johnson had walked in the room. "And I didn't kill that kid on Okinawa either. Just so you know."

That stung Johnson. Uncommonly at a loss for words, he just stood there, looking at the man whose life had been ruined by a decision he'd been a part of.

Spires brought things back around. He asked Johnson, "Have you called Colonel Nagatamura?"

"I have."

Spires grew impatient with that incomplete answer. "And?"

"And he corroborated what you've told us about the letter and about Fujiwara and Yamamoto. How did you escape Thai authorities?"

"I have a friend in Thailand who helped me. He shall remain nameless. I think you can understand why, Sir."

Johnson looked at him and nodded, then turned to Greene. "Major General Paul Stanley is the director of logistics and security assistance for US Pacific Command. I looked him up."

Greene whistled. "So, he had a lot to do with this shipment to Vietnam?"

"Sure did. I googled information on this arms sale. Found an old *CNN* story in which Paul Stanley was mentioned as the staff principal at Pacific Command (PACOM) that coordinated the sale."

Greene looked at Spires and then back to Johnson. "So, there is something going on here."

Johnson nodded, "Yeah, good possibility. Where's your secure line? I should call General Hurley."

# 30

## CHAIN OF COMMAND

**B**rigadier General Chuck Hurley, commander of the United States Special Forces Command, Pacific, wasn't a big man in stature and that made him somewhat of an anomaly in the world of special operations. But what he lacked in size, he made up for in craftiness. Three years ago, in Afghanistan, he'd captured twenty-five Taliban fighters with a force of only four Army Green Berets, including himself. A local tribal leader had told them of a nearby village where the Taliban had killed all the men and were now holding the women hostage. Hurley and his small band surrounded the village—or, at least, that is what they'd made the Taliban fighters believe—simply by placing weapons around the village and then scurrying from gun emplacement to gun emplacement, delivering volleys of fire. As the firefight raged and the Taliban started to take casualties, they were given a choice: surrender or face complete annihilation. The Taliban surrendered, but Hurley's team was then faced with another problem. They needed someone to guard the nineteen or so prisoners, while his team regrouped and treated the wounded. There were about forty women remaining in the village. Hurley called them all together and, through an interpreter, told them he needed their help. Producing about a dozen 9 mm pistols, he gave them a quick lesson in how they worked. Then he made the prisoners sit in front of a wall facing their guards, the women they'd been abusing. Hurley told the women to shoot any of them that moved. When one of them decided to test the women's resolve, a shot rang out. It didn't kill the Taliban fighter; in fact, it nearly missed him altogether, but it sent a clear warning to the rest of the prisoners that the women were more than willing to follow their last order. Several of them were later interviewed, their stories appearing across the US on the national news. All of them praised Allah and Hurley for their rescue.

As the C-17 carrying Johnson and Cleve rolled to a stop at the military airlift command's terminal on Hickham Air Force Base, Oahu, Hawaii, Hurley exited his sedan and waited on them to deplane. As the two approached, he asked, "Any trouble?"

Lucas replied, "Not after you talked to the commander at Kadena. They just weren't going to let him on this flight ahead of the others who'd already checked in. There's one pissed-off retired air force colonel still sitting at Kadena, but I guess he'll get over it. Thanks, sir."

"Well, I'm glad I could help," Hurley said.

"General Hurley, this is Sergeant Maj— . . ." *Dammit! I did it again.* "This is Cleveland Spires."

"Spires, you've gotten yourself into quite a mess, I hear."

Cleve nodded as they shook hands. "Yes, Sir."

They moved to the sedan to make the short, thirty-minute drive to Hurley's command center at Fort Schafter. Johnson and

Hurley, who had served together in previous assignments, made small talk along the way. Cleve sat in the back, silent.

Cleve had been inside this headquarters before, but things had changed. Troops clad in digitally camouflaged fatigues sat in front of laptop computers poring over data. There was no smoking inside the facility and, perhaps Cleve's biggest surprise, many of the troops were female. The formerly all-male world of special operations had certainly changed. Hurley led them into a conference room, closed the door, and flipped a switch that illuminated two signs outside the room's entrance. TOP SECRET. DO NOT ENTER. As Johnson and Cleve settled into chairs, Hurley began, "We have a briefing with Lieutenant General Kinney, deputy commander of the US Pacific Command, and Admiral McKeever this afternoon at 1400. In the meantime, let's go over some ground rules. Who knows about Spires being here in Hawaii?"

Lucas went down the short list.

"OK, good. That list needs to stay short until we can determine what, if anything, we are dealing with here."

Cleve disliked the words, "if anything," but decided to keep his mouth shut and let these two set the pace for the time being at least. For the next hour, they discussed exactly how they were going to justify bringing a known fugitive into Pacific Command (PACOM) headquarters and, perhaps even more importantly, that McKeever had a two-star general on his staff that was behaving suspiciously.

"Everything I'm going to tell you now is top secret, compartmental. Only Kinney and McKeever can override me in determining who knows about this." Hurley looked directly at Spires. "Understand?"

Cleve nodded, "Yes, Sir."

Hurley persisted. "This is important. You are going to see and hear some things while you are here that you can't talk about . . . ever. I'm sticking my neck out with you. You don't have any kind of security clearance, and we don't have time to get you one. So, again, you can't talk about any of this, to anyone. Understand?"

"Yes, Sir. I understand."

"OK, then. Let's get into it. I was curious to see if and when Paul Stanley might have been in Japan, since it seems he and Yamamoto are buddies and Stanley's talking about moving there, post-retirement. I asked a contact at the Department of Homeland Security to run Stanley's image against TSA security camera footage at Honolulu International Airport using some sophisticated facial recognition software." He glanced over at Spires. "That's the kind of thing that you can't ever talk about."

Cleve nodded.

"We got a hit. Six weeks ago, he boarded a flight out of Honolulu to Anchorage, Alaska. Then I asked them to run Anchorage footage through the same software. We got another hit. It seems General Stanley flew from Anchorage to Tokyo."

Lucas offered, "It's not unusual for someone on the Pacific Command staff to go to Tokyo, is it, sir?"

"No, it's not, but why fly all the way back to Alaska? I don't know what kind of business a PACOM staff guy would have in Anchorage, and there are plenty of flights out of Honolulu to Tokyo. For that matter, there are a lot of flights out of Hickham to Yakota Air Base in Tokyo. It just didn't make sense to me. Unless, of course, McKeever or Kinney can give us a logical reason."

"Have you asked them?" Lucas asked.

"It will be one of the first questions we get to this afternoon."

LIEUTENANT GENERAL LYNN Kinney and Admiral Chet McKeever were all business as Hurley, Johnson, and Spires walked into the secure conference room. Hurley had arranged this meeting at the last minute, and it was crammed between two other high-level briefings that McKeever had on his calendar. But when Hurley told McKeever's exec that the subject was highly classified and had possible national security interests, he'd found this time on the admiral's schedule. Kinney had had to cancel another meeting, but McKeever wanted him here. As they settled into seats, the admiral wasted no time, "OK, Paul, what's this all about? You know I should have MPs waiting outside that door, don't you?" He looked at Spires.

"Yes, Sir. I appreciate your trust. But we think that something may be up with the Vietnam arms sale."

"Really. What does he have to do with that?" This time McKeever pointed to Spires.

"He's the one that's brought us the information, Sir. Take a look at this." Hurley handed him the letter from Stanley to Yamamoto.

McKeever read it, passed it to Kinney, and asked, "Who's this guy Yamamoto?"

"Don't know, sir. But Spires thinks that Driscoll's death, Cato Fujiwara, Major General Stanley, and Seito Yamamoto are all somehow connected."

"What do you think?" asked Kinney before McKeever had the chance.

"I think it's worth looking into, Sir."

McKeever asked, "How do you know this letter is legitimate?"

"We have confirmed through a colonel in the Japanese Ground Self-Defense Force that he assisted Spires in Tokyo and that this letter was taken from a mailbox on the estate of Seito Yamamoto. My staff has checked out Colonel Yoshii Nagatamura. He is a trusted source."

Kinney queried, "What does Cato Fujiwara have to do with this? We know he's a global dealer in drugs and human trafficking. Now you're going to tell me he's an arms dealer?"

"Well, Sir, we don't know exactly what his interest is, but he regularly visits Yamamoto at his estate just outside of Tokyo. So, we think there's a distinct possibility they might be planning on hijacking some or all of these shipments to Vietnam."

"OK. Any idea what Stanley's connection is to Yamamoto?"

"None, at this point, sir. But I'd like to ask you if you know why Paul Stanley might have recently flown to Tokyo via Anchorage, Alaska. Was it official business?"

McKeever thought for a moment. "He took leave a while back. Said he was going to be in the Alaskan wilderness and out of contact. I approved it . . . didn't like one of my staff principals out of touch like that, but he's done a good job. He deserved the time off."

"But did you know the same day he arrived in Anchorage, he boarded another flight to Tokyo?"

McKeever shook his head. The room fell silent for a while, and then Kinney glanced at McKeever. "It does look odd, Sir."

It didn't take any of them very long to see that McKeever was pissed over the deception. "OK, then let's get his ass in here and see what he has to say for himself."

Hurley had worked with McKeever long enough to know that the admiral could have a short fuse, but he knew Kinney was more patient and could reason with him, so he glanced at Kinney and then advised McKeever, "Uh, Admiral, I think we should hold off for a while on that. There's still too much we don't know and if we get him in here and tip our hand, it gives him more time to fill in the blanks his way."

Kinney calmly offered, "I think General Hurley may be right on that point, Sir."

McKeever didn't like it. He squirmed in his chair, but when he spoke, it was what they wanted to hear, "OK. So what's next, Chuck?"

Inwardly, Hurley breathed a sigh of relief, "Well, Sir. I think we need to do a little snooping on Yamamoto's Tokyo estate."

"Spires, tell the admiral and the general what you saw on the grounds there."

"Satellite dishes, Sir. Big ones. Seven of them, each one about eight feet in diameter. I don't know who this guy is talking to, but he's got a communications set-up at that estate that rivals yours here at PACOM."

Hurley looked at McKeever. "So, Sir, here's where we need your help. We need to get the Defense Intelligence Agency to eavesdrop on these satellite dishes and see what kind of traffic is going back and forth between Yamamoto's Tokyo estate and whoever he is talking to."

"What about Stanley? I could get the JAG to request a wiretap on his phones. It'd be nice to know who he's talking to and what he's saying."

Hurley offered, "Let him go at this point, Sir. If you go to your JAG, then he'll know about this op and so will whoever he has to coordinate the wiretap with. Until we know more about who Yamamoto's talking to and what they are saying, the fewer who know anything at all about this, the better, it seems to me." There was a pause and then Hurley added, lest anyone forget, "And let's keep an eye on the arms shipments to Vietnam."

McKeever offered, "Two ships have already sailed from Sunny Point, North Carolina. Two more are scheduled at the end of the month, and the last two are out of Port Hueneme, California, by the middle of May. Stanley briefed me just yesterday."

"Well, we could also use some satellite time to check in on these ships and make sure that piracy isn't part of any plan. Fujiwara, for one, is certainly capable of hijacking them, if he wanted to," Hurley said.

McKeever offered cautiously, "You know, I'm going to have to brief the chairman of the joint chiefs on this in order to get the satellite time."

"Yes, Sir. I understand. But you and I both know we need to keep this op highly compartmentalized. At this point, if the chairman can just direct the DIA to eavesdrop and provide transcripts to us, I think we can do our own analysis."

McKeever was fully on board now. "Agreed. I'll advise the chairman. I'll have him direct the DIA to deliver all transcripts directly to your headquarters at Fort Schafter, Chuck. The fewer on my staff that know about this, the better. Paul Stanley is well-liked around here. I don't want somebody to put friendship over professionalism and tip him off. Keep Lynn and me in the loop, will you? I'll let my exec know that if you call and need to see me, that you get right in. If I'm out of town, then brief Lynn. He'll keep me up to date. Anything else?"

"No, sir. I'll let you know what we find out."

# 31

## THE LISTS

Cleve felt like he was a prisoner again. His cell was more spacious this time around. Hurley's headquarters was well-hidden and secure within the boundaries of Fort Schafter. It certainly was busier than his jail cell at Fort Leavenworth, full of uniformed soldiers hustling about. But because Hurley had told him, "You cannot leave this headquarters unless you hear it directly from me," Cleve felt confined. Yet, as frustrating as all of this was, he understood why he'd been given that order. Hurley had held up a bulletin from the Joint Intelligence Center, Pacific at Hickham Air Force Base, and said to him, "You're famous, but not in a good way." He had read the bulletin aloud to Cleve:

*Cleveland A. Spires, an American citizen, is wanted in Thailand for the murder of CSM (USA) William Driscoll. Spires was last seen in Bangkok, Thailand. However, Thai authorities believe he may have escaped the country. Spires has a previous conviction for murder.*
*INTERPOL requests assistance in locating this fugitive. In the*

*event he is seen, notify the Joint Intelligence Center, Pacific (JICPAC) immediately. PACOM UNITS ARE ADVISED NOT TO ATTEMPT APPREHENSION OR DETENTION. SPIRES IS CONSIDERED ARMED AND DANGEROUS.*
*Signed*
*WHITWORTH*
*COLONEL, USMC*
*JICPAC WATCH OFFICER*

The bulletin contained Cleve's picture obtained from security camera footage at Don Muang Airport in Bangkok.

"This isn't because I mistrust you, but, if I let you walk around, and someone recognizes you . . . well . . . your cover . . . our cover would be blown. I wouldn't be able to keep you out of the authorities' hands. We will do everything we can to make you comfortable here, but, make no mistake, you are under house arrest. Is that clear?"

It was crystal clear. Yet, despite everyone's efforts, the last week seemed like a month to him. The only saving grace had been that Hurley had allowed him to work with the intelligence analyst tasked with assembling all of the data intercepted from the satellite dishes at Yamamoto's estate and analyzing it. She was a bright, young Marine staff sergeant by the name of Emily Youst. Together they had prepared the briefing she was about to give.

Hurley was fidgety from the moment he'd sat down. "OK, Youst, let's cut to the chase. Who is this guy talking to?"

She'd briefed him before. She knew he liked the bottom line upfront and after that the briefing needed to be sufficiently flexible. She would need to be able to move from point to point based on any questions he might ask. "Message traffic is between Tokyo and seven other countries, Sir. They are China, Vietnam, Thailand, Malaysia, South Korea, the Philippines, and North Korea . . ."

Hurley interrupted, "Wait a minute. Did you say North Korea?"

"Yes, sir."

"Who? Who specifically in North Korea?"

"General Pak Jung Yi, sir, North Korea's minister of foreign relations."

Hurley held up both hands in front of him and waved them back and forth, disbelieving. "Youst, are you sure?"

"Absolutely, Sir. There is a direct satellite link between Yi and Yamamoto in Tokyo. They flow through a commercial satellite that someone . . . we presume it to be Yamamoto . . . has purchased bandwidth on. The data running on the link is encrypted, but the folks at Langley didn't take long in developing the software that cracked the code. We've been following the traffic between each country and Tokyo for over five days now."

"So, this isn't some kind of inter-governmental communication link?"

"No, Sir. Strictly private. The dishes on the other end are all located on the grounds of private residences. The DIA analysts collecting the data said they'd never seen anything quite like this. Everyone except Yamamoto, the guy in Tokyo, is some kind of government minister, but this communication equipment . . . well . . . they're not connected to any government operation that we have been able to detect."

"OK." Hurley paused for a minute to make a note or two. "So, what do we know about this guy Yamamoto that we didn't know a week ago?"

Youst was ready for this question. "Well, Sir, based on the way traffic flows . . ."

Hurley interrupted, "How does it flow?"

Ninety percent of it flows into Tokyo. There's only the occasional message between Tokyo and the outlying countries, Sir.

So, we think that means Tokyo is some kind of headquarters. We also think Tokyo . . . Yamamoto . . . is the focal point for something called Operation Light Switch."

"And what exactly is Operation Light Switch?"

She looked at Cleve, swallowed hard, and said, "We have had to do some reading between the lines to answer that one, Sir, but we believe it is a series of *coups d' etat.*"

Hurley caught the multiple use of the pronoun "we" and the subtle interaction between his analyst and Spires. "We? Who's 'we', Youst?"

"Umm . . . Mr. Spires and me, Sir."

Hurley looked at Cleve, nodded, and said, "Go on. *Coups d' etat,* eh?" Hurley glanced again at Cleve and then back to his briefer. "That's some pretty serious stuff, Youst. What've you got to back that idea up?"

This was it, time to prove to Hurley that they knew what they were talking about. Cleve could tell Youst was a little unsure of herself, but he fought off the urge to help out. She was good at her job. They'd discussed all of this. Youst knew what to say next; she just had to overcome some jitters first. She'd never worked on something quite this earth-shattering before. She straightened up a little more, as if gathering her resolve, and simply said, "Lists, sir."

Hurley chuckled. "Lists!"

"Yes, Sir. Each country, within the last several days has submitted a series of lists entitled *Trusted, Unsure,* and *To Be Eliminated.* We haven't verified every name on each list, but the ones we have . . ." Youst paused for just a moment, "Well, Sir, they are all members of the military in these countries and many of them are general officers or admirals." She picked up a bundle of papers and passed them across the table to him. "Here they are, Sir."

He quickly thumbed through the lists and said, "I'd be interested in hearing what you make of these lists, Youst."

"Yes, Sir. We think the *Trusted* lists are names of personnel that will remain in authority after the coups. The *Unsure* lists are people whose loyalty might be in question. And the *To Be Eliminated* lists are people that cannot be trusted and are consequently marked for elimination." Youst looked at Cleve and nodded.

"Eliminated?" Hurley wasn't naïve, but the sheer brutality of publishing lists of people to be . . . what? Executed? He was having trouble getting his head wrapped around that. "What do you think they mean by that?"

Cleve spoke up for the first time. "Killed, Sir. And you're not going to believe whose name is on the *To Be Eliminated* lists from six of the seven countries."

"Who?"

"Paul Stanley, Sir. North Korea was the only country that didn't have him on their *To Be Eliminated* list."

"Shit!" was all Hurley could unapologetically say.

Cleve wasn't finished. "This morning, Yamamoto or someone from the estate in Tokyo sent Japan's lists to the other seven countries . . ."

"Wait. Stop. So Japan is planning a coup as well?"

"We believe so. Yes, Sir. Oddly, the lists from Japan contain no names of military personnel. But the *To Be Eliminated* list from Tokyo included Paul Stanley's name as well as Cato Fujiwara's." The room fell silent for a moment and then Cleve managed to put into words what everyone else was thinking, "This is one ruthless bunch we are dealing with here, Sir."

Hurley was stunned. All he could do was nod.

# 32

## PRE-TRIAL CONFINEMENT

W ithin two hours of Hurley's briefing, Hurley, Youst, and Spires sat nervously waiting in a secure conference room at Pacific Command headquarters at Camp H.M. Smith, Hawaii. Admiral Chet McKeever and Lieutenant General Lynn Kinney swept into the room fifteen minutes late. There were no introductions. Everyone knew everyone else except Staff Sergeant Youst, and she would take care of that detail as she began, directing her remarks to McKeever, the senior officer in the room. "Sir, I am Staff Sergeant Emily Youst. I am an intelligence analyst for the United States Special Forces Command, Pacific. This briefing is classified Top Secret, Compartmentalized, No Foreign Dissemination and has been compiled from information provided by the Central Intelligence Agency, the Defense Intelligence Agency, and Cleveland A. Spires."

McKeever nodded. "Nice to meet you Sergeant. Please proceed."

Youst went through the briefing she had just given to Hurley. Predictably, many of the questions were the same as Hurley had asked. What no one in the room could have predicted, however, was McKeever's reaction when he heard that Major General Paul Stanley, his director of logistics and security assistance, was so heavily involved and now, apparently, marked for elimination. It was like an Atlas rocket had ignited within the small conference room. As the profanity and the smoke cleared, McKeever glared at his deputy and sputtered, "Eliminated, my ass! If anyone is going to eliminate him, it's going to be me. Lynn, get that bastard in here right now. Grab a couple of MPs and take them with you. I want that sonuvabitch put in pre-trial confinement and court-martialed for treason."

No one moved, and that seemed to anger the four-star admiral further. "Well, what the hell is everyone waiting on? We've got the proof. We've got him by the balls. I want him in the brig by sundown."

Hurley was the first to speak, "Uh, sir, if I might suggest, there's still a lot we don't know about what's going on, and Stanley could likely fill in some gaps for us. For example, it would be nice to know the dates when Operation Light Switch will begin. We haven't been able to pull that off the satellite communications yet. No one disagrees that he's guilty as hell, but, right now, he's an intelligence asset that could be of high value to us."

McKeever, still seething at Stanley's deception, said, "So, what are you suggesting, Chuck? You want me to mollycoddle this guy hoping he'll roll our way? He doesn't deserve it. He deserves jail . . . for the rest of his fu— . . ." McKeever caught himself, realizing there was a female present, "for the rest of his life!"

Now Kinney weighed in. "Admiral, Chuck's right. We need Stanley's cooperation now more than we need his incarceration.

Give me first crack at him. I was on the selection board that picked him for his first star, so I'm feeling very deceived myself right now."

McKeever looked to Hurley, who was nodding in agreement. The room was quiet while McKeever collected himself. "OK, Lynn. You win. But I want this handled by the book. I don't want him to wiggle out of prosecution because we fumbled some legality. Read him his rights and when you are finished, I want him in the brig."

Kinney looked at McKeever and then to Hurley. "What do we want to tell his deputy, Jay Chance? He'll wonder where his boss is. We can't tell him the truth."

Hurley looked at his watch. "It's 1600. Is Stanley still in his office?"

"I assume so. He's usually here until after 1800," Kinney offered.

"How about Captain Chance? What time does he usually unplug for the day?"

Kinney said, "It varies, but I don't think he's around that late. Jay's got a bunch of kids, so he's got volleyball, soccer, swimming, all that stuff. He tries to get to as much of that as he can."

Hurley scratched his head. "OK. Here's the deal. We need to be as discreet as possible in getting Stanley out of here after you talk with him, General. That means we've got to wait until the place is as empty as possible and then the MPs escort him to Pearl Harbor with as little fanfare as needed . . . no handcuffs, no restraining him. It's got to look like he's just leaving for the day and is walking out with a couple of MPs."

Kinney nodded in agreement.

"Then, sir, I suggest you give Captain Chance a call at home this evening. Give him some story about a medical emergency.

Tell him that Stanley was taken by ambulance to Tripler, but they decided it was serious enough that they needed to evacuate him to Bethesda Naval Hospital. That way his staff won't show up at Tripler looking to visit him. I will take responsibility for covering this story with Bethesda in case Chance or anybody else should call them asking about his health. He will be "in intensive care and unable to receive phone calls or visitors."

The last order of business with McKeever and Kinney was to go over who knew about any of this. The list had not grown very much. Staff Sergeant Youst was the only real addition. Analysts back in Virginia who'd seen the photos and transcripts were told only to collect, not analyze. Analysis was Youst's job. McKeever offered, "I owe the chairman a call. I won't do that until I hear from you, Lynn, but call me at home tonight on the secure line after you've talked with Stanley. I want to know what he's got to say."

"Aye, aye, Sir." Kinney acknowledged.

THE PHONE ON Stanley's desk rang just before 6:00 p.m. Caller ID told him it was the deputy commanding general. "Stanley, Sir. You just caught me. I was closing up for the day."

"Paul, I've got something I need to discuss with you. It's classified. Can you come to my office?"

"Yes, Sir. Be right there."

From an antechamber off to the side of Kinney's office, two MPs watched Stanley enter. As soon as Kinney had closed the door, they took up their designated positions on either side of the only doorway into the office.

Kinney was neither brusque nor sophomoric as he asked, "Paul, how long have we known one another?"

The question surprised him. His relationship with Lynn Kinney had always been friendly, but professional, so he was not prepared for this start to their conversation.

"Uh, well, let me think, Sir. It must be seven or eight years now, isn't it?"

"Yeah, that's about what I was thinking." Kinney leaned back in his desk chair, looked at him, and said, "That's long enough that you should trust me by now. Right?"

Stanley had no idea where any of this was going, but he was growing more and more uncomfortable. "Uh, well, yes, Sir. I've always trusted your judgment."

Kinney decided he'd pussyfooted around things long enough. "Then, Paul, trust me when I tell you, you are in some serious trouble." Kinney reached into the center drawer of his desk and took out a laminated card about the size of a business card. From it, he read Stanley his rights. As part of this Kinney was required to disclose the crime he was suspected of and the maximum punishment possible under the Uniform Code of Military Justice. The crime was treason; the maximum possible punishment, death.

Stanley sat there half-paralyzed by the jolt of adrenaline that had just surged through his body. He thought, *How? How could they have found out? I've been so careful. They've been so careful.* His voice was weak, unconvincing, "Sir, I don't know . . ."

Kinney slid the letter Stanley had written to Yamamoto across the desk. "I'm telling you this now as a friend, Paul. We've got you solidly in cahoots with at least eight other people and we know you are planning coups in at least eight Asian countries. It appears to me that you now have a choice to make. You can cooperate with us and tell us everything you know, or you can keep your mouth shut, be labeled a traitor, face a general court-martial and be the only man that goes down with the ship. Oh, yes, and while you are deciding, you might want to consider this." Kinney slid the intercepted lists from Japan over to him. "The last page is the most interesting," Kinney told him. "It's a *To Be Eliminated* list that Yamamoto, or someone from his estate in Tokyo, sent out this morning to the other seven countries involved in your scheme. Just so you understand the type of people you are dealing with here, Paul, your name and Cato Fujiwara's name are on that last page."

Stanley sat there, blankly staring at Kinney.

"Go ahead. Take a look. I want you to know that I'm not just shitting you about any of this, Paul. And, just so we are clear, there are two MPs outside that door," Kinney pointed to it. "They are going to take you to the brig at Pearl as soon as you and I are finished here. You will be held in solitary pre-trial confinement until your trial date. Do you understand the bind you are in?" Kinney was surprised to see a tear form in the corner of Stanley's eye.

# 33

## THE TANK

The phone rang at 2200 hours at Chuck Hurley's quarters. "Good evening, Sir."

Chet McKeever was to the point on this unsecure phone line. "Paul, meet me planeside at Hickham at 1100 hours tomorrow. Bring Youst and the gentleman she's been working with. Plan on being gone a couple of days for meetings at the Pentagon."

"He cooperated?" Hurley asked.

"Sure did. I'll brief you on the plane."

THEY LANDED AT Andrews Air Force Base just outside of Washington, D.C. at 0400 hours on May 15. It was already hot and humid in northern Virginia, and the air conditioner in the late-model Chevy Tahoe was cranked to full blast, a good thing, because the power windows in the heavily armored vehicle had been rendered inoperable. Traffic at that early hour was light.

At 0445 hours, they pulled up to the Pentagon's west portico. Ascending the wide stone stairway to the entrance, McKeever told everyone, "We're briefing in the Tank. It will be the chairman, the chief of staff of the army, the chief of naval operations, the chief of staff of the air force, the commandant of the marine corps and, Chuck, your boss, the commanding general of the US special forces command . . . just them. I told the chairman this was highly compartmentalized so the dwarfs weren't invited." The dwarfs, as they were jokingly called, were the executive officers to each of these four-star generals and admirals. It was customary for them to attend briefings with their boss. Turning to Staff Sergeant Youst, he asked, "Have you ever briefed in the Tank before?"

She had not, but she refused to let him see her jitters. "No, Sir, but I'm ready."

Smiling, he said, "Just give them the same briefing you gave me. Add in the things that Stanley has given us and you will be fine."

"Yes, Sir."

The group proceeded through four separate security check points before reaching the door that opened into the Tank. The others went in, but McKeever stepped aside and pulled Cleve over to him. "Listen, Spires, I'm not sure what kind of a reception you are going to get in there. The chairman has advised me that the chief of staff of the army thinks you should be bound over to the police. I've told the chairman that would be a very big mistake." McKeever put his hand on Cleve's shoulder. "I told him that he needed to run interference for you and me. We wouldn't have the foggiest fucking clue as to what these guys are up to if it weren't for you. So, don't take any of what might happen in there personally. The chairman and I have your back."

Cleve nodded. "Thank you, Sir."

MCKEEVER WAS RIGHT. Cleve could feel the army chief of staff's steely stare from the moment he entered the Tank behind McKeever. However, as things progressed and the army's highest-ranking officer discovered he apparently had a rogue general on his hands, the four-star's attention shifted. When Youst was finished, he asked, "Where's Stanley now?"

Youst knew the answer, but looked at McKeever, who said, "He's in solitary pre-trial confinement at the brig in Pearl Harbor."

Curtly the four-star replied, "You gonna court-martial the sonuvabitch or am I?"

The question riled McKeever because it missed the point, but he controlled his anger. After all, it was just yesterday that he'd been the one asking the same type of question. "Listen, Chief, I know how you feel about this deception. I was right where you are now twenty-four hours ago. Trust me, I'll see that Paul Stanley gets everything that's coming to him. But right now, everyone in this room needs to pay attention to two questions. One, what can we do to find out when this operation is going to kick off? And, two, what do we do next with the information we have?"

The army chief looked over at General Jonas Pastor, the chairman of the joint chiefs of staff, who was nodding in agreement, and then turned back to McKeever. "Yeah, you're right, Chet." He looked at Youst and asked, "Are we still monitoring those satellite dishes?"

"Yes, sir. I get transcripts from Langley four times a day. So far there's been nothing about a start date."

Pastor looked to McKeever. "Stanley doesn't know the date?"

"Claims he doesn't. Says he was told by Yamamoto himself that he didn't need to know that piece of information. I believe him."

Pastor nodded. The chairman's next question wasn't so easy. "So, how do we find out?"

Youst knew someone in the room had an answer to that, but she kept her mouth shut as she looked to Cleve.

He caught her glance, nodded, then turned to Hurley. "Sir, if I may."

Hurley exclaimed, "Absolutely, Sergeant Major," this time not retracting the incorrect use of Cleve's former rank.

Hearing it stung Cleve, but there were more important things in front of them. "Let me begin with an observation. These guys have kept this operation a secret for a long time, thirty years or more. Their entire scheme depends on the element of surprise. Now their cover is blown, but they don't know that. Whatever we do, we can't tip them off that we know what they are up to. I also think we have to assume that they are in a position to trigger Operation Light Switch today, if they thought their secret had been compromised." He glanced around the room. A few heads were nodding. "So we have to avoid confronting any of the eight men that Stanley has implicated as belonging to this thing called The Association. But there is one person that we might confront. He's vulnerable because he's on their *To Be Eliminated* list and he doesn't know that. He's also vulnerable because we know his routine. He goes every other day to visit Yamamoto at that estate just outside of Tokyo. He takes the same route every time to get there. The only other person with him is the driver. There's an opportunity to get to him at some point along that route. Maybe, just maybe, Cato Fujiwara knows when Operation Light Switch is going to start. If we can convince him of Yamamoto's double-cross, maybe we can turn him."

"This is absurd," came the response from the army chief of staff.

Cleve was pretty sure that acerbic reaction was because he was the one who had suggested it. There had been a time when Cleve would have treaded more lightly. However, that time was long since passed, he had nothing to lose at this point, and, quite frankly, the army chief of staff's attitude pissed him off. He looked at the four-star, reached down inside of himself and said, "With all due respect, General, I'm willing to hear your ideas."

It was getting nasty fast. The army chief of staff spluttered something unintelligible except for its profanity.

At that point, General Pastor intervened. "Gentlemen," he said as he looked around the room, "the sergeant major is right. If anyone has a better idea, now's the time to put it out there."

The army chief of staff persisted. Looking at Cleve, he asked, "Are you suggesting we give this Fujiwara guy a pass on his role in this debacle?"

Cleve looked first to Hurley and then to McKeever, who nodded. "Yes, sir. If we do this right and it all plays out the way I think it will, there won't be anything to prosecute. The coups in Japan won't happen if we can convince Fujiwara to pull his support out from under Yamamoto."

The room fell silent except for a few hushed conversations. Finally, General Pastor looked to McKeever and said, "Chet, you know the next move has to be to get this in front of the president's national security team. I can't OK this move on Fujiwara without talking to Tim Munson."

McKeever nodded, "Yeah, I agree. How quickly can we get to him?"

"I dunno. He's in town, I believe. Today; tomorrow at the latest."

Then McKeever offered, "Then I guess it's time we talk about the elephant in the room."

The pachyderm Pastor and McKeever had talked about was huge. Now it was time to get the service chiefs involved in the discussion. Pastor nodded, "OK. Gents, let's talk about need-to-know." The service chiefs looked at one another as if somewhat confused. Pastor proceeded, "Chet and I aren't sure we want to get too many involved in this, given that the element of surprise is so key."

No one said anything, until, finally, Hurley's boss, the commanding general of the US special forces command, spoke up. "Are you suggesting what I think you are? Are you suggesting *we* pick and choose who we are going to tell about this nightmare?"

This rocked every one of the service chiefs back in their chairs.

The chief of staff of the air force was the first to speak. "If we are talking about even the slightest chance that we put troops overseas in harm's way, the president is going to have to go to Congress. The Constitution . . . The War Powers Act requires it."

McKeever spoke up. "And if he goes to Congress, and someone leaks what we know about Operation Light Switch to the press . . ." He didn't need to complete the thought.

The commandant of the marine corps, a tough old guy who'd risen all the way through the ranks from private to four-star general, bluntly asked, "What are you suggesting, Chet?"

"The chairman and I have talked about it. We don't trust the vice president, the secretary of defense, or the secretary of state to keep their mouths shut. The VP and the defense secretary are pure political animals, and they won't put their asses on the line. The secretary of state is a self-indulged, naive academic who believes everything can be solved by sitting down and talking about it. Any one of them would leak what we know about

Operation Light Switch even before the president could get to Congress. We think we need to tell the president that he can't involve them and that he must be prepared to commit troops clandestinely."

The chief of staff of the army asked, "So, are you suggesting we go straight to the president with this thing?"

McKeever cleared his throat and said, "Not exactly." He cleared his throat again. "Tim Munson's the only one General Pastor or I trust. We convince Munson that this is our only option, then we make a run at the president."

"Jesus, Mother, and Mary," exclaimed the chief of naval operations, "it's political suicide for all of us."

Pastor fixed a steely glance on the four-star admiral, but it was McKeever, a Naval Academy classmate of the navy chief's, that spoke up. "That could well be, but, as Sergeant Major Spires has suggested, if anyone else has a better option, now's the time to put it on the table." Everyone looked around the room. No one spoke up.

Pastor concluded, "So, gents, it's either all in or nothing at all. I need to hear it from each of you." One by one, each indicated their agreement.

"OK," Pastor said. "All of us will need to be present when we meet with Munson. Keep your calendars flexible. No one leave town. I'll let you know when we are scheduled."

McKeever said, "In the meantime, if it's OK, I'd like to turn Chuck Hurley loose on drawing up a plan for the raid on Fujiwara. Munson will want details on that before he asks the president to meet with us. We should be prepared to give him those details." There were nods all around.

# 34

## TRAFFIC STOP

It was pre-dawn on the morning of June 1 as the C-17 settled down onto Honolulu International's Reef Runway. Chuck Hurley called his wife to let her know he was back on the island, but then went straight to his office. The secure phone on his desk rang once. He was expecting the call.

"Chuck, McKeever here. You are a go. Sorry, but General Pastor wants you with us here."

Hurley, just off of an eight-hour plane ride from Washington, hung his head and shook it, but didn't say anything.

"As soon as you have your arrival information, send it to me. I will have a car waiting for you."

"Roger, Sir." There was no sense in protesting. Hurley knew the meetings between McKeever, Pastor, Munson, the national security advisor, and Wilson Glover, the president of the United States, would be tense. If he were the president, he'd want as many knowledgeable people as possible around him as well. The military was going to run a military op in Japan that would essentially hijack a Japanese citizen, even if his detention was to be only momentary. To further complicate matters, the military was asking the president to approve the operation without telling anyone on his national security team except Munson, and no one in Congress. Hell, the prime minister of Japan didn't even know what was about to go down. They were on a very slippery slope and, now that he'd been ordered to the White House Command Center, Hurley knew full well what that meant. All involved parties and who-the hell-knew-who-else were going to be watching the entire operation play out in real time via a secure satellite link. He could only hope that the president or one of the others didn't decide that they should start calling the shots from half a world away.

Lucas Johnson would be in charge of operations on the ground. Along with him would be three other hand-chosen special operators from the First Special Forces Group, Colonel Yoshii Nagatamura of the Japanese Ground Self-Defense Force, who was, crucially, acting entirely on his own in this delicate little op, and one civilian, Cleve Spires, who had pled his case convincingly to Lucas Johnson. But the buck on this somewhat controversial decision had not stopped at Johnson, who'd had to be equally convincing with everybody up his chain of command.

The plan to waylay Cato Fujiwara was a simple one, but, like all plans, could become quickly complicated if it didn't go exactly as designed. For example, what would happen if Fujiwara or his driver pulled a gun? Shots fired on a public street would not go unnoticed. The police and the press would certainly get involved and, not necessarily in that particular order. If they were caught, the US's advantage of surprise would be lost forever. Paul Stanley, who'd been asked during his interrogation, "Are they prepared to launch Operation Light Switch today?"

had responded, "What do you think? If they've put together lists of who they can trust and who they can't, then wouldn't you assume they are ready?"

DAWN WAS JUST breaking in the Land of the Rising Sun on June 3 when Colonel Yoshii Nagatamura pulled his car into a parking spot in front of United States Forces, Japan (USFJ) headquarters on Yakota Air Force Base. Ironically, the US base was only about five miles as the crow flies from Yamamoto's estate on the western fringes of Tokyo. Once cleared by the security police at the building's main entrance, he was escorted to a secure briefing room.

He was very curious about what was going on. The text to his phone came from an unknown number. *You are invited to a classified briefing at USFJ headquarters at 0500 hours, June 3. Your attendance is completely voluntary. Do not respond to this text.* After receiving it, he'd checked his phone a few minutes later. The message was gone.

Cleve was the first to greet him. "Colonel, it is good to see you again, my friend."

Nagatamura was stunned. "How did you . . ." He glanced around the room. "I . . . I . . . don't know how you . . ."

Chuckling, Cleve said, "Well, it's a long story, Sir. Sit down and let us fill you in."

They went through it chapter and verse. To say he was astounded would be an understatement. *Coups . . . eight countries . . . a United States of Asia cut off from the rest of the world . . . my own country controlled by The Yakuza,* he thought. When the briefing was finished, Johnson asked, "Colonel Nagatamura, you are familiar with the route that Fujiwara takes?"

"Yes."

"Can you lead us on that route?"

"Yes, yes, I can."

Cleve nodded and smiled at Johnson. "I told you he'd be up for this."

Johnson looked at Nagatamura. "I am obligated to tell you that no one in your country's government knows we are here. No one knows what we are planning. If something goes wrong, I cannot protect you from your government's inquiry, and, I must tell you, there is every likelihood there will be an inquiry at some point."

Nagatamura looked around the room. Cleve's eyes were on him like lasers. Turning to Johnson, Nagatamura calmly asked, "What can I do to help?"

Johnson stepped to a magnetic white board with four toy cars attached to it. "It's pretty simple really. This is Fujiwara's car . . ." It didn't take long to lay it out for him.

"How soon?" Nagatamura asked.

"This afternoon," Johnson replied.


THE STRETCH OF road was a scant two kilometers long. Traffic was light and Fujiwara's car was clipping along at about sixty miles per hour. Nagatamura said into his mouthpiece, "Intercept is just ahead. I am going to pass now," and he eased his foot down on the accelerator. In the rearview mirror, he saw the other two cars keeping up with him. He glanced over at Fujiwara's driver who never took his eyes off the road ahead as Nagatamura passed him and moved into the lane just in front of Fujiwara's car. Within only a few seconds, Johnson's car that had been closely following Nagatamura pulled alongside Fujiwara's. The driver kept even with it. Behind Lucas's car, a third one containing two soldiers moved up to a spot just behind Fujiwara.

Over their headsets, everyone on the team heard Nagatamura say, "Slowing now."

Johnson, in the car alongside Fujiwara's, rolled down the passenger side window and held up a sign lettered in Kanji.

*Cato Fujiwara, we wish you no harm. We are US soldiers on a US sanctioned mission. We know about Operation Light Switch. You are in danger. We wish to help you. Please stop your car.*

Nagatamura, in the car directly in front of Fujiwara's, slowed and then rolled to a stop. Johnson's driver stopped his car alongside Fujiwara's, preventing it from pulling out and passing Nagatamura. The trailing car moved to a position immediately behind, stopped, and a US soldier riding in the passenger seat got out. Walking up to Fujiwara's car, he said in perfect Japanese, "Cato Fujiwara, we only want to talk. Roll down your window, please."

Nothing happened immediately. The windows in the back seat of Fujiwara's car were blacked out, but they could see the driver looking and then turning around as if talking to or receiving directions from Fujiwara in the back seat. Johnson, Cleve, and the soldiers with them strained to see signs of a gun. Every one of them had their hands on theirs, but no one pulled their weapon from its holster. Finally, after what seemed an interminably long time, the back seat window nearest Johnson rolled down and Fujiwara asked in excellent English, "Who is in charge?"

Lucas opened the back passenger door at the same time that Cleve opened the front passenger side door. Both men got out. Lucas said, "I am Colonel Lucas Johnson, US Army. I suspect you already know who this is," he said pointing to Cleve. "Cleveland Spires. He and I have some important information for you, Mr. Fujiwara."

Fujiwara noticed the cameras mounted on the shoulder straps of their backpacks. Suspiciously, he asked, "Who else is watching?"

Lucas replied, "This operation is sanctioned by the highest level of the US government."

"So, who is that? Your President? President Glover? Well, hello, President Glover. If you know about Operation Light Switch, then you know it won't be long before you and I must establish . . . what shall we call them . . . diplomatic relations . . . Mr. President." His tone was scoffing.

AT THE COMMAND Center in the White House, President Wilson Glover bit his tongue.

LUCAS SAID, "MR. Fujiwara, we only have limited time. You must stay on schedule on your visit to Seito Yamamoto, but before we send you along, there are some things that you should know and that is why we are here. Things are not as they may seem, Mr. Fujiwara."

"What do you know of it, Colonel?"

"Well, actually, I know quite a bit more than you." Quickly, Lucas laid out the plans for the coups in the other seven countries. Fujiwara was noncommittal. Lucas explained about the intercepted lists and when he was finished he handed them to Fujjiwara. "You will be interested in knowing you are on the list of Japanese to be eliminated following the coups, the very coups which Yamamoto is counting on you to pull off for him. Not a very fitting reward for such a loyal soldier, is it, Mr. Fujiwara?"

As everyone looked on, Fujiwara slowly thumbed through

the pages, stopping on the last page—the one that contained his name.

Lucas rhetorically asked him, "How many of your lieutenants are on that list, Mr. Fujiwara? I'm sure Yamamoto isn't planning on risking any leftover loyalty to spoil his ascension to power here in Japan or in the rest of this United States of Asia for that matter." Lucas gave that a moment to sink in and then asked, "Am I right, Mr. Fujiwara?"

They had been stopped along the road for about four minutes. Traffic was light, but not nonexistent. One of the soldiers had moved the car carrying Johnson and Cleve to the side of the road in front of Nagatamura's car, so it appeared that these were simply four cars pulled to the curb, one behind the other. Yet time remained of the essence. Fujiwara's arrival at Yamamoto's estate had to be kept on schedule in order to avoid raising eyebrows.

Lucas could tell from his expression that he was spot on, but Fujiwara wasn't totally convinced. "How do I know these lists are not just some fabrication by your government?"

"Well, you can't be sure about that, but let me ask you, if we know about Operation Light Switch and have taken the trouble, not to mention the risk of coming here to tell you about what we know, why would we fabricate these lists? We could have simply just notified your prime minister about your plot against his government and let him handle it."

"So, why didn't you just do that, Colonel?"

"Because, Mr. Fujiwara, your country's government isn't the only one in this part of the world that we care about. And there is at least one piece of vital information we are lacking that we think you might know."

"And what is that?"

"The start date. When will Operation Light Switch kick off?"

"Ah, yes, I can see where knowing that piece of information would be helpful to you."

"I am authorized to offer you a deal, Mr. Fujiwara."

"A deal, Colonel. I have done nothing wrong. Why should I need a deal?"

"Well, yes, you can refuse to tell us what we want to know. If you choose to roll the dice, we will leave you here today to your own devices. But before you make that decision, I should tell you that my government has no intention of allowing these coups to occur. We will act in some way, swiftly, and then you can figure out a way to wriggle out of your actions when your government comes calling on you to explain your treasonous role." He gave that a moment and then proceeded, "Or, Mr. Fujiwara, you can tell me what I want to know, and, provided you and your men stand down, meaning there is no coups in Japan, your government does not need to know anything about your involvement. Or at least they will never hear it from my government, the US government."

Fujiwara was considering, but the clock was ticking. Lucas urged, "Consider carefully. The element of surprise has shifted, Mr. Fujiwara, from your side to ours. Your chances of success are now seriously degraded."

"What if I don't know when this Operation Light Switch is to begin?"

"Then we will be forced to act based on what we know up to this point and that is what the president of the United States will share with your prime minister . . . that a coup is imminent, that the Yakuza is intimately involved and that the leader of the Yakuza . . . you, Mr. Fujiwara, are a principal planner."

Lucas glanced at his watch. Seven minutes had elapsed. Fujiwara, a master of intimidation, refused to show any sign of weakness as he thumbed through the pages of lists Lucas had given him. Then Lucas heard in his headset, "Put a headset on this dirt bag. I want to talk directly to him."

Tim Munson advised, "Mr. President, I'm not sure that's a very good idea."

"Bullshit. Colonel, get this guy up on the air."

Lucas happened to agree with Munson, but was in no position to refuse the president's order. "Yes, Sir," he said, directing Cleve, who was sitting next to him in the back seat of Fujiwara's car, to give him his headset.

Fujiwara no sooner had it in place than President Glover let go. "Listen, Fujiwara, we aren't going to fuck around forever while you decide what you are going to do. You've got exactly ten seconds to tell us anything you know about Operation Light Switch or I will direct my men to leave you right where you are. After that you can go fuck yourself for all I care. Now you only have five seconds. What's it going to be?" The last five seconds passed in the blink of an eye. "OK, Colonel, pack . . ."

"Operation Light Switch will begin on July 4."

Then calmly, coolly, both Johnson and Fujiwara heard the president say, "OK, Colonel. Come on home. Good job. The White House is clear."

But there was one more order of business that Johnson and Cleve wanted to conduct. They waited until they were sure the White House channel was clear and then Lucas directed, "OK, gents. Shut down communications. Spires and I have one more little bit of information we need. Wait for us."

He got a "Roger, Sir," from everyone on his team and then he removed his headset and took back Cleve's from Fujiwara.

"What now?" Fujiwara asked disgustedly.

"Now, Mr. Fujiwara," Lucas said, "I want you to tell us about Billy Driscoll."

"Who?"

"Don't be coy with me, Cato, or I will have your driver removed from the car, I will leave, and you may deal directly with Mr. Spires."

"What is your connection to Billy Driscoll?" Lucas asked again.

"I do not know of anyone by that name."

Cleve piped up, "Fujiwara, dying men don't waste words and they don't lie. So why were the last two words out of Driscoll's mouth *Yakuza* and *Fujiwara*?"

"How should I know?"

Lucas said to Cleve, "OK. Let me out of the car. He's all yours."

Cleve opened the door and moved to let Lucas get around him, but before he'd even put a foot on the ground, Fujiwara relented.

"OK . . . OK. He works for us in Bangkok. He is . . . he is one of our suppliers."

Cleve closed the car door. Lucas said, "OK, that's a start. Who killed him?"

Fujiwara looked over at Cleve. "He did."

Cleve reached past Lucas, grabbed Fujiwara by the lapel of his expensive suit jacket, and pulled him to him while balling the other hand into a fist. Fujiwara's driver made a move to help his boss, but Johnson, whose pistol was at the ready, leveled it at him and made it clear that if he tried to intervene, it would not go well.

Fujiwara was, for the first time in a long time, defenseless. The intimidator was now the intimidated. Fear showed in his eyes and his voice trembled as he sputtered, "No . . . no . . . I mean . . . that is what they say . . . I don't know who killed him. Driscoll has many enemies. All I know is that he killed a man on Okinawa a long time ago and then blamed it on him." He pointed to Spires.

That answer stunned Johnson.

Cleve asked, "Why was Tetsu Agaki following me in Cleveland?"

Fujiwara was overflowing with information now because Cleve still had hold of his lapel. "I don't know why. Maybe he was afraid you were going to come after him. Look at what has happened. It was a reasonable fear after all, wasn't it?" Fujiwara had thrown them a bone. Then he tossed another one. "Tetsu is a friend of mine, but I did not hire him to follow you. Driscoll did that."

"Did you know I was going to Bangkok to see Driscoll about Agaki?"

"Now, how would I know that? You were never a threat to me. What happened to you happened because Driscoll needed someone to blame the murder in Okinawa on. I had nothing to do with any of that. It was all Driscoll. He even bragged to one of my associates that it had cost him fifty thousand dollars to frame you. He said it was the best fifty thousand he'd ever spent."

There it was. The lie uncovered. Cleve, stunned by the truth to the point of near exhaustion, let go of Fujiwara, opened the car door and returned to the other car.

Though Lucas, too, was stunned, he kept his wits about him and issued Fujiwara a final warning. "None of this ever happened. If you deceive us and reveal to anyone what we have told you today or if you participate in the coups, the president will offer military assistance to your prime minister. If that happens, I will personally come and hunt you down like the criminal that you are. Do you understand?" As Lucas slid across the seat and out of the car, he could see Fujiwara straightening his jacket and hear him scolding his driver.

The team sat there alongside the road until Fujiwara departed, headed in the direction of the estate. Then one by one they each did a U-turn and returned to Yakota.


THAT NIGHT AS the C-17 climbed to its assigned cruising altitude somewhere over the Sea of Japan, heading back to Hickham Air Force Base, Hawaii, Johnson and Cleve found a quiet spot alone on the huge airlifter. "Listen, Sergeant Major, I don't know what to say. I can't give you back those ten years, but I can see that you get your rank and your reputation back. At this point, it seems to me the government owes you at least that . . . and a huge apology."

Cleve looked at Johnson, "You know, during the court-martial, I thought Driscoll seemed a little too smooth, a little too rehearsed, but I gave up suspecting him. I'd read the *Army Times* while I was in prison. I'd see him get promoted to first sergeant, then to command sergeant major. I told myself he couldn't have anything to do with it. If he were guilty of something, the army would figure it out and nail him. But they never did. All those lives he's ruined . . . that security policeman on Okinawa . . . all those Thai women he's used . . . the addicts whose lives were ruined by his smuggled drugs . . . and, then, there's me."

Lucas could only nod.

After a lull in their conversation, Cleve broke the monotony of the sonorous hum of the huge airlifter's turbine engines. "But, you know what, Colonel, he's dead and I'm alive. I can get bitter or I can get better. I choose *better*. When this whole thing with Operation Light Switch is over, I'm going back to Chuk Ra Met, Thailand, and see my wife and son. If you really want to help me . . . if the government really wants to help . . . it's Driscoll's murder in Bangkok that I want to be cleared of, so I can go back there and be with my family."

Again, all Lucas could do was nod.

"So what's next?" Cleve asked.

"That's going to be up to the president. General Hurley wants us to wait at his headquarters. So that's what we will do. I expect they are talking next steps right now in Washington.

# 35

## A SECRET OPTION

Twelve hours after the raid on Fujiwara in Tokyo, it appeared that Fujiwara had kept his mouth shut. There were no reported coup attempts in Japan or anywhere else in that part of the world. Things, however, were about to get very heated in Washington.

Tim Munson slammed his fist down on the conference table in the White House's Command Center. "You do not have the right to dictate those terms to the president, General. You do not dictate what he can or can't tell Congress."

Jonas Pastor's nostrils flared and his gaze drilled holes through the national security advisor. "Mr. Munson, I am well aware that what I am proposing is not politically correct and depending on how closely one wants to interpret the Constitution and the War Powers Act, may be illegal. However, I am at the point where I must choose between the law and my responsibility to protect the lives of America's fighting men and women. The only military option we have depends on the element of surprise. You know as well as I that Washington has as many leaks as a bouquet of birthday balloons at a porcupine ranch. If the president marches over to the Capitol and asks Congress for their permission to deploy troops overseas to defend against these coups, as the law says he must, we will very likely lose the only thing we have going for us. All anyone in Congress who happens to disagree with him has to do is leak one word of this to the press and our plan falls apart. Our one single advantage is lost. At that point, there are no viable military options. So, while you may not like it, that is the choice the president must make and if he chooses to go to Congress, then my colleagues and I withdraw our support for the plan and we will resign before we put troops in a situation where we know they cannot win."

Munson looked around the table. All of the joint chiefs of staff were nodding. "You bastards! You realize that what you are proposing is political suicide for the president and what you are doing is nothing short of mutiny?"

"We do. But putting the entire world economy at risk by leaving these eight countries to their own devices is just as suicidal."

Munson countered, "But we don't know that these governments couldn't prevail over their enemy. We have the lists. Why not just give them their list of traitors and let them deal with it? These coups are nothing short of civil wars. I would think that after Vietnam, Afghanistan, Iraq, and Syria, you, of all people, would want to avoid sticking your noses into another country's civil war."

Pastor looked to Chet McKeever for support; the admiral wasn't bashful. These coups were going to happen in his area of operations. Within this room he was the avowed military expert on these countries. There was no other military person present who better understood the politics and the role of the military in each of these countries, but, as McKeever began to speak, he waved his hand around the table at his military colleagues trying to show Munson they were a united front. "We agree that leaving some countries to their own devices to solve their internal problems is the right thing to do. China will survive under that plan. Is there anyone in this room who doesn't think the Chinese premier, with only a minimum of advance notice, could act swiftly enough to purge the revolting generals from his army and replace them with the next crop of power hungry up-and-comers?" He gave it a moment to see if anyone might disagree and when he saw no one did, McKeever moved on. "The same is true of Vietnam. Then there's Malaysia and the Philippines, countries that are best described as neither friend nor foe. It is unlikely either would accept military assistance even if we were to offer it, especially the Philippines. Their president has his own agenda, and it doesn't seem to include the United States. The joint chiefs and I agree that all we can do in these four countries is advise them of what is going to happen and the rest will be up to them."

McKeever paused momentarily, unable to read Munson's reaction, then continued, "So, that leaves us with Japan, Thailand, South Korea, and North Korea. Japan is a true ally, a huge trade partner, and a country in the region whose friendship the US can ill afford to lose. Cato Fujiwara remains under close surveillance. The DIA and the CIA have his phones tapped. He continues to meet with Yamamoto at the estate. He is keeping up appearances. So far he has not communicated anything about Operation Light Switch to any of his subordinates and we are within thirty days of the kick-off. But we don't think there will be a coup in Japan. However, the ringleader of all of this is Seito Yamamoto, a Japanese citizen. We want the president to authorize the insertion of a Special Forces team to take him into custody on July 4 . . ."

Munson was shaking his head. "That's fucking nuts. What do you propose we do with him after we barge into a foreign country where there is no coup and take one of its citizens as a prisoner?"

"Sir, with all due respect," McKeever asked, "what would we have done with Osama Bin Laden had we not killed him during the raid on his home in Pakistan?"

"That's not the same," Munson shot back. "Bin Laden was a terrorist. He killed three thousand people at the World Trade Center, Admiral. It's not the same . . . just not the same."

"Sir, surely you don't see Yamamoto as anything other than a terrorist. He will kill many more than three thousand people if he and his associates succeed, to say nothing of the economic havoc they will wreak around the world."

Munson just sat there. His job was to shoot holes in their plans, to find options, to advise the president on the best course of action. But he had nothing to come back with.

McKeever continued, "Let's talk about Thailand. As you know, the country is currently under military rule after a coup in 2014. Looking at the lists intercepted from Yamamoto's estate, it isn't hard to see that this is little more than a complete power grab by the ruling junta of military generals. If we do nothing in Thailand, it will become another Myanmar. They will likely kill the king, oppress the general population, and rape the country's treasury. But we have a plan to intervene . . ."

Derisively, Munson said, "Yeah. I bet you do."

The tension in the room was like a pressure cooker and Munson's attitude blew McKeever's lid off. "Dammit, Munson! For once put politics aside and think about something besides political survivability."

Munson jumped to his feet and for the briefest of moments it looked as if he was about to physically attack the admiral until

Pastor stepped between the two of them. "Gentlemen, we have just under two hours before the president joins us. We have the obligation to have discussed all options before he gets here. So it's time to put away the personal animosity."

Munson returned to his seat. McKeever loosened his tie and began again, "Cleveland Spires . . ."

Munson refused to quiet down. "Come on! He's a wanted felon."

McKeever glanced at the chairman, who was shaking his head, and bit his tongue. Clearing his throat, he said, "He is the one who exposed this entire plot, Sir. He is credible. He tells us that there is a unit in the Korat area that he is sure is not part of the plot in Thailand. He personally knows the unit's commander, a Colonel Pramrashorn Saraveet. We have background on Saraveet. He is a graduate of ICAF. We believe that with Saraveet's cooperation and the element of surprise, his unit could provide adequate resistance against the coup in Thailand. If we can save the king and then gain his endorsement of new leadership, Thailand could become a more democratic nation. Once that happens, the US can more fully justify our support of them as an ally in the region."

Munson asked, "So you aren't suggesting any US troops be committed to Thailand?"

McKeever cleared his throat, again. "Uh . . . um . . . we would offer some Special Forces to Colonel Saraveet. It would be up to him to accept them or not."

Munson shook his head, but said nothing.

"South Korea is a much thornier problem. From the lists we've seen, it isn't difficult to see that the South Korean military is riddled with revolutionaries. So whatever we do, it must be done at the last minute, must be decisive and must preserve those certain members of the existing government that are not part of the coup there."

"We have a well-equipped infantry regiment on the demilitarized zone (DMZ). Can we redeploy them?" Munson asked.

"We can. But the minute that unit begins moving from the DMZ into the heart of Seoul, everyone in Korea will know that something is up."

"So what do you suggest, Admiral?"

"We are proposing that we leave them on the DMZ and use them only as reserves. We propose inserting the 2nd Battalion, First Special Forces Group from Fort Lewis, Washington, into Seoul and placing them at key government offices and other locations of strategic importance like airports, seaports, and media outlets. We can also use the 51st Fighter Wing at Osan Air Base to fly overhead cover for these locations. We especially want to defend Cheong Wa Dae."

Munson had been there. Cheong Wa Dae, or the Blue House, is the residence of the president of the Republic of South Korea.

"So, save the president, save the republic?"

McKeever had the momentary thought that perhaps this asshole was finally coming around. He responded respectively, "Yes, Sir."

Munson glanced at his watch. They had just a little over an hour before the president would join them and expect to be briefed on what his options were. "OK. What about North Korea?"

McKeever merely shook his head. "We do nothing. Let the revolutionaries try their luck at killing off that inbred sack of crap who runs that country. We anticipate getting nothing worse than what we already have. Optimistically, Paul Stanley has said, their Minister of Foreign Relatons, Pak Jung Yi, who's running the revolt in North Korea, is talking about reunification. So, if he perseveres, we might get a regime that is willing to talk about reunification with the south for the betterment of the people of that godforsaken place."

There really was no other military option that could work other than the one the joint chiefs were proposing. And everyone in the room knew it depended on complete surprise. Forty-five minutes before the president was to join them, Munson put his palms flat on the table. "OK, gents. I get why you don't want to just let them fight this out on the ground. The global economy is at stake. But I don't even pretend to know what the president is likely to say to your plans. Jonas," he said turning to the chairman of the joint chiefs, "you and McKeever talk him through this. I'll put my two cents in where I think I need to. We'll see what the boss wants to do."

For the next forty-five minutes, secure phone lines buzzed between the White House, Hawaii, and the CIA headquarters in Langley, Virginia. Nothing had appeared to change. Fujiwara was still playing by the rules. Yamamoto and his associates were still communicating as if they were completely undetected. The US's secret still appeared to be exactly that--a secret.

# 36

## INDEPENDENCE DAY

*Tienanmen Square, Beijing, China, 0600 Hours,*
*China Standard Time, July 4*

Apiss-yellow sky hung over the city. It was always noisy here. Twenty-two million people called Beijing home. But this morning the noise was different. Diesel engines roared, tracks clanked as tanks, and armored personnel carriers full of armed soldiers maneuvered into positions around the square's perimeter. Shots rang out, some seemingly quite random, others in a kind of scheduled cadence. The air, usually an acrid mix of exhaust fumes, garbage, industrial pollution, and cooking odors this morning contained gun smoke and, as one got closer to the square's center, the smell of blood.

President Wilson Glover had given the Chinese premier less than twenty-four hours' notice of the coup coming his way. As it turned out, it was more advance notice than was needed. It seems that in the particularly paranoid world of Chinese politics, this premier, like premiers before him, had a contingency plan for this very situation. The premier had a list of his own, one that he had carefully prepared over the last five years of his reign as China's most powerful man. All he had to do was check his list against the lists provided by the White House Command Center. When he found no matches, he activated his list of loyalists.

The purge began with the minister of banks and securities, who was the Chinese representative to Yamamoto's Association. He, his wife, and three children had been rousted from their home, shackled, and then chained together. The home, along with its now infamous satellite dish, was set ablaze. The family was marched through the streets to the center of Tienanmen Square proceeded by a loud speaker truck blaring, "Follow us and witness what happens to traitors." By the time the procession reached the square, there was a throng of curiosity seekers that wrapped themselves up to five deep around the huge square. The crowd expected a public execution, but few were prepared for the horror that was about to unfold in front of them.

The minister was made to stand at the bottom of a gallows and witness, first, the hanging of his youngest child, a daughter, who had just turned seven, followed by the hanging of his twelve- and fourteen-year-old sons. Finally, before the last bit of life had gone from the eldest boy, his wife was strung up. The crowd was offered no proof of their guilt, but apparently needed none. They roared each time the trap door fell from under the hangman's victim.

Then it was the minister's turn. While his family hung lifeless in front of him, a microphone was thrust out. He was ordered, "Admit to your crime and your end will be swift. Deny or remain silent and you will beg for death to come."

Paralyzed by the horror of what he'd been made to watch, he tried to speak, but nothing came out. His tormentor persisted,

"Admit your crime." There was a loud thump as the microphone was jammed against his lips. When he said nothing, a soldier nudged him hard in the middle of the back with his rifle.

Tightly shackled, he knew he couldn't fight back, but he hated these people, all of them, his tormentors and every one of the wild pack of jackals that ringed the square and had just cheered the deaths of his innocent family. The soldier nudged him again, even harder this time. The doomed minister managed to sputter, "I regret nothing." The crowd booed him.

Four large draught horses were led by separate handlers into the square's center. He struggled with his captors, but his situation was hopeless, and he was too sorrowful to persist for long. Ropes of equal length were attached first to each of his wrists and then to his ankles. The other end of each rope was attached to a collar on the draught horse. Once the minister was lashed down, a command was given to move the horses slowly in four different directions. When the minister could scream no louder, each horse was whipped on its hind quarters and he was pulled apart into five different pieces as the crowd, once again, roared its approval.

No attempt was made to remove the hanging victims. The body parts that once were the minister were shoveled into a heap below his dead family. A banner was hung from the gallows that read, *Death to all Traitors*, and the carnage continued.

At first there was no schedule. Later in the morning, as larger and larger numbers of suspected traitors were assembled into hastily configured cages on the square's edge, a more orderly schedule was necessitated. There was not even the semblance of a trial for those rounded up. They arrived by the truckload, many of them high-ranking military members. There was no sorting, only shackling and chaining them together into lots of twelve. When it was time for the next lot to move, they were prodded by soldiers with rifles and bayonets into a death march toward the square's center. Occasionally one or two would attempt to run away, but their shackles and chains made that a futile effort. These few were summarily executed with a bullet to the head. When this happened, the chain was not broken; instead, the man or woman on either side of the corpse was forced to carry it to the firing line. There everyone was made to kneel. A soldier with a hand gun would take up a position directly behind them and on command, fire a bullet into the back of each traitor's head. The crowd around the square, now massive, cheered with each volley. Bodies of those executed were stacked like cordwood at one end of the square to be picked up later and hauled away by the truckload to mass graves where they were unceremoniously dumped and then covered with lye. A western reporter who had infiltrated the crowd would liken the carnage to the days of the coliseum in ancient Rome. The premier's purge of his government's enemies went on for three full days before tapering off to only a few dozen a day for the next month.

All of this took a heavy toll on the premier's military. His expansionist plans for the South China Sea would have to be put on hold while he repaired the damage that he'd necessarily had to do to his army, air force and navy. But his hold on power had been preserved. Time was on his side. He could become a patient man, if he had to.

*Hanoi, Vietnam, 0900 hours, Indochina Time Zone, July 4*
VIETNAM'S PRIME MINISTER had received his call from President Glover a scant five hours earlier. It was purely by coincidence that he had a cabinet meeting scheduled for seven o'clock this morning, necessitated by a scheduled mid-morn-

ing ceremony that day in Dalat, a city in the central highlands. The one-hour plane ride was scheduled to leave at 8:30 a.m. But Glover's phone call caused him to make some changes to his schedule. There was no need, however, to alter the scheduled cabinet meeting. It would be one that none of his cabinet would soon forget.

The prime minister had been a soldier once in the great war of liberation against the American enemy. In fact, he'd acquitted himself so well on the battlefield that when the reunification of the two Vietnams began to progress after April of 1975, he was one of a handful of leaders chosen to conduct the reeducation of the citizens of the former South Vietnam, a process that could only be described as ruthlessly efficient. He had done this so well that he'd risen through the Communist Party ranks to minister of defense before becoming the prime minister two years ago.

On the list given to him by Glover were two of his cabinet members. Nguyen Van Thuy, his minister of culture, had been identified by the US president as Vietnam's member of Yamamoto's Association. His minister of defense was also identified as one of the revolutionaries. Both of these men had been very vocal in their support of the two recent arms sales to Vietnam by the US government. Now the prime minister understood why they had been such aggressive advocates.

"Good morning, gentlemen," he began quite cordially. "I trust all of you have had as good a week as I have had." Heads around the room nodded as he stood up and began to move about the large conference room. "I guess it would be appropriate to begin with an update on the arms sale from the US. We have received everything, if I understand correctly."

The minister of defense responded, "We have. The last ship

completed unloading in Haiphong last weekend. The cargo will have cleared the port this week and will be available to our air force."

Toying now with him, the prime minister asked, "And how long before you expect to begin using items from these new shipments?"

The minister of defense, still confident that the secret coup remained on schedule and that all hell was about to break loose across all of Vietnam, smiled, and then lied, "Current stocks will see us through the year. These newer stocks will keep us supplied until we can begin producing our own."

The prime minister stepped behind Thuy, Yamamoto's associate. "So, with that, let me ask our distinguished minister of culture, did you really think you could get away with it?" The question stunned everyone in the room.

Without turning around and despite the jolt of adrenaline that riddled his body and the rising panic he felt, Thuy managed to play dumb. "Get away with what, Mr. Prime Minister?"

The prime minister smiled down on him, an enigmatic smile that both mocked and derided Thuy. He reached behind his back and pulled a pistol from the waistband of his trousers. He raised his right arm, leveling the weapon at Thuy's head. The shot pierced everyone's ears in the room. Thuy fell forward, his chest, shoulders and what was left of his head slumping onto the table in front of him. Everyone else except the prime minister and the minister of defense dove for cover under the huge teakwood conference table.

As the minister of defense bolted for the door, the prime minister warned, "It's useless to try and escape." His warning fell on deaf ears. As soon as the minister of defense opened the conference room's door, he was taken into custody by two security guards purposefully stationed there. He motioned for them to bring him back into the room.

Calling the other cabinet members out from under the table, he said, "Gentlemen, gentlemen, please. The excitement is over. It seems that we have one dead and one live traitor among us. Perhaps it is best if you hear of their traitorous plans from the one that can still talk. Tell us, sir, of your treachery and I will be lenient with you."

When he didn't speak, the prime minister directed the two security guards to "loosen him up." He made his cabinet watch all of this until a bloodied Minister of Defense spilled his guts to them. When he was finished, the prime minister stepped in front of him and asked, "Do you know what else Thuy had planned?" He grabbed him by the hair and jerked his head up. "Well, do you?"

The minister of defense, barely conscious at this point, managed to shake his head.

"I thought that might be the case. So know this: the second part of his plan, after the coup, was to collaborate with a person in Japan and turn Vietnam into a lackey of Japan and China." He grabbed him by the hair again. "You would do this after Vietnam has struggled for so many years to become free of foreign colonialists? You don't deserve to live any longer!"

"I . . . I . . . I didn't know . . ."

"Of course you didn't. And that is why I will be lenient with you." The prime minister motioned for the two security guards to force the minister of defense to his knees. When he was in position, he met the same brutal fate as his colleague.

More prepared this time, the other cabinet members stayed in their seats, a few of them covering their ears to the tremendous blast of the powerful hand gun in the small room. The prime minister told the two guards, "Get these two pieces of dung out of here." They did as they were told, leaving in their wake a trail of blood.

Turning to his comrades, he laid the pistol on the table and muttered to no one in particular, "You fucking pricks. You should have suffered more." Then he composed himself, straightened the lapels of his suit jacket, and said, "Now, let us discuss how we rebuild the government." He tossed copies of a list onto the conference table in front of him. "As we speak, executions of thousands of other revolutionaries are underway here in Hanoi and in Ho Chi Minh City. Let's get busy identifying their replacements."

*Kuala Lumpur, Malaysia, July 4 and 5*

THE COUP IN Malaysia was nearly bloodless and by the late evening of July 5, the elected government had succumbed to the rebels, but by this time, the minister of foreign trade, Yamamoto's accomplice, knew that coups in China and Vietnam had failed. He had tried to communicate with Yamamoto, but feared the worst when he received no reply to his communiques. He was now in charge of his country's government. He'd spent years developing the lists he'd supplied to Yamamoto. He knew who he could trust and who he could not. Quickly evaluating where he stood, he decided that, no, there would not be a United States of Asia as he and his colleagues had hoped, but he would now rule Malaysia and he would be a better ruler that the others had been.

What he was not prepared for was one of the rebel generals barging through his office door and demanding an explanation. In his hand, he held the lists that had been sent to the recently overthrown President by the U.S. "What is this?" he shouted. "We found these lists in the old president's office. He said the US president had given them to him. I am on the list marked for elimination." A gun came out of the general's holster. "Get up. I have assembled a group of us on this elimination list. We want to talk to you. We want answers. Now!"

*Manilla, the Philippines, July 4 and 5*

IN THE PHILIPPINES, no clear winner could be identified after two days of fighting. The president was in hiding, but still managed to control significant numbers of the military and the national police. He had been quoted in the press as saying, "I will never surrender." Thousands of innocent men, women, and children had been killed or wounded in hundreds of different skirmishes occurring in the capital city. It would be three months before a clear winner could be identified. By that time, it really didn't matter who won. The country had broken down into dozens of different factions with their only commonality being the violence they were willing to use to prove their point. The clear losers, however, were the poor, innocent civilian citizens of this third-world country.

*Bangkok, Thailand, 0400 hours, Indochina Time, July 4*

THE ARMORED COLUMN progressed unimpeded down the broad boulevard toward the king's palace. Loudspeakers, usually used to broadcast morning prayers, blared, and media outlets warned citizens to stay off the streets. A revolution was underway and the best way for them to avoid injury was to stay inside for at least the next twenty-four hours. Nearly everyone complied; everyone, that is, except Colonel Pramrashorn Sara-veet and the thousand or so soldiers belonging to his Tiger Bri-gade.

Well camouflaged and placed at key locations along the armored column's route of march, they watched the tanks and armored personnel carriers progress. All they were waiting for was the word from their leader to open fire. When Saraveet gave it over the radio, a hundred anti-tank weapons let loose, most of them finding their mark and utterly stopping the lethal proces-sion in its tracks.

No one had been expecting any resistance. A few tank com-manders began to swivel the turrets of their tanks in the direc-tion of smoke trails left by the anti-tank weapons. Then came a second volley of anti-tank fire. The entire procession was stalled, its progress blocked by burning tanks or personnel car-riers. Troops piled out only to meet a withering hail of bullets fired from the rifles of Tiger Brigade soldiers who picked the revolutionaries off like targets at an arcade.

The ambush had been perfectly executed except for one kill that came just a few seconds too late. The commander of the column managed to get off a mayday call. "Cobra Six, this is King's Palace Six. We are discovered. We are stopped. Request air support. Ambush on either side of our column. Over." He didn't live long enough to get a response to his call as the ammu-nition stored in the racks behind him exploded with a dynamic force that scattered his tank over a hundred yards.

Five minutes later, Saraveet heard the first plane approach. "Pushback 1, this is Pushback 6," he said into his radio's micro-phone. "Fast movers approaching from west. Cleared to fire air-to-ground cover. Over."

Darrel Greene, commander of the First Special Forces Battal-ion, was Pushback 1. He had visited Pramrashorn Saraveet at his Korat headquarters at the direction of his boss, Lucas Johnson, a little over a week ago. The visit's purpose was to fill Saraveet in on what was happening in Bangkok and to determine if he would relocate the Tiger Brigade clandestinely from Korat to Bangkok for the purpose of foiling the coup in Thailand. During that visit, Greene offered up one other important bit of information. "I've been authorized by our government to offer you any military assistance you may require."

Saraveet had taken a minute to ponder the offer before answering and then said, "I have no organic anti-aircraft defense. Can you provide that?"

"Six, this is One. Roger, out," Greene responded before relaying the message to his air-to-ground missile operators. The shoulder-fired, Hellcat missiles were laser guided and extremely accurate. The problem was that a shoot-down over crowded Bangkok would result in tremendous collateral damage. Greene reminded his missileers, "OK, catch them coming or going, but let's try and keep them out of the city."

"Roger, sir," came the short response from his team chief.

Five aircraft came after the Tiger Brigade. All five were shot down and all but one crashed on the outskirts of the city. One, however, turned back toward the city center after taking a direct hit in the cockpit and killing the pilot. It crashed into a splinter village occupied by several thousand or so workers who were employed building two nearby skyscrapers. The death toll was incalculable because no one knew exactly how many workers and how many wives and children lived here in these miserable conditions, and, up until now, no one apparently cared. Later, the king of Thailand would tour the area with tears in his eyes, placing wreaths everywhere and reciting a Buddhist prayer for the lives that were lost in the ensuing inferno.

The armored column that had been advancing on the King's

Palace was stopped cold. The danger now was to secure the column as quickly as possible so that firefighters could get to the burning tanks and armored personnel carriers before the ammunition inside them started to cook off. Saraveet's men quickly moved from their well-hidden ambush positions along the route to round up the rebel soldiers. The rebels had lost their will to resist. Firefighters were on the scene within the hour, pouring water onto the burning vehicles and eliminating the danger of secondary explosions. The coup was essentially over. Announcements over public address systems, radio, and television changed to offers of forgiveness for those officers and soldiers that voluntarily stood down. No questions asked. During the weeks immediately following the failed coup, the Tiger Brigade, under Saraveet's steady hand, rounded up the revolutionaries on the lists provided by the US. Most of the rebels were incarcerated. Some of them were later executed, but only after a trial by an impartial tribunal at which they were allowed to defend themselves.

*Seoul, South Korea, 0500 hours, Korea Standard Time, July 4*

PERHAPS AMERICA'S STAUNCHEST ally in the region, South Korea's government, ironically, was the most riddled with revolutionaries. But, as had been the case in most of the other countries, the revolutionaries were overly confident and the Second Battalion, First Special Forces Group would use this to quickly stem the tide of the coup. Interrogations of Paul Stanley had yielded a long list of targets in South Korea that the revolutionaries were going to hit. The attackers, expecting virtually no resistance, were armed almost entirely with handguns. What they were met with, on the other hand, were well-trained, well-armed US Army Special Forces operators who stood nose-to-nose in opposition. Some of the revolutionaries died, and more were wounded; most, however, fled back into the streets from which they'd come, not prepared to pay the ultimate price for their cause. Casualties to US forces, on the other hand, were nonexistent.

To the majority of Seoul's twenty-eight million inhabitants, it appeared that the coup in and around the city never happened, except for one key point of resistance: the presidential residence, known as Cheong Wa Dae (the Blue House). As it had been in Bangkok, it was to be so in Seoul; an airplane crash would cause the largest number of fatalities of the entire coup.

Approaching ground forces headed for the residence were easily and quickly turned back. But someone managed to get a call in for air support and it wasn't long before a South Korean F-16 with a rebel pilot in control was headed directly for the Blue House. It had managed to get off the ground at Osan before the fighters of the 51st Fighter Wing could be ordered into the air to keep other South Korean aircraft from launching in support of the rebels.

Staff Sergeant (SSG) Bernard Flanagan, standing on an east-facing balcony of Cheong Wa Dae, aimed his Hellcat missile at the inbound fighter, heard the steady tone in his headset that told him the laser had acquired the target, and pulled the trigger. The quick forward thrust of the missile's launch pushed him back, but the steady tone continued in his ear. He flew the missile directly into the side of the approaching aircraft. The now-doomed pilot, however, had apparently decided that he should die a martyr's death. He pushed the fighter's throttles to full, lowered the nose of the aircraft until Cheong Wa Dae was in the middle of his cockpit's canopy, and flew his aircraft directly into the front of the residence. A fireball erupted, killing SSG Flanagan, a dozen other US soldiers, and the South Korean president and his family.

In a country in which the majority of its population and most of its government sat a mere twenty-five miles from a regime that vowed to destroy South Korea, planning for the continuity of government was an ongoing, important government function. The prime minister stepped flawlessly into power, while the South Korean National Police purged their own ranks from the lists provided by the White House, and then rounded up the remaining rebels. But the nation's period of mourning the loss of a beloved president would take months.

The tragic events at Cheong Wa Dae would haunt President Glover as well. Prophetically, when he was told of the incident, Glover said to Tim Munson, "I might have survived if this hadn't happened. Now Washington's vultures will pick my political carcass clean."

*Pyong Yang, North Korea, 0200 hours, Korea Standard Time, July 4*

"HE IS ASLEEP. He will not wake before nine or ten o'clock."

Pak Jung Yi, North Korea's minister of foreign relations, had been waiting for this word from the North Korean dictator's personal valet. He placed a call, turned on the nearby television and waited. At 0215 it happened.

The chief of staff of the North Korean army could be seen striding onto the television's news set. The news anchor, surprised, followed the general's direction to get up and leave. The general took his place, looked into the camera, and began, "Citizens of North Korea, today begins a new time in our history. The rule of the dictator is over. To see for yourself, come this morning at eight o'clock to Kim Il-sung Square, which after today will be called the People's Square. Witness the end of our repression as a people. Witness the birth of a new nation, a nation free of fear, a nation that is ready to reunite with our brothers and sisters to the south." He read from prepared remarks that explained exactly what was to happen this morning. When he was finished, the cameras stayed on him while he refreshed himself with a drink of water and then he began anew. The general stayed in front of the cameras until 0730 and then departed for the square himself. The broadcast switched from the studio to a remote hookup with cameras trained on the center of the newly-named People's Square which by now was teeming with people.

At precisely 0730 Pak Jung Yi was led to the dictator's bedroom by the valet.

"He will be groggy," the valet explained. "I doubled the dose of sleep aid I gave him last night."

They entered the bedroom: Yi, two guards, and the valet. They made no attempt to be particularly quiet. The dictator did not stir. Yi stood there for a moment over the bed of the man whose family for the past three generations had raped this country until it was one of the poorest in the entire world and certainly the most suppressed. Nudging the sleeping dictator, he said, "Wake up. It is time for you to pay your penance."

Nothing. Yi prodded him again. This time he rolled over. "What? What's that you say? Why are you here?"

Yi ripped the covers back and told the two soldiers next to him, "Get him on his feet." They complied, easily overcoming the chubby man's uncoordinated efforts to resist them. "Bring him along."

He led them to a balcony where the dictator had presided over numerous military parades and other shows of pretentious but phony national unity. On the packed square in front of them loud speakers began blaring, "Today marks a new beginning of prosperity for the people of our country. Today marks the end of a tyrant's rule."

The frightened little man began appealing to some of the generals gathered on the balcony with him. He offered them bribes, money, if they would take the minister into custody. The generals only glared at him.

"They won't help you. They side with me. They side with a fresh start. They relish your death." He directed the guards to hold the dictator still. He pulled a gun from his waistband and brandished it before the crowd. They roared as the public address system kept repeating, "Today marks a new beginning . . ." The minister stepped behind the dictator, pulled the trigger, and ended their country's long period of suffering.

Yi turned to the generals gathered with him on the balcony and announced, "Tomorrow I shall head to Seoul to begin reunification talks with our comrades to the south." All nodded their approval. Their plans had been careful. A hearse awaited the dictator's corpse. He was taken to a nearby crematorium and within an hour of his execution he was rendered into ashes which nobody wanted. They were spread in a nearby flower bed. The man spreading them said, "Fertilizer! Finally you have done something good for your country."

The minister's trip to South Korea was, of course, delayed. Things had not played out as he had anticipated and, at first, the failed coups elsewhere had caused him some concern. It was, however, only a matter of a few days before he realized that even though The Association's plans had failed miserably, he was still in power and prepared to begin reunification talks. Even before the flowers fertilized by the old dictator began to bloom, Yi had made his way to Seoul. Despite the south's terrible loss and upheaval, Yi and the new government of South Korea had begun reunification talks.

*Seito Yamamoto's estate, west of Tokyo, 0500 hours, Japan Standard Time, July 4*

THERE WAS NO coup attempt in Japan. Cato Fujiwara held true to his word and did not activate his men. However, there was the matter of Seito Yamamoto to be dealt with. Wilson Glover and his counterpart in Japan, the prime minister, had spent much time on the phone hashing out how he was to be handled. While Yamamoto might technically be guilty of conspiracy, for that to happen Glover would have to disclose what he'd learned from Fujiwara. The US had basically offered him immunity if he stayed out of it and since he'd done just that, Glover never disclosed to Japan's prime minister what Fujiwara's potential role might have been. Both leaders, however, agreed that Yamamoto needed to be held accountable for the havoc he'd wreaked on seven other Asian countries. It was finally decided that he would be tried in the World Court in The Hague, The Netherlands. He would be brought there by a joint force of American and Japanese soldiers that would descend upon his estate, take him into custody, and then transport him.

So Colonel Lucas Johnson, Colonel Yoshii Nagatamura, and two other Special Forces operators from the First Special Forces Group burst through the front door of Yamamoto's estate. What they found would simultaneously surprise and disappoint them

In the entrance hallway lay Fukora, Yamamoto's manservant. He'd been shot once through the head and once through the heart, apparently for good measure. A pool of blood encircled the upper half of his body. Across the dead man's legs lay a doberman pinscher, its forelegs outstretched, its head cradled on them. Every now and then, the dog whimpered softly.

Johnson said to the others, "It's OK. Spires mentioned there might be a dog in here and that he's friendly."

Nagatamura bent down and stroked the dog's head, "It's OK, boy. He was your master? Sorry we were too late." He stood up. "Stay here." The dog seemed to take solace from his gentle words and did not move.

Leaving the dog and getting back to business, the team moved through the house, clearing each room and hallway they came to until they reached the back. There they stood at the entrance to what appeared to be a library, but along the back wall, one of the shelves was pushed to the side, revealing a doorway into another room. At this concealed door, they peered into a large command center. One wall blinked with lights, switches, and levers. Below that was an array of desktop computers. In a chair in front of one of the computers sat Seito Yamamoto, his back to them.

In Japanese, Nagatamura said, "Seito Yamamoto, put your hands up. You are under arrest. Put your hands where we can see them."

Nothing.

Lucas walked to the chair, spun it around, and nearly vomited at what he saw. Yamamoto's throat had been cut, his heart was cut out and lying on the floor in front of the chair, and his bowels were eviscerated and spread over his lap. Johnson motioned for Nagatamura to come over and then said, "Ask the prime minister if he is seeing this."

Over their headsets, they heard the prime minister answer in Japanese and Nagatamura translated that he was watching and would like to know who would do such a gruesome thing.

Lucas, without hesitation, knew exactly who would do something like this, but, again, because Fujiwara had been granted immunity, Johnson could not respond. Nagatamura, who also knew who would do something like this, almost broke the silence, but a quick glance from Johnson and a shake of his head caused him to reconsider.

Leaving Yamamoto's corpse, they spread out through the estate. It wasn't long before the team heard one of their members say, "Colonel, back here, off the kitchen. In the basement. You aren't going to believe this!"

BY NOON ON July 4, Johnson, Nagatamura, and the rest of the team sent to take Yamamoto in to custody was back at Yakota Air Force Base. The doberman sat at Johnson's side in the secure conference room, already seemingly adjusted to its new master. Nagatamura sat across the table from him.

"It's not right, Lucas," Nagatamura said solemnly.

"What's not?"

"Fujiwara gets away."

"I know, but at the same time, it's one of the things I admire most about President Glover. He struck a deal. It worked out well for everyone, but especially for Japan."

"I suppose you're right," Nagatamura said, "but I'd sure like to see that sonuvabitch suffer a little bit."

Lucas looked at him and smiled, "I have an idea. Let's give him a call. Do you have a number?"

Nagatamura shook his head, but then smiled, "I have a friend in intelligence, another colonel. He owes me a favor or two. Give me a couple of minutes." While Lucas tended to the details of coordinating with the crew of the C-17 that was to return the other Americans and the dog to Hawaii, Nagatamura worked his magic.

THE CALLER ID on Yamamoto's cell phone indicated the caller was from something called PACAF. Fujiwara wanted to ignore it but was both curious and afraid to, given the events of the morning. He answered in English, "Yes."

"Cato, it's Lucas Johnson. Remember me?"

"Yes . . . yes, I do. It's *Colonel* Johnson isn't it?"

"It is, but, please, call me Lucas."

Fujiwara wasn't fooled at all by the friendly banter. This call had a purpose and he was pretty sure he wasn't going to like whatever that purpose might be. "All right, Lucas. What can I do for you today?"

"Just calling to ask a question or two."

"About?"

"Were you afraid Yamamoto would rat you out if we took him alive?"

Fujiwara gave a devious smile, which, of course, no one could see. "I've been watching the news. Dreadful that you had to kill the man . . . and his manservant, I understand. But, I'm glad you weren't injured."

Lucas changed his tone. "Cut the crap, Cato. You know as well as I do that we didn't kill that sonuvabitch."

"No . . . well, when I heard on the news that he was killed, I just assumed that you . . . Well, if it wasn't you, then, who do you think did it?" He wanted to chuckle, but stifled the impulse.

"Yeah, well, I thought you might take that approach, but I did want to call and let you know about something you and your men missed."

"Me and my men?" he repeated. Why, Lucas, I don't know what you are talking about."

"Gold, Cato. I'm talking about gold. Several thousands of ingots, I'm guessing. All neatly stacked in rows in the basement of Yamamoto's estate."

There was silence on the other end.

"Yeah, keep watching the news. Your government will make an announcement as soon as they have it all under lock and key. But it was there, right under your nose when you were killing Yamamoto and his man. You should have looked around. I don't think anybody knew it was there. You could have taken it and nobody would have ever been the wiser. Guess you were in just too big of a hurry, huh?"

More silence.

"Well, listen, it's been very nice talking with you, but I've got to be going. Have a good day, Cato." Johnson hung up.

Nagatamura looked at him smiling broadly. "Bravo, Lucas, bravo!"


THE NEXT MORNING, July 5, word of the fortune in gold found at Yamamoto's estate broke in the news. Fujiwara summoned his chief counsel to his office. "You have heard the news?"

"About the gold?"

"Of course about the gold, you fool. How could you overlook such a thing?"

"But it was in the basement, Fujiwara-san. We had no reason to go . . ."

"Why did you not think to look around? Do you realize what I would have paid you for such a find as that?"

The chief counsel grew angry. "You did not send us there

to look around. You sent us there to kill Yamamoto and that is exactly what we did. If you wanted me to look around you should have told me to do that."

Sitting at his desk, without looking down, Fujiwara opened the middle desk drawer and felt for the revolver. He'd had enough of this man's incompetence which was now compounded by a bad attitude.

# 37

## GOVERNMENT FALLOUT

News of what was going on in Asia began to hit the US's twenty-four-hour news cycle just before the 11:00 p.m. newscasts on July 3. Ida Spires had turned in early. It had become her habit as she coped with the fatigue caused by worry. She had not heard from her son since he'd left for Thailand. When the phone rang at 10:45, it both woke and scared her.

Cleve had been kept in seclusion at Brigadier General Chuck Hurley's headquarters, US Special Operations Command, Pacific, for the month since his return from the trip to Japan and the detainment of Fujiwara. It seemed like a year to him. Hurley, however, had just told him that the news channels had picked up the story and it would be broadcast everywhere within the next several hours. Cleve asked if he could, at least, call home and let his mother know that he was OK. Hurley had approved. Cleve could sense the fear in his mother's voice as she'd answered the phone. "Mom, it's me."

"Oh, thank God, Cleveland. Are you all right? Where are you? I'll come as soon as I can. Just tell me where you are . . ."

"Mom, I'm OK. It's a long story. A lot has happened. If you turn on the television, you will see reports of revolts throughout Asia. I didn't want you to worry about me when you begin hearing the news. I'm in Hawaii. I'm not sure when they will allow me to leave, but it shouldn't be too much longer."

"Hawaii? But, I thought you were in Thailand. How . . .?"

"Again, long story, but I will fill you in when I see you. Just don't worry. I'm fine."

"What about Liott and Daniel, Cleveland. Have you seen them? Are they all right?"

"That's my next call, Mom, but they were fine when I saw them last. There was a coup attempt in Thailand, but it failed. Most of the action was in Bangkok, far away from where they are, but I will call a good friend and check on them. Don't worry."

"Cleveland, that detective from the Cleveland police was here a while ago asking about you. He still thinks you had something to do with that man's death the night of the bus accident down the street."

In the tense excitement of the last few days, Cleve had suppressed his thinking about Tetsu Agaki, Billy Driscoll's death, and Cato Fujiwara's startling admission that Driscoll was actually the one that killed the security policeman on Okinawa. Any sense of relief he had felt was completely overshadowed by the tense international situation they had been facing. But now, his mother's concerns allowed him to refocus on his own situation. "It's OK, Mom. That'll work out somehow. I know it will. I've got to go, but I will call again as soon as I know more."

After hanging up, Cleve fished in his pocket for a small notebook. Finding the number he was looking for, he dialed it. After two rings, he heard, "Saraveet."

"Pram, it's Cleve."

"Good to hear your voice, my friend. Where are you?"

"Hawaii. I've been following your exploits. Good work."

"Yes, well the rebels are contained. We are still fighting the fires in Bangkok, but within the next few hours, they will be under control. How are you?"

"Fine. Just fine. Are Liott and Daniel OK?"

"They are. I'm sure they are. The revolt was concentrated here in Bangkok. Korat was not impacted, so I can't see how anything could be wrong at Chuk Ra Met. I'm rather busy here these days, so you will probably get home to see them before I will, Cleve."

"Uh, yeah, well, about that, Pram. Do the National Police still have a warrant out for my arrest?"

"They do, but, believe me when I tell you that you are not their priority today, nor will you be in the immediate future. The king has directed that they work for me as we go about rounding up the rebels. Thanks to the lists provided by your president, we know who the leaders are. We will go from there. Once I get that organized, I have an idea that I want to try out, but it will take me a week or so before I am able to get to it. I'm sorry, Cleve, I hope you understand."

"I do, my friend. When you are able . . . when you are able. Until then, take good care of yourself, General."

Saraveet laughed. "So, you've heard the news."

"Oh, yes. The king is a wise man, my friend, a very wise man."

IN WASHINGTON, THE vice president and the secretary

of defense stood in front of Tim Munson's desk demanding answers. Munson wondered why it had taken them so long to get to him.

Charles Randall was from the great state of Texas. Before becoming Wilson Glover's running mate in the last presidential race, he had been the governor. Randall was ambitious and made few bones about it. He practiced politics under the belief that, in Washington, one has no friends, only political allies and enemies—allies one kept around as long as they were useful, and enemies one got even with. When President Glover cut him out of the loop on what was going down in Asia, the president became one of Randall's enemies. Leaning over the edge of Munson's desk he demanded, "Just exactly what did you and the joint chiefs think you were doing making an end run around the rest of the Security Council and the Constitution?"

Munson, who hadn't closed his eyes in the last thirty-six hours, just wanted to go home, hug his wife and kids, and get some shuteye. He was not going to let this prick get to him at this point. "Mr. Vice President, the military option that presented itself, the only military option we had, by the way, had to be kept an absolute secret. No one, not me, not the joint chiefs, not the president, was willing to take the chance that our secret would be compromised. So we made a conscious decision to limit to an absolute minimum the number of people who knew what was going to happen and when. You and the secretary of defense were not in that group. Neither was either house of Congress."

Randall shot back, "You realize that the other party, the majority party in Congress, I might add, is already talking impeachment."

Munson caught the secretary of defense standing next to Randall nodding his head up and down like a bobble-head doll.

*The joint chiefs were right about these two . . . pure political animals,* he thought. And, no, he hadn't heard the rumblings about impeachment. He had been solely focused on events happening half a world away and it hadn't been but just a few hours since it had broken in the news. He looked Randall straight in the eye, "The president is a big boy. He knew exactly what he was doing and he knew the political toll it might take. Whether you two and Congress can get past your egos and admit that he did the right thing is not something I am going to lose sleep over. We did the right thing. Time will prove that."

Randall looked at the secretary of defense and jerked his head toward the door. As they were leaving, he turned to Munson with a sneer on his face and said, "Time, Mr. Munson, may be the one thing that the president does not have on his side."

# 38

## SETTING THE RECORD STRAIGHT

General Pramrashorn Saraveet was tired. Exhausted was probably a better word to describe his physical condition at this point, but he changed into freshly starched fatigues, polished up his four-star insignia of rank, strapped on the pearl-handled 9 mm pistol given to him personally by the king of Thailand, and headed out the door. It was July 9, less than a week after the ill-fated coup attempt, and he had decided it was time to go ahead and make his move on behalf of Cleve Spires.

By now, he was a household name in Thailand, but that was not necessarily a good thing in Bangkok's notorious sex districts. His procession of five official sedans swung onto Soi Cowboy's narrow pavement, prompting a number of working girls in the various bars along with their customers to step into open doorways and spill out onto the sidewalk. The drivers pulled their cars to a stop along the curb in front of Club Exotica. Car doors swung open and five uniformed officials, led by

Saraveet, walked into the noisy, dingy bar. No one approached them. In fact, most of the club's girls headed for the back rooms and out of sight. Customers fled onto the street and disappeared into other bars, not wanting to be anywhere near so much brass. Saraveet picked out Mama-san and motioned for her to come to him. "Turn the music off and the lights up. You and I have to talk."

As the place became quiet and brightened even more than he'd hoped for, Mama-san returned to him. "Come with me." He walked out the door onto the street, which was now eerily empty. "It doesn't look like we are very good for business, does it?" he asked her.

She shook her head.

He led her back inside and introduced her to his colleagues, a couple of other army generals and two top officials from the national police. All of them were wearing side arms. "Here's the deal, Mama-san," he began in a no-nonsense manner. "I'm going to ask you some questions about the death of Billy Driscoll. If you don't answer or if I get the feeling that you are lying to me, we will be back . . . often . . . much more often than will be good for your business or any of the other businesses on this street. Do I make myself clear?"

She nodded.

"OK, then, you've told the police that you saw this man kill Billy Driscoll." He showed her a picture of Cleve Spires. "Is that the truth? Did you see this man do that?"

She took a long time to answer and that gave him a hint as to the answer he could expect, but while she was thinking, he gave her something else to consider. "You should probably think about the other business owners on Soi Cowboy before you answer. I'm guessing that if I spread the word up and down the street that I won't leave you alone until I get the truth, they might make your life miserable for a while. Don't you think, so?"

Ruefully, she nodded.

Tapping Cleve's picture, he asked, "So, is this the man that killed Driscoll, or not?"

Still avoiding eye contact, she said, "No, he didn't kill Beelee."

Saraveet rocked back in his chair across the table from her. "Who did?"

"I don't know . . . some other man . . . younger . . . a Thai. He was waiting." She pointed to the bar stool where the assassin had sat. She pointed to Cleve's picture. "As soon as he came in, the killer stepped over and shot Beelee. Then he ran out the back."

"So why did you lie to the police?"

She didn't answer right away. The bartender had given the others a cold beer. Pram looked over at them and said, "This is a nice place isn't it, gentlemen? We could get used to it, couldn't we?" They smiled and raised their beers to him.

Mama-san spoke up. "A man paid me to say it was him." She pointed to the picture again.

"I see. So who is this man that paid you?"

"I don't know. He's Japanese. He hasn't been back here since that night. I heard he works for the Yakuza, but I don't know. He told me to tell the police that it was that man that killed Beelee." Again her bony index finger pointed to Cleve's picture.

Saraveet smiled at her. "OK." He fished in his shirt pocket for his card and handed it to her. "If the Japanese man comes in here again or if you see him on the street, you call me. I want to talk to him. In the meantime, we will leave you alone." He joined the others for a cold beer, and when they were finished, they left. He'd gotten what he'd come for.

Within twenty-four hours the national police cancelled their warrant for Cleveland A. Spires, as did Interpol. Saraveet phoned the new commander of the Tiger Brigade and asked him to go to Chuk Ra Met and deliver a message. The commander was new to the Korat area, so Saraveet had to give him directions on how to find the remote village, but he said he was happy to do as the general asked.

Saraveet's next call was to the headquarters of the US Special Operations Command, Pacific in Hawaii. He asked to speak with Cleveland Spires and was surprised to be told that Mr. Spires was not there because he was on his way home to Cleveland, Ohio.

FOR LUCAS JOHNSON, the week following July 4 had been a long one. While the other Americans on Lucas's team had departed on the fourth, both he and Yoshii Nagatamura had spent two days debriefing the Japanese prime minister, his minister of defense, and the chief of staff of the Japanese Ground Self-Defense Force. He had hoped that he could simply go home to his wife and daughters from there, but that was not to be the case. The secretary of defense and the vice president of the United States wanted debriefings as to what had exactly taken place.

Fortunately for Johnson, the army chief of staff intercepted him before that scheduled meeting. The general filled him in on the political infighting that was now going on. "Lucas, I can't tell you what to say when you talk with these two. Both of their security clearances are certainly high enough to know everything that went on. Trust me when I tell you that General Pastor has already given them nearly all of the details."

"Nearly all, Sir?" Lucas cautiously asked.

The chief of staff liked Lucas's insightfulness. "You caught that. I'm glad."

Lucas merely nodded.

The chief of staff explained, "We have not disclosed anything about Cato Fujiwara's involvement in any of this with either the Japanese prime minister or the vice president, or the secretary of defense or Congress." The army chief of staff raised his eyebrows. "All of the joint chiefs have talked about it." He shrugged his shoulders. "Some would argue that we are withholding vital information, but, honestly, none of us give a shit. The president made a courageous decision knowing that the shit was eventually going to hit the fan. It appears that it has. There are impeachment rumblings on the hill, but those of us who know what took place aren't going to run scared and neither is the president."

Lucas said, "Thanks for the heads up, Sir. I won't mention Fujiwara."

There was a long pause and the chief of staff sensed Lucas had something else on his mind. "Lucas, I'm not telling you to avoid . . ."

Lucas realized it was impolite to interrupt, but the chief had it wrong. "No . . . no, Sir. That's not it. Fujiwara is an asshole, but I understand why we have to keep his role in all of this confidential. But there is one thing I'd like to ask."

"What's that, Lucas?"

"It's about Cleve Spires. Fujiwara admitted to me that Spires did not commit the crime that he was sent to prison for. Spires was right there and heard it, along with a master sergeant that works for me. Master Sergeant Baron will attest to what I'm telling you." Lucas paused for a moment.

The chief of staff shook his head, but didn't say anything.

"Sir, I was the president of the court-martial board that sent Spires to prison, and we made a terrible mistake that we can never fully fix. The man lost ten years of his life. But I would like for the secretary of defense to set aside his conviction, reinstate his rank, and give him the back pay he deserves."

"Hmmm, I see. And you believe Fujiwara?"

Lucas nodded, "I can see no reason for him to lie about this. It was Billy Driscoll, the guy you asked me to investigate when I took command at the First Special Forces Group. He killed a security policeman on Okinawa and then managed to frame Spires for the murder." Lucas gave it a moment for this all to sink in and then added, "I believe Fujiwara had Driscoll killed just so he could hang that one on Spires as well, but I can't prove that. But, I'd like to see the record set straight on who killed that kid on Okinawa. It wasn't Spires. We've screwed his life up enough, Sir. We need to do something to make it up to him."

The army chief of staff stroked his chin and then said, "OK. But don't say anything to the secretary of defense. He and the vice president are up to something and no one on the joint chiefs thinks they can be trusted to do the right thing. Let me see what else I can do."

Lucas nodded, "Thank you, Sir."

# 39

## REUNITED . . . AGAIN

Cleve knew it was risky to go to Cleveland with an Interpol warrant still out on him and Bergstrom still lurking around, but he felt he owed it to his mother to go home and see her. He would not stay in Cleveland. He longed to be with Liott and Daniel in Chuk Ra Met. On July 9, both Brigadier General Hurley and Staff Sergeant Youst had delivered him to the Honolulu Airport for the long trip home.

"Sergeant Major . . ."

Cleve held up his hand. "Sir, you know that isn't . . ."

Hurley nodded, "Yeah, I know. We're working on that."

That comment intrigued Cleve and he wanted to ask what he meant by it, but he also trusted Hurley sufficiently to know that if the general had more information than that, he would have offered it up.

Hurley continued, "Sergeant Major, you didn't have to do what you did. It was a huge risk. The nation owes you a deep debt, and it is unfortunate that security classifications will keep it from being acknowledged. But know that those of us who know the details know that none of this would have turned out as well as it did, without your stepping forward."

"Thanks, Sir. That means a lot to me." He looked at Youst, who was tearing up. "General, look at what you did. You made a marine cry." Everyone chuckled, even Youst through her veil of tears. "It was a pleasure working with you, Sergeant Youst," Cleve said to her. "You will go a long way in the Marine Corps. Good for you. Good for them."

She stepped forward and hugged him.

It surprised Cleve and caused him to tear up.

Hurley laughed and said, "Staff Sergeant Youst, look at what you did. You made the sergeant major cry." It was a good note to end on. Cleve shook Hurley's and Youst's hands, turned on his heel, and headed for the security checkpoint.

On the flight home, Cleve worked carefully through the details he could share with his mother and with Detective Bergstrom. As he did that, it gave him more reassurance that it would all work itself out. He'd done the right thing. There were lots of people that would verify he wasn't a murderer. His plan was to surprise Ida. He'd catch a cab at the Cleveland airport and simply appear at her doorstep.

IT WAS ABOUT 6:00 p.m. when he knocked on his mother's front door. The only difference between now and that bleak day in February when he'd returned home from prison was that it was daylight this time, it was hot as hell in Cleveland, and he was optimistic Saraveet would make it so he could return to Chuk Ra Met to be with his family.

He heard Ida gasp as she looked through the slats of the blinds to see who it was. But when the door opened, Ida had stayed behind it. In front of him, not five feet away, stood Liott, her arms outstretched. Without a word, they stepped into one another, kissed, and then fell into a hug that brought applause from Ida and Daniel, who joined the two after they'd had a moment to enjoy the warmth of their reunion. Cleve sputtered, "How did you two . . .? I never in my wildest dreams expected . . ." He nuzzled deep into Liott's shoulder and pulled her even closer to him.

"Pram sent word. When we heard, Daniel and I decided we'd come home. We wanted to be here when you got here. This is where we knew you'd come first. "

"When did you . . .?"

"Just a few hours ago," Liott said. "I am so glad all of this is behind us, my darling." She felt him tense up.

"Liott, it isn't exactly behind us. I still have a warrant out for my arrest, and there's a detective here in Cleveland that would just as soon see me in jail."

She was shaking her head. "You don't know do you? You haven't spoken to Pram?"

"Not since July 4 or 5. He was up to his eyeballs in rebels in Bangkok . . ."

"Well, let me fill you in. Charges against you have been dropped. Pram talked to the mama-san at that bar in Bangkok where Driscoll was killed. She lied to the police about you. Someone paid her to say it was you. They haven't found the real killer yet. Pram doesn't think they ever will. But the important thing is that everyone knows you didn't kill him."

Cleve suddenly felt very tired, as if the weight of the world had just been lifted off of his shoulders. He looked at his mother, who was crying. "What about Bergstrom?"

Ida shrugged her shoulders. "What about him? I already told

him that you went out that night to see why you were being followed. He said, 'Then your son lied to me.' I told him that if you hadn't lied, that he might have arrested you and you'd never be able to prove your innocence. He didn't like it very much, but he knows he doesn't have a case against you. Besides, Wanda says Mr. Shaw would take your case in a heartbeat. He says Bergstrom has no case. You're free, Son, free and clear of all charges."

Cleve sat down and put his head in his hands. Liott stood next to him with her arm around his shoulder. Daniel said, "Papa, tell us what happened . . . what happened after you left Chuk Ra Met? I asked Uncle Pram. He says that I should ask you."

Cleve looked up at his son, chuckled, and then said, "I played a small part in stopping the coup in Thailand."

"What about in the other countries?" Daniel wasn't going to let it go.

Cleve smiled at his son, held his thumb and index finger up about an inch apart, and said, "A small part . . . and I probably shouldn't have even said that much."

The boy's expression clouded over, "Have you heard about the president's impeachment?"

"I have heard those rumors. Yes."

Daniel nodded. "I don't get it, Papa. Most of the people here in America think the president did the right thing. So why are they trying to impeach him?"

"It's politics, son and it can sometimes be ugly. There is a vice president and a secretary of defense that were left out of the discussion. There are four hundred and thirty-five representatives and one hundred senators who were left out as well. They claim it's a constitutional question, but I think their feelings and their pride are hurt and they aren't listening right now to the people that sent them to Washington in the first place. The president did a heroic thing, but he stepped on a lot of people's toes in doing it. We'll just have to wait and see what happens."

# 40

## THE DEAL

*10:00 a.m., Eastern Standard Time, August 10, The Capitol, Washington, D.C.*

**D**espite public opinion polls showing a 75/25 split not to impeach, the House voted to move forward and sent three Articles of Impeachment to the US Senate for trial. They were:

- *That the President of the United States, Wilson W. Glover, did intentionally violate the Constitution of the United States of America and the War Powers Act of 1973 by committing US troops to combat operations in Thailand on July 4 of the current year without proper Congressional authority.*

- *That the President of the United States, Wilson W. Glover, did intentionally violate the Constitution of the United States of America and the War Powers Act of 1973 by committing US troops to combat operations in the Republic of South Korea on July 4 of the current year without proper Congressional authority.*

- *That the President of the United States, Wilson W. Glover, did intentionally violate the Constitution of the United States of America and the War Powers Act of 1973 by committing US troops to combat operations in Japan on July 4 of the current year without proper Congressional authority.*

*10:00 p.m., Eastern Standard Time, August 10, the White House, Washington, D.C.*

WILSON GLOVER SAT behind his desk in the Oval Office, his chair turned to face out the window overlooking the well-lit White House grounds. With him was his national security advisor, Tim Munson. He heard the door open and his chief of staff announce Vice President Randall. Glover spun around and smiled at his chief of staff. "Thanks, Bill. Do me a favor and make sure no one interrupts us, will you?"

"Yes, of course, Mr. President." The door closed and the president turned his attention to the vice president. Randall's look was smug. Glover hated him right now. He had never been Glover's first choice for the job, but two and a half years ago, when he was running for president, he knew he needed votes in the southern tier of states. Randall had been the means to that end. "Charley, wipe that smug look off of your face and sit down." Glover knew he insisted on being called Charles, but tonight in this game of one-upsmanship, he was going to be called Charley, like it or not.

"Mr. President, I didn't come here to . . ."

Glover raised a hand to silence him, "You're here because I

asked you to be here. So shut the fuck up and listen. I'm tired, Charley."

"These are trying times for all of us, Mr. President."

"No, I don't mean physically tired. I'm tired of your deceitfulness. I'm tired of not being able to trust you any further than I can throw you. So, I'm prepared to offer you a deal."

"A deal, Mr. President?" Randall cast a cautious glance toward Munson and then said, "You are the one that, I would think, should be looking for a deal."

"Yeah, well, before you get too cocky, you might want to listen to what I have to offer. You want to be the next president and I think you will do everything you can to see that I'm impeached. But what would you say if I told you that Tim Munson and I are ready to resign right now . . . well, perhaps tomorrow . . . and let you just succeed me as the next president. You can appoint anybody you want to as your national security advisor. I mean, why drag the country through a long and difficult impeachment trial that pits you and Congress against the American people? So what if I just step down and let you have all the marbles?"

Randall had to get a shot in somewhere and this seemed like the right time. "So, what has happened to Wilson Glover, whom the Japanese prime minister calls America's most courageous President?" He had a sneer to his voice. "Is he really going to just leave America to twist in the wind at this most crucial time in her history?"

Glover wanted to step over and cold cock the bastard, but instead he shot back, "Here's the thing, Charley," returning the sneer, "I think America will survive the remaining two years of my current term in spite of you. You will run in the next presidential election, but you won't be elected. You may win in the south, but people in the east, the west, and the heartland won't vote for you. The guy that brung you to the dance, is leavin' town, Charley. And your prospects for another date are slim to none."

Glover had scored. Randall managed to stammer, "Screw you, Mr. President. You are about to be impeached."

"Well, so you say, Charley. Maybe so, maybe not. You know the Senate isn't the push-over that the House of Representatives is. Are you willing to take the chance that the Senate won't find me guilty and won't impeach me? Remember, Charley, it appears in the polls that the people are on my side, even if you boys here in Washington aren't. Do you think that maybe a few senators from the other party won't roll my way because they don't want to piss off the people back home? Better think about it, Charley. I'm offering you a sure thing."

"And what do you want from me?"

"Not anything that I think you will have any trouble living with. First, I want you to guarantee me that the names of all the special operators that were involved in deflecting these coups in Asia will forever remain classified."

"Um, well, I thought that was standard policy within the Department of Defense."

"It is, Charley, but remember, I don't trust your fucking ass, so I need your promise."

Randall nodded.

The president prodded, "I need you to say it, Charley. Say you promise."

Randall rolled his eyes but said, "Yeah, OK. I fucking promise, Wilson. What else do you want?"

"Do you know who Cato Fujiwara is?"

Randall thought for a moment and then shook his head.

"He's the head of the Yakuza."

"OK. I don't know why he's important, but I'll play along."

"Well, let's just say that he played a role in everything that has happened over the past couple of months in Asia. His cooperation actually helped us avoid a coup in Japan and gave us some important information we were lacking."

Randall whistled. "Wow, you've been playing fast and loose with organized crime, Mr. President."

"Think what you will, Charley, but part of our little deal is that you will not disclose Fujiwara's involvement in what has just happened in Asia."

"You must have a reason."

"I do, but it may not be one you would understand. I gave my word that if he provided us certain information and then played along with us, he would not be exposed to his government as possibly having a role in any coup in Japan."

"And your word is your bond, eh, Mr. President."

"See Charley, I told you, you wouldn't understand."

"OK, Mr. President, spare me any more insults. Is that all?"

"No, there's one more thing. I have this evening signed a pardon for Cleveland A. Spires. I've pardoned him of a murder that he didn't commit but which cost him ten years of his life in prison. I intend to return him to his original rank of command sergeant major and to pay him retroactively for all those lost years. I do not want you to comment or in any other way challenge my pardoning of Spires. You are to keep your mouth absolutely shut about this matter and that puppet of yours, the secretary of defense, must do the same."

"Who is he?"

"Suffice it to say, that we would not have known anything about what happened in Asia if it hadn't been for Command Sergeant Major Spires."

Randall sat in the chair in front of the president's desk and looked around the room. He coveted this office and all of the power that went with it. Wilson Glover knew he had his fish hooked.

Randall looked at the president and said, "OK, Mr. President, I accept your offer. What time tomorrow shall we make the announcement?"

Glover looked at Tim Munson, who was smiling and nodded. "Charley, let's let our staffs work out the details. My chief of staff will be in touch with yours within the hour. It will be a sleepless night for them and, likely, you. Tim and I, however, will sleep like babies."

Randall got up to leave, but before he reached the office door Glover called to him. "Oh, Charley, there is one other thing."

Randall stopped and turned to face the president. "What now, Wilson?"

"I've recorded this entire conversation." He pulled a cell phone from his pocket and flourished it in front of the vice president. "If you break faith with any of the terms of our deal, I will make sure this gets to every major news outlet in the country. Don't fuck with me on this, Charley, unless you want the horns."

# 41

## A DISTANT GOODBYE

Cleve and Liott Spires were wealthy people by Thai standards. After the presidential pardon, the Defense Finance and Accounting Service had direct-deposited nearly three-quarters of a million after-tax dollars into Cleve's bank account. They'd spent almost a month traveling with Ida and Daniel around Ohio, Pennsylvania, Indiana, and Illinois visiting whatever sight struck their fancy. When they weren't travelling, Cleve was on the phone with a civil engineering firm in Bangkok. Part of the money was going to be used to bring electricity to Chuk Ra Met and that required planning the grid, purchasing the equipment, installing it, and then getting it up and running.

Two weeks ago, Liott and Cleve had said goodbye to Ida and their son. Daniel was going to spend another two weeks with his grandmother. On their way home, the couple spent two nights in Bangkok putting the finishing touches on the electrical plans with the engineering firm. Now that it was up and running, Cleve envisioned the day that he wouldn't have to go into Korat to find a telephone. Perhaps a cell phone tower close to the village would even net them service in Chuk Ra Met. Modernity was coming to this place and Cleve had pondered whether or not that was really a wise thing.

On the morning of September 15, he'd made his way into the bus station in Korat. From there he would make his way to Bangkok to meet Daniel's flight home, but a planned phone call to his mother was prudent just to make sure all travel plans were on schedule.

In Cleveland, Ohio, when the phone rang right on time, Daniel answered, "Hello, Papa."

"Hello, Son, how are you?"

There was a certain hesitancy in his answer that gave Cleve some pause. "Everything OK, there?"

"Just fine . . . yes, everything is fine."

Again the hesitancy, but Cleve tried to gloss over it. "OK, I am on my way to Bangkok . . ."

"Papa . . ."

Now Cleve knew something was wrong. "What is it, Son. Is your flight delayed?"

There was no easy way for Daniel to break the news. He had not discussed it with any of them. It was something he'd been thinking about for the last couple of months. The recruiter had been able to get him everything he'd wanted; one-station unit training to become an infantryman, then onto Airborne School at Fort Benning, Georgia, Ranger training after that, and a shot at Special Forces if he earned his Ranger tab. Daniel decided he just needed to lay it out there. "Papa, I'm not coming home."

The words stung Cleve. "But, Daniel . . . I don't . . ."

"I've enlisted in the army, Papa. I report in two weeks to Fort Jackson. I'm going to be an infantryman."

It was as if someone had gut punched him. Cleve dropped the

phone's receiver to his side. He could hear Daniel saying, "Papa . . . Papa . . . are you there, Papa?" He returned the receiver to his ear. "Yes . . . yes, son. I'm here. What am I going to tell your mother?"

"Papa, I know you don't understand. I know Mama won't either. But . . . but this is something that I have to do."

"Is your Grandmother there?" Cleve asked.

Ida was sitting at the kitchen table just behind Daniel. The two of them had discussed what Cleve's reaction to the news might be. He handed her the phone. "He wants to talk to you."

"Hello, Cleveland."

"Mom, did you know he was going . . ."

"No. He didn't tell me until today after he'd signed the papers." She looked across the kitchen at her grandson whose concerned look was smeared all over his face. "He told me he didn't want anyone to try and talk him out of this."

Cleve gathered himself. His son was a man, capable of making his own decisions, but the sudden unexpectedness of this one had truly caught him by surprise. "I wasn't expecting . . ."

"No. None of us were." She paused to wipe away a tear. *Why am I crying? I'm proud of the boy!* She didn't want either of them to think she was disappointed. Turning to look at Daniel, who'd taken a seat at the kitchen table, she smiled and said, "Cleveland, Daniel is a good boy . . . a good man. He's just like you Cleveland . . . the same kind of man. Don't you or Liott worry. He's done a good thing. He's done the right thing."

On the other side of the world, Cleve considered his mother's words. He knew she was right. But still, after all that had happened to him. He heard his mother ask, "Cleveland, are you there?"

"Yeah, Mom, I'm here." He needed to set things right with his son. "Can you put Daniel back on the phone?"

He heard Ida say, "He wants to talk to you, Daniel," and then Cleve heard, "Papa, please don't be angry. This is something I have to do."

Tears stained Cleve's cheeks, but they weren't tears of anger. "Listen, son. There was a boy once, from Cleveland. In fact, he was named after that very city. He'd felt the need to go and serve, just like you, and so he did. It wasn't always easy for him. In fact, there were some years that he felt like he'd lost everything. But I know that boy pretty well, and he would tell you that it's an honorable thing you are doing. So go and do it. Do it well. Do it to the very best of your ability and never forget that your grandmother, your mother, and I are all very proud of you, Daniel. I love you, son."

"I love you, Papa."

There was nothing else to be said. Cleve wiped the tears from his eyes and placed the receiver back on the phone with both hands, allowing them to linger there as if he was trying to make this goodbye last a moment longer, as if he was trying to hold on for just a second longer to the boy he'd missed seeing grow into a man. He walked outside into the heat of Korat's mid-day and stopped across the street in front of the bus station. He stood there and watched the bus for Bangkok depart. In his pocket, he could feel his ticket. Liott would be surprised to see him back home so soon. She would think there had been a flight delay, or some other simple reason for his early return. He pulled himself together. He had done many hard things in his life. None would be as hard as telling Liott that her son was to become a soldier, like him.

# ACKNOWLEDGMENTS

I SERVED IN the US Army for nearly twenty-seven years. In that time I was privileged to work with dynamic leaders and alongside soldiers and civilians whose dedicated service to their jobs inspired me daily. This book could not have been possible without those friendships.

Another inspiration is my daughter, Brynn. A true "military brat," she loves me to this day even though her roots were pulled from under her every two or three years when it was time to move to the next duty station. Brynn, this book is for you and every "military brat" like you.

I owe my wife, Diane, more than I will ever be able to give back to her. She encouraged me to write the first version of this book back in 2003. Since then she has encouraged my writing life. She is the first editor of anything that I write. She endures my grumbling and grousing at her comments and never says, "I told you so!" when my editors, more often than not, pick up on the very same point. Diane, I can never thank you enough for all of your support.

Finally, I want to thank the people at Mission Point Press from whom I have learned so much about the process of getting a book ready for the marketplace. Doug Weaver, Mission Point

Press's business manager, is patient, thorough, encouraging, and thoughtful, a resource I could not do without. Similarly, Heather Shaw, a talented writer herself, excels at graphic design and is, simply put, indispensable. She designed the cover that first drew you to this book among all the others on the shelf or table. I would not like the marketing aspect of selling books nearly as much if I did not have Heather in my court. I worked with two editors from Mission Point Press, John Pahl and Tanya Muzumdar. John helped me polish the book. Tanya made it sparkle. I extend to each of them my sincerest thanks for their friendship and their professionalism. Finally, to Anne Stanton, the editorial director at Mission Point Press and the executive director of the National Writers Series in Traverse City, Michigan, I want to say thank you. Anne and her husband, Doug Stanton, a New York Times best-selling author, are turning the northwest corner of Michigan's lower peninsula into a regional hub for writers.

I hope everyone enjoys the read as much as I did in getting it ready for you to read!

JOHN WEMLINGER IS a retired U.S. Army Colonel with 27 years of service. He lives now in Onekama, Michigan, with his wife, Diane, close to the Lake Michigan shore. When he and their border collie, Sydney, aren't roaming the beaches or nearby hiking trails, he is playing golf, pickleball, working on his next novel or creating an unusual piece of original art from the drift-wood, rocks and beach glass that he finds along the shoreline. One of the true joys of his life is talking with people about his books and his art. He can be contacted at www.JohnWemlinger. com or on Facebook.

# ALSO FROM JOHN WEMLINGER

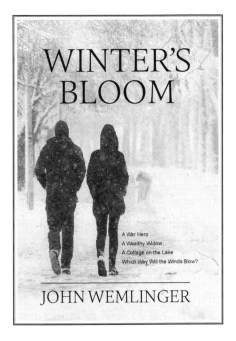

PRAISE FOR **WINTER'S BLOOM**:

FOR OVER THREE decades, Rock Graham has carried the physical and emotional scars from a tour in Vietnam. He is a decorated war hero, but guilt from what happened one dark night in a steaming southeast Asia jungle is always lying in ambush, waiting for an unguarded moment to set his demons free. When he tries to find solitude at a cottage on Lake Michigan in the dead of winter, a chance encounter on the desolate, frozen shoreline changes his life forever.

JOHN WEMLINGER HAS written a powerful novel about a veteran suffering from PTSD and the unlikely path that leads to his salvation. *Winter's Bloom* is a poignant tale of loss, love and redemption that will keep you turning the pages.

— Frank P. Slaughter, author of *The Veteran* and *Brotherhood of Iron*